## A DECLARATION OF LOVE

"He has offered for you, has he not, Diana?"

She did not insult Nicholas's intelligence by pretending to misunderstand. "How did you know?"

"I would have to be blind not to see it," he said, grasping her shoulders and compelling her to face him. "What did you tell him?"

"Nothing. It was too soon," she said.

"You can't marry him!"

"I fail to see what business it is of yours, Nicholas," she said defiantly.

"He doesn't love you. You are nothing to him but another decorative object to display with the rest of his trophies!"

She turned her face away. "I know it," she whispered.

"Then why didn't you refuse him outright?" he asked angrily. "Surely you aren't entertaining his proposal. He's twenty years older than you. You can't do it!"

"Why can't I?" she cried, her voice throbbing with indignation.

He bent his head and his demanding lips met hers. She lifted her hands to push him away, but instead her fingers curled against him, twisting in the thin fabric of his fine cambric shirt to draw him even closer as she responded passionately to his kiss. . . .

Books by Kate Huntington

THE CAPTAIN'S COURTSHIP

THE LIEUTENANT'S LADY

LADY DIANA'S DARLINGS

Published by Zebra Books

# LADY DIANA'S DARLINGS

## Kate Huntington

Zebra Books
KENSINGTON PUBLISHING CORP.
http://www.zebrabooks.com

ZEBRA BOOKS are published by

Kensington Publishing Corp.
850 Third Avenue
New York, NY 10022

Copyright © 2000 by Kathy Chwedyk

Zebra and the Z logo Reg. U.S. Pat. & TM Off.

First Printing: July, 2000
10 9 8 7 6 5 4 3 2 1

Printed in the United States of America

To Robert Chwedyk, Jake Elwell and
John Scognamiglio, my heroes

# One

It had cost Caroline Benningham a small fortune, even when one considered her lavish income, to rent the romantic villa on the Tyrrhenian Sea that summer.

She might just as well have gone to Bath and spent her days drinking those abysmal waters and listening to the dowagers grumble about their gout, she reflected bitterly.

Seeking comfort, the wealthy widow paused before an oblong mirror held on the wall by two coy gilded cupids to assure herself that every strand of her sleek, dark coiffeur was in place.

Caroline was on the shady side of thirty and still remarkably handsome. Everyone told her so, perhaps a little too emphatically.

A reigning toast in her salad days, Caroline had a lifelong habit of staring into mirrors for reassurance at every opportunity, and of late this formerly gratifying experience invariably surprised a slightly pained expression on her face, as if a prankster had painted those infinitesimal lines at the corners of her eyes and lips in order to vex her.

Which, in a manner of speaking, explained what she was doing in Naples.

Time was running out.

Caroline estimated that she had perhaps another five years

before she would be forced to rig herself out in turbans and little ruffs to conceal her sagging chin line while she waited to cock up her toes. She was determined to have one grand adventure before she attained the venerable age of forty, and she intended to have it far from the censorious eyes of London society.

The moment she saw the little villa with its classical statuary of undraped gods and goddesses, cool red tile floors, gilded plasterwork and garden fountain sparkling in the hot Neapolitan sun, she knew it was a perfect setting for her last stand against decrepitude.

That had been a month ago, and, to her disgust, her only experience in Naples that remotely might be described as an adventure had occurred when an urchin attempted to snatch her reticule as she listlessly examined ugly ceramic pots in the marketplace.

"My dear Diana, admit it," Caroline said, impatiently pacing the grand salon as she turned reproachful eyes on the lady she rashly had invited to accompany her to Naples. "You're as bored as I am."

"Bored? I thought we were having a lovely time," said her companion, sounding conscience-stricken.

Lady Diana, the daughter of an earl and the widow of Viscount Dunwood, made a pretty picture as she sat on the white brocade sofa, her lovely golden head bent as her long, elegant fingers continued their mundane occupation of knotting a fringe. Occasionally she bent and bestowed a caress on her eighteen-month-old son, Stephen, who lay on a little rug at his mother's feet drooling over the front of his little frilled shirt.

Despite the fact that her son was the only charge in a nursery tended by a veritable army of nursemaids at the late Lord Dunwood's estate in Kent, Diana had categorically refused to abandon him to the tender mercies of his less-than-affectionate paternal grandmother and the rather taciturn nurse who reigned over the manor's nursery apartments. The dowager Lady Dunwood made no secret of the fact that she considered Stephen an unsatisfactory heir to her late son's honors.

Despite Caroline's initial skepticism about traveling with so young a child, she had to admit the boy was no trouble. He was quiet and rather inclined to lie about listlessly instead of toddling all over the place getting into mischief like other boys his age, a fact that Caroline knew caused Diana no end of concern. Although Diana rarely complained of her mother-in-law, Caroline decided the old bat must have ice in her veins not to appreciate a child with so sweet a smile and so gentle a disposition.

While Diana fretted over her child's health, Caroline worried about Diana herself.

Although she was only twenty years old, the formerly high-spirited Diana had become docile, soft-spoken and polite, the very soul of feminine virtue since her husband's death a year ago. No wonder Caroline was worried about her mental state!

Worse, she utterly refused to accompany Caroline to masquerades, balls, casinos or, in short, anywhere Caroline might have been expected to meet one of the tall, dark, exotic strangers she had been misled into thinking were so plentiful in Naples.

If Caroline had been blessed with Diana's youth, beauty and magnificent Junoesque figure, *she* certainly wouldn't be wasting her entire stay in Naples knotting *fringes,* of all the dispiriting things.

"It's unnatural for a beautiful young woman to waste all this time in mourning," Caroline grumbled.

"Half-mourning," Diana pointed out as a twinkle lurked in her melting cornflower blue eyes. She smoothed the skirt of her modish lavender damask gown complacently.

"Don't quibble! It's the same thing if you're going to refuse to have any fun while we're in Naples. I can't imagine what Rupert Milton ever did to deserve such devotion to his memory."

"He died," Diana said half to herself as the laughter faded from her eyes.

"So did mine," said Caroline, unimpressed, "but you don't see *me* getting all maudlin about it."

This vastly improper sentiment had the effect of bringing the laughter back.

"No, love," Diana agreed, her lips twitching.

Caroline had made it clear to all her acquaintances that the only kind thing her unsatisfactory spouse did for her during the six hideous years of their marriage was to make her a widow.

That was ten years ago, and Caroline had been celebrating her freedom with what some condemned as unseemly enthusiasm ever since. She had utterly refused to go into mourning, denouncing as barbarous any convention that requires one to wear black for such a rotter of a husband. ("Too *depressing*, darling," she had told her scandalized acquaintances airily a bare month after her husband's demise. "And I do most sincerely hope there is an afterlife because I'd like to think Giles *knows* I'm wearing a carmine red gown at this very moment!")

"I remember when you were ripe for any mad scheme that promised entertainment," Caroline said with a sigh.

"I was younger then," Diana said.

"Living with Rupert and his mother would be enough to make anyone feel old," Caroline observed.

"You never liked Rupert."

"No," Caroline agreed. "And you know perfectly well the feeling was mutual, so don't try to make me feel guilty about it now that he's dead. He was *beastly* to you."

"He was not always kind," Diana said carefully, "but some might say he was sorely provoked."

"Humbug," scoffed Caroline, remembering how Rupert frequently humiliated his bride in public for quite innocent offenses, and how he punished her for minor indiscretions by banishing her to his ancestral pile in Kent as if she were a naughty schoolgirl.

"I never thought you would be so poor-spirited," Caroline said aloud, picking up the thread of their argument. "All I am proposing is a simple evening excursion."

"Get thee behind me, Satan," Diana said, laughing. "It is cruel of you to tease me, for you know I am dying to see the inside of Count Zarcone's palace."

"This may be your only chance."

Naked desire shone on Diana's face as she struggled to resist temptation.

Diana had a passion for art and antiquities that Caroline, resentful at being dragged on tours of musty old churches to look at molding tombstones and ugly effigies, sternly warned Diana that this would earn her an undesirable reputation as a bluestocking if she wasn't careful.

According to the gossip, the count's domicile was decorated in a style so fanciful that it made the Prince Regent's Royal Pavilion under perpetual renovation in Brighton look like a farmer's cottage.

The count also was reputed to be the possessor of a fine collection of Etruscan artifacts, which caused Diana to suspect that a gentleman of such discriminating tastes could not possibly be the soulless libertine of his reputation.

Caroline encouraged this naive assessment of the count's character, although personally Caroline hoped Diana was wrong. It would be the outside of enough for Caroline to go to the count's palace in search of a grand adventure only to find him a dull dog of respectability.

Unfortunately, it was not easy for two English gentlewomen unacquainted with the bachelor count to procure an invitation to see the palace for themselves. One rarely met him in good society, because the gentleman preferred more nocturnal pursuits and less refined companions, but he was reputed to be devastatingly handsome.

Caroline, for one, intended to find out if this was true by seeing the count for herself. Further, she was determined to persuade Diana to go with her.

The count was patron to a group of artists, some of them Englishmen, and the only females invited to his parties were the working girls of Naples euphemistically referred to as models. According to rumor, the girls posed for the artists while the count and his intimates looked on.

Caroline and Diana would simply gain entry to the palace by posing as two of these models.

"We would be *ruined* if we were to participate in anything

so improper!" Diana exclaimed. "What if someone recognizes us?"

"We will satisfy our curiosity and slip out before anything truly scandalous occurs," Caroline promised. "How could anyone recognize us? The few Englishmen among the count's guests will hardly be the sort of people we would encounter in society, and the count's friends are probably all fat, nearsighted old men whose idea of excitement is trying to pinch one's bottom."

"Now, *that* sounds like a high treat!" Diana said dryly.

*"Please,* Diana," Caroline pleaded, unscrupulously exploiting Diana's soft heart. "If you refuse to go, my whole trip to Naples will be ruined."

"All right," Diana said, as Caroline knew she would. "I will go with you."

"I knew you wouldn't fail me," Caroline gloated.

"There is a condition."

"Anything!" vowed Caroline.

"You must go with me to the ruins tomorrow."

Caroline made a face, but Diana merely smiled at her.

"I *hate* ruins," Caroline pouted. "They're so *dispiriting."*

"No cultured English traveler would neglect to visit the excavations at Pompeii while in Naples."

"I never claimed to be cultured, love," Caroline said with a sigh.

"The frescoes unearthed in the city are supposed to be very fine," Diana pointed out. "Will you go with me or not?"

"I will go," Caroline said wryly.

"Good."

"Now for your part of the bargain," said Caroline with gentle malice.

"No!" Diana exclaimed in horror as Caroline's serving woman held up a thin, cheap white blouse and a full skirt in a garish shade of red. "I wouldn't be caught *dead* in such horrid things!"

"Nonsense," Caroline said briskly.

She quickly unhooked Diana's demure muslin gown and

pulled it down over Diana's slim hips. Then she began to remove the chemise.

"What are you doing?" asked Diana, alarmed, as she clutched the thin undergarment to her bosom.

"The blouse will look better without it," Caroline said, firmly removing the chemise from Diana's clutching fingers.

"Oh, good heavens," Diana wailed.

Laughing, Caroline slipped the blouse over Diana's head and hitched up the skirt. Then she unpinned Diana's hair and let it hang down her back in golden waves.

"It's positively indecent," said Diana, not entirely unadmiring of the result. The blouse was cut to ride low on the bosom and shoulders. It was no more revealing than a ball dress, but the red skirt clearly exposed Diana's ankles. Her loosened hair did make her look rather abandoned.

"Here," Caroline said, handing her friend a triangle of fabric. "You wear this kerchief pinned around the shoulders, see?"

"Well, that's a little better," said Diana, arranging the kerchief to hide as much of her bosom as possible.

After Caroline was dressed in an equally disreputable-looking costume and Stephen was given to his nursemaid, the two women joined several others whom Caroline had cultivated for the purpose. These girls, who had modeled for the count's artists before, had told their benefactors they would be bringing friends to join the party, Caroline explained.

Diana's eyes grew round later that evening when she entered the large reception rooms of the palace, and they nearly popped out of her head when she saw the cavernous ballroom where the party was in progress. More than one gentleman broke off his conversation with his cronies to stare at the newcomers.

*"Molta bella,"* sighed one of them ingratiatingly as Diana passed him.

Ignoring him, Diana feasted her eyes on the ornate Italian Renaissance plasterwork that bordered the ceilings and the mammoth frescoes that lined the mellow parchment-colored walls. The staircase and floors were made of pure, cool, white Carrara marble.

There were paintings set on easels about the room as well, but Diana dismissed them disdainfully as being unworthy of this splendid room. She could not be expected to appreciate the renderings of voluptuous houris with wanton expressions on their simpering faces, sprawled in ungainly abandon on richly colored cushions. She assumed these paintings were the result of previous sessions similar to this one, and her optimistic assessment of the count's aesthetic tastes went down several degrees.

"Where do you suppose he keeps the Etruscan artifacts?" Diana asked.

"Shhh. We're supposed to be *Italian*," Caroline whispered in an impatient undervoice.

Laughing young artists and their dissipated-looking patrons lounged on thick carpets and pillow-laden couches. It had amused the count to transform the magnificent ballroom that had been built during the Italian Renaissance into a Turkish seraglio, and Diana thought disapprovingly that if *she* owned this room the first thing she'd do would be to set every servant to sweeping the carpets.

These were apparently Oriental in origin, quite old and obviously valuable. They might even have been brought from the Orient during the Crusades by one of the count's ancestors, Diana speculated with a thrill of excitement.

Perhaps the Etruscan artifacts were under glass somewhere.

She was so caught up in wondering how she might get away from the company to look for them that she didn't see the leering young man approach her. Obviously, she and Caroline had been naive in assuming the gentlemen would begin the evening in relative sobriety.

"Come here, sweetheart, and give us a kiss," said the man as he hooked a friendly arm around her.

*"Bacio,"* he added as an afterthought, obviously expecting her to comply.

Diana jumped nervously. He reeked of liquor, and his hands were stained with some dark substance. Obviously, he was one of the English artists. Just as obviously, judging from the look in his eyes when they rested on Diana, his mind was not on his work.

"No," gasped Diana, backing away.

*"Timida,"* Caroline hurriedly explained to the man, seeing the look of panic on Diana's face.

The accommodating artist shrugged, put his arm around Caroline and led her away instead. Diana gave her friend a look of dismay, for she had been about to suggest that they leave.

Now that Caroline's reassuring presence was gone, the enormity of what she had done in consenting to accompany her on this scandalous excursion burst upon Diana as she helplessly observed the behavior of the count's guests. Most of the girls already had paired off with the artists or their patrons and were accepting their fondling with every appearance of complaisance.

The high-pitched coquettish squeals of the models told Diana that Caroline had been right about the fondness of the count's friends for pinching feminine bottoms. Diana was careful to keep her back to the wall.

Soon a young Englishman with a pleasant face, who, unlike his companions, looked both sober and clean, indicated that she should sit on the carpet. He spoke to her in Italian, and, to Diana's relief, her almost forgotten schoolgirl study of that language came to her aid and she was able to follow his conversation a little. Fortunately, he primarily required her to remain still while he worked. Caroline, Diana could see, was laughing and playfully trying to extricate herself from her companion's loose embrace. Reassured that they would leave as soon as Caroline returned to her, Diana decided she would humor the innocuous-seeming artist until then.

Diana arranged her skirts modestly about her limbs and sat on the floor in the place the artist indicated, regarding him warily. He seated himself next to her, drew a pad of paper across his knees, and indicated that she was to face to the side so he could draw her profile.

Caroline sent her a concerned glance, and Diana smiled at

her. Apparently reassured that Diana was content for the moment, Caroline accepted a glass of spirits from her companion and resumed her conversation with him.

Several artists were dabbing paints about, getting more on their persons than on the canvases. One bold young woman stroked an artist's arm. He responded by removing her blouse. Diana hastily looked away.

Diana's companion touched her shoulder, and she jumped, but he only wanted to show her the finished sketch of her profile. She smiled in relief and obeyed when he indicated that she was to look directly at him so he could do a front view of her face. Apparently, he was not interested in the rest of her anatomy.

Even so, she was becoming alarmed by the drama on the other side of the room that she watched from the corner of her eye.

The artist who had removed the model's blouse was pushing her against a wall, fondling her thoroughly in the process. The virtually nude girl shivered with excitement in her thin undergarments. Diana gasped.

The patrons began throwing coins at some of the other girls, and Diana realized that this was their way of encouraging them to follow the half-naked model's example. Diana was horrified when several coins struck her own bosom. She saw that a handsome, olive-skinned man dressed in rich garments was leering at her, and she instinctively recoiled from the devilish glint in his eye.

She looked to Caroline for guidance, but Caroline was sitting on the floor with her legs akimbo, giggling helplessly as she gathered coins into her skirt.

Caroline never did have much of a head for spirits, Diana reflected sadly.

The leering gentleman, seeing that Diana was not taking the hint to disrobe, grinned and seized her with the obvious intention of undressing her with his own hands.

Diana screamed and instinctively brought her knee up to break his hold. He easily dodged her effort to unman him, and the other gentlemen laughed. He imprisoned her in his arms and tried to kiss her, paying no attention when the artist who had been drawing her face sought to remonstrate with him. Caroline had started forward, but she was hampered by the amorous embrace of her companion.

At that moment, Diana heard a male voice rap out a command in Italian, and Diana found herself abruptly released. The dark-haired, powerfully built newcomer approached and exchanged a few words with Diana's captor, who spread his hands out in an expansive gesture. Then, sprawling at ease on an ornate sofa, the olive-skinned man imperiously beckoned to two other women, who eagerly joined him.

Diana jumped when her rescuer spun her around to face him and recoiled at the anger in his dark eyes. Her words of gratitude died on her lips.

Although Diana was five feet nine inches tall in her stockinged feet, she had to look up into a face that would have been classically handsome except for its disdainful expression.

Diana screamed when he suddenly seized her, threw her over one broad shoulder and walked out the doorway as if she weighed nothing at all.

Terrified, she began pounding her fists on his back as the other men's laughter followed them.

"You've got a hellcat there," one of the Englishmen shouted from the doorway, raising his glass in a mock salute. "She probably bites."

"She won't bite *me*," he replied grimly.

As Diana desperately attempted to free herself from the steel bands of the man's sinewy arms, a whisper reached her panicked brain.

"Stop that," her captor said furiously under his breath, "or I'll hand you over to those swine. You'll fare better with me, I promise you."

Diana didn't believe him for a minute. Nearly mindless with panic, she struggled all the harder.

# Two

Nicholas Rivers, Lord Arnside, had been inclined to take his quarrelsome Aunt Edith's complaints about her daughter-in-law, Lady Diana, with a generous pinch of salt until he saw the lovely blond noblewoman disporting herself among the depraved Count Zarcone's intimates.

It was a good thing, it seemed, that Nicholas had impulsively decided to avail himself of the count's invitation to join the company tonight. With luck, he could take his cousin by marriage away from here before her reputation was quite ruined.

Not that the little hoyden seemed inclined to cooperate. The blows she landed on his back were not the halfhearted ones of a lady making a token protest.

Nicholas carried the struggling woman into a room equipped with a bed and threw her upon it in an undignified jumble of skirts. She tossed her head back sharply to get her disheveled hair out of her eyes and faced him on her knees with bared teeth, looking frightened but prepared for battle.

"Admirable, my dear, but quite unnecessary," he said dryly. "I haven't the remotest intention of molesting you."

"You will let me go?" she asked, sounding surprised.

"Yes. Chivalrous of me, is it not?"

"If you really mean it, I can only be grateful," she said, watching him warily.

"Save your gratitude. I am not doing it for you," he said, "but out of respect for my poor cousin Rupert's memory."

"You are Rupert's cousin?" she asked in horror.

"I hadn't thought you remembered me. I attended your wedding while I was on leave from the army. Nicholas Rivers, at your service."

"Rupert's cousin," she repeated faintly. "Lord Arnside. Of course."

"Listen, my girl," he said impatiently. "If you weren't connected with my family, I'd let you take your chances with Count Zarcone. His pleasures are said to be a trifle unusual. And painful for his partners."

Lady Diana shuddered and regarded him with wide, terror-stricken eyes.

"Almost you convince me, but it is rather too late to play the innocent now," he said contemptuously, wishing the woman didn't look so outrageously beautiful in those appalling clothes.

Sternly he reminded himself that the notorious Lady Diana, daughter of an actress fortunate enough to trap a callow young heir to an earldom into marriage before maturity and his horrified parents could intervene, probably inherited her mother's histrionic talent and had used it often to dupe poor Rupert.

"My congratulations. Your pose of frightened virtue certainly is effective," he said coldly, suppressing a chivalrous impulse to assure her that he would defend her from those who would harm her with his last breath. Her lovely blue eyes had the most unfortunate effect on him.

Her chin came up at that.

"How dare you!" she said. "What did you tell the count? You didn't tell him who I am, did you?"

"No. I merely said we are acquaintances of long standing, and I wished to converse with you in private."

"You *didn't!*" she said with a gasp. "Now he thinks—"

"No doubt. But even that is preferable, you would agree, to telling him you are an English noblewoman who entered his home under false pretenses as a lark. It would amuse him to entertain the Englishmen of his acquaintance with the tale, no doubt. He might even be tempted to try the virtue of such an adventuresome lady.

"It is perfectly all right to scream," he added when she

gasped and covered her mouth with a trembling hand. She really did it quite well. "They quite expect it."

"You are insufferable, sir," she said in an injured tone.

"You have no one to blame but yourself," he pointed out. "No lady of refinement would be caught dead in this place."

"I notice that *you* appear to be quite at home here!" she said with some spirit.

"Hardly. I would not have called on the count if my cousin, Bernard Rivers, did not happen to be in his employ. I must say this snug little gathering is quite as distasteful as I anticipated."

"I have never seen anything so disgusting in my life," she agreed vehemently.

She seemed to mean it. Nicholas began to wonder if she was more foolish than depraved.

"Quite," he agreed in a milder tone. "Perhaps you would like to tell me how you came to be here."

"No, I would not," she said. Her chin was lifted in challenge, showing off the sculptured grace of her jawbone and long, slender neck. "Since you obviously are determined to despise me, I may as well save my breath."

"As you please," he said with a creditable assumption of indifference. "Perhaps you should go now. Who is to say the count might not desire to join in our play? And I, being his guest, could hardly refuse to share—"

*"Must* you be so odious?" Lady Diana demanded. "I refuse to listen to your insults for another moment."

She bounced off the bed and started for the door with her back ramrod straight.

"Wait!"

She turned to look at him.

"The streets are no safer here than in London," he said, surprising himself with his concern for her safety.

"I can manage," she said, giving him a look of pure loathing.

"Nonsense," he said. "My carriage is outside. I will send you home in it."

"But I came with someone," she objected. "I cannot leave Caroline here alone."

"Caroline?" he asked. Then the concerned face of the pretty brunette he had noticed when he first entered the room flashed across his mind. Of course. Mrs. Caroline Benningham, the dashing widow who had led his cousin's young wife into many a scrape and rendered Rupert's life miserable. He had thought she looked familiar. "If half of what one hears about the lady is true, she can take care of herself."

"I cannot just leave her without—"

"As you wish," he said with a sigh of resignation. "I will fetch Mrs. Benningham."

A few moments later he was bundling Lady Diana into his carriage. Mrs. Benningham had come outside at Nicholas's request to speak to her friend and seemed relieved that no harm had come to her, but she insisted that she was not ready to leave and could get to the villa perfectly well on her own now that she was assured that Diana was safe.

"I thank you, my lord, for your consideration," Lady Diana said almost meekly after Mrs. Benningham had gone back inside.

"As I said before," he said harshly, his conscience pricked by her gratitude, "I'm not doing it for you."

A truly considerate man would escort her personally, but he had no intention of dancing attendance on his late cousin's frivolous wife.

After he ordered the coachman to drive on, Arnside strolled back into the ballroom and dropped to the floor beside his cousin Bernard. Bernard looked up reproachfully, and Arnside stole a glance at the paper he was sketching.

"Pretty creature, isn't she?" Nicholas said as he admired the delicate bone structure of Lady Diana's face in the sketch. Bernard had outlined the rest of the figure. Nicholas had to acknowledge that Bernard had talent, but he could only deplore his otherwise sensible cousin's insistence upon remaining in the count's employ instead of returning to England with Nicholas.

Bernard merely grunted.

"Don't sulk, cawker," Nicholas said. "I didn't touch the girl.

I merely put her in my carriage and sent her home. *Her* home, that is."

"I'm glad." Bernard looked up from his sketch in relief. "Anyone could see she was no lightskirt."

*That shows what you know,* Arnside thought, recalling some of the wilder tales he'd heard about Lady Diana from her mother-in-law. It wouldn't do to tell Bernard about the lady's true identity, however. The fewer who knew about this business, the better.

"Yes," Nicholas said deliberately. "She didn't belong here any more than you do."

"Nick, I am not going to run tamely back to England just because my mother begged you to save her innocent child from the heathenish influence of a lot of unwholesome foreigners. I know exactly how she thinks, so don't bother to deny it."

"I do deny it," Nicholas said. "I will admit that I wish you would return to England with me. But you're a grown man, and you have to make your living the way you see fit."

"So you didn't come to Naples to drag me home?"

"No," Nicholas said, keeping his tone even. "I came because after my father died and I had to resign my commission to discharge my obligation to my remaining family and my father's estate, I couldn't bear the thought of either spending the summer at a fashionable resort or remaining another week in Surrey. Every brick of the manor house speaks of him, Bernard. I don't know if I will ever accept the fact that I will never see him again."

Bernard's eyes softened, and Nicholas looked away. He didn't want his cousin's pity.

"But it's time I went home," Nicholas added. "And it's time you came home as well."

"To do what? Starve for my art? I am extremely fortunate to have Count Zarcone as my patron, even if he does have peculiar tastes in entertainment. Don't worry that I will develop a taste for these sordid little evenings. They bore me senseless. If that girl hadn't arrived, this would have been a complete waste of my time."

He bent his head to study the sketch.

"See here, you aren't interested in that girl, are you?" asked Nicholas with some asperity.

"Only as a model. You know I'm not in the petticoat line, Nick. I can't afford to be," Bernard said ruefully. "I felt sorry for her. She looked like a lost soul, and I didn't care for the way our host forced himself on her. I would guess she was talked into coming here by her friend over there."

Caroline Benningham. A notorious woman ripe for any mischief. Lady Diana couldn't help being the daughter of an actress, but she certainly *did* have the power to choose her friends more wisely.

Mrs. Benningham was sitting on the floor, giggling idiotically. At some point she had started throwing coins back at the men. Unlike most of the females in the room, however, she still had all of her clothes on. Nicholas supposed that was *something* that could be said in her favor.

All of the artists except for Bernard had dropped any pretense of work and were participating in the bacchanal.

"She was a beautiful woman," said Bernard, looking critically at his sketch. Nicholas was staring straight ahead, his brow creased in thought.

"Too bad she won't be back," Bernard added. "She's just the model I need for one of the count's nastier commissions. But I suppose I will do well enough from memory."

"Yes," Nicholas said absently.

# Three

"Haven't I suffered enough?" asked Caroline plaintively as she tripped along the broken stone streets of the excavated city of Pompeii in her unsuitable slippers, trying valiantly to keep up with her energetic friend's longer strides.

"We've only just arrived," Diana said, consulting the little black book she carried in one gloved hand. The other held a white parasol to protect her complexion.

"My head is pounding," Caroline wailed.

"Don't sulk, love," replied her heartless companion. "This," she added impressively, stopping before a ruined edifice with fluted columns, "is the Temple of Isis."

"I shouldn't be at all surprised," said Caroline, refusing to encourage Diana by pretending interest. She looked with loathing at Diana's guidebook. "Must you quote to me from that appalling object?"

"The Roman senate issued decrees banning the worship of the Egyptian goddess four times within ten years," Diana continued. "Emperor Augustus and, after him, Tiberius also issued orders to suppress the cult."

"Well, good for them," Caroline muttered dryly. "I say, Diana. If you poke me one more time with that infernal parasol, I am going to give you such a clout! If you *must* walk along with your nose buried in that ridiculous little book, at least watch what you are doing."

"I'm sorry," said Diana, transferring her parasol to her other side so it would be farther away from her friend. "How can you not be interested in all this *history?*"

"Very easily," Caroline said dryly. "You had better take care, my girl, or next you will be having people say you're *bookish!*"

"That *would* be shocking," Diana murmured.

"Oh, look! Isn't that Lord Arnside? Yes, I am certain it is he. There is no mistaking those *magnificent* shoulders, and those wicked, *dangerous* eyes."

Diana peered in the direction of Caroline's pointing finger and saw Lord Arnside approach them. She flushed with embarrassment. What must he think of her after last night? The alarming thought occurred to her that since he was one of her son's trustees, he might decide she was an unfit mother and try to remove Stephen from her care. But if he did, she thought bitterly, it would be the first time any of Rupert's stuffy relations took an interest in her son.

"Good afternoon, Lady Diana," he said mildly, tipping his hat to the ladies. "Mrs. Benningham."

"Cousin Nicholas," Diana said cautiously. "How are you enjoying the ruins?"

"They are most interesting," he said, looking at her a little askance. After last night, he probably thought she spent all of her time at wild parties, Diana thought in despair.

"We were about to go to the House of the Vettii," she said. "According to the guidebook, it contains some rather remarkable frescoes."

"Not *I,* my girl!" Caroline interjected. "Now that your cousin is here, he can escort you to the House of the Vettii to look at sadly deteriorating walls. I am going to find a place in the shade to rest."

She retreated to the shadows of a thick, sadly damaged column and seated herself on a dusty step, much to the peril of her low-cut jonquil sarcenet gown. The matching plumes of her stylish bonnet drooped dispiritedly.

"Oh, Caroline," Diana called. "Are you sure?"

"Perfectly sure. Do run along and enjoy yourselves. Remember not to throw any rocks at one another. They must all be saved for posterity, you know."

She turned to Lord Arnside.

"You must forgive me, my lord. Perhaps by the time you return I will be more pleasant company. I am too hot and uncomfortable to be charming now."

Lord Arnside bowed to her and took Diana's elbow.

"I am at your service, Cousin," he said in a neutral tone. For a moment Diana could have sworn the taciturn gentleman was amused, but it must have been a trick of the bright sunlight. None of the Riverses had a sense of humor.

"I would not dream of imposing on you," she said, embarrassed by the way Caroline had thrown them together. The man already thought she was shockingly *fast*.

They proceeded in awkward silence to another house, and Diana felt a thrill of anticipation as she stepped inside the low doorway.

When her eyes adjusted to the semidarkness of the building, Diana was astonished to see the depiction of a stately, classically beautiful woman engaged in an act so profane that her face flamed immediately. She averted her eyes from this sordid but fascinating rendering only to observe one every bit as shocking on the opposite wall. It was not safe to allow one's gaze to rest *anywhere!*

To her surprise, Lord Arnside seemed just as embarrassed as she was.

"Cousin Diana, I assure you I had no idea . . ." he began in apology.

Then the glow of an approaching lantern illuminated the faces of two men who were walking toward them from another room. Lord Arnside grabbed Diana's arm and quickly ushered her back outside.

"What is it?" she asked, blinking against the sunlight.

"My cousin is in there with the count."

"Dear heavens!" she gasped, putting one hand to her throat in dismay. If she was recognized from having attended a party in Count Zarcone's palace, she would be utterly ruined. "Do you think they saw me?"

"No. I am certain they did not. I knew Bernard meant to visit the ruins today, but I did not think the count would be with him. Bernard has been commissioned to do a painting for the count based on some of the frescoes here."

"*Those* frescoes?" she asked, shocked.

"Most probably," he said, his face bland. "Perhaps we should join Mrs. Benningham."

"Yes," Diana said. She looked wistfully at the house. "Such a disappointment. But there are many wonderful things to see here. Are you interested in antiquities, Cousin Nicholas?"

"Only as the veriest dilettante. Rupert's father has a magnificent library of antiquarian books at his estate in Kent. But you know this because you live there."

"Yes. That library kept me sane during my period of mourning for Rupert."

Lord Arnside gave her a suspicious look as if he thought she might be roasting him. Well, she could hardly blame him for thinking the worst of her, she thought sadly.

Count Antonio Zarcone gave a sigh of satisfaction as he examined the sketch that Bernard had drawn of the pretty Italian girl at the party. A pity that Lord Arnside had staked his claim to the girl, and as a good host the count had no choice but to give in graciously.

"Yes," the count said in appreciation. "A veritable goddess." He looked about and pointed to the fresco before him. "This one, I think. In just this pose, if you please, my dear Mr. Rivers. I fancy it as one of a group to adorn my bedchamber."

"An excellent choice," said Bernard, trying to conceal his distaste. He sighed and began sketching the fresco.

Count Zarcone paid him well, but as an artist Bernard had to question the wisdom of wasting his time creating work that could never be shown in respectable company.

However, Bernard was committed to do this painting, regretful as he was to use the innocent Italian girl's image for such a purpose. It seemed, somehow, as if he were profaning the girl herself. But he would execute the work to the best of his ability because he was a professional, and as such he had his own peculiar kind of pride.

\* \* \*

"Thank you for your escort, Lord Arnside," Diana said in a tone of unmistakable dismissal once they were some distance away from the House of the Vettii. "I will wish you a pleasant stay in Naples. Stephen and I are returning to England tomorrow so I am unlikely to see you again."

"So soon?"

"Yes. Stephen is not thriving in all this heat. I only hope that in our absence my dear mother-in-law has not burned my clothes or thrown my furniture into the cow pasture."

Nicholas was not quite sure what to say to this. It was most improper for her to speak so critically about his aunt in his presence; however, he had to acknowledge that his aunt had said many worse things about Lady Diana.

"Rupert's death was a great shock," he said carefully, feeling obliged to offer excuses for his aunt's acrimony.

Lady Diana gave him a straight look.

"I suppose she told you that I murdered him," she said in a tone of resignation.

"You can hardly blame Aunt Edith for suspecting foul play when you left with Rupert for Greece rather suddenly on a holiday and accompanied his body home to England a few months later."

She deliberately turned her back on him.

"What *really* happened to Rupert?" he asked. "The truth cannot be any worse than the rumors that were flying around at the time. I have heard various tales, including that you poisoned him and that he was killed in a duel after calling out a man he suspected of being your lover."

"Yes. I have heard those as well," Diana said quietly. "Lord Arnside, I have no intention of discussing this matter with you or anyone. The end was very painful and . . . not sudden. Some people enjoy dwelling on that sort of misery. I don't happen to be one of their number. Let my poor husband rest in peace."

He would have questioned her further, but at that moment the count came out of the House of the Vettii and approached them as Caroline, obviously bored, approached from the other direction.

"Damnation," said Nicholas under his breath. "There goes all hope of hiding your identity from the count."

"Maybe he will not recognize me."

"Not recognize a long meg like you?" Nicholas scoffed. "You towered above all the other females at the party like a blond beacon."

Nicholas saw no reason to add that the count had asked him all about her after he sent her home last night. The count had, indeed, assumed she was Nicholas's mistress, and he made it clear that he would be interested in taking her under his own protection once Nicholas departed for England. The count was not pleased when Nicholas categorically refused to facilitate the proper introduction.

Now Count Zarcone would know the truth—that Lady Diana was an English noblewoman who kept fast company for amusement. *That* would do her reputation and poor Rupert's memory a world of good! He could just imagine how Aunt Edith would receive *this* choice tidbit of gossip.

"Well, what a delightful surprise," the count said as his eyes devoured Diana from the crown of her becoming straw hat to her lavender kid half boots. "I don't believe we were properly introduced last night."

The smirk on his face told Nicholas that he definitely had designs on the lady. Nicholas hoped he wouldn't be obliged to defend Lady Diana's questionable virtue on the dueling field.

The things a man did for his family!

"Count Antonio Zarcone," said Arnside reluctantly, "permit me to present my cousin by marriage, Lady Diana. She was married to my late cousin Rupert Milton, Viscount Dunwood."

"Charmed," said the count, taking Diana's gloved hand in his.

Diana smiled mechanically at him and extricated her hand rather hastily. He leered at her, and then he glanced at Caroline, who had been standing by watching them with avid interest.

"And who is this?" he asked sardonically as he apparently recognized her as well. *"Another* cousin?"

"Caroline Benningham," said Caroline, casting a flirtatious look at him from under her lashes as he bowed over her hand and muttered a careless greeting.

The count gave Caroline a cool, dismissive glance and turned away from her to address Diana.

"You must permit me to call on you, my lady," he said. "You are staying—"

"I am afraid that will not be possible," Diana said. "I will leave Naples tomorrow."

*"I* will be staying for another month," Caroline said, batting her eyelashes at the count.

"You are not going home together?" Nicholas said, surprised. "Surely, Cousin Diana, you don't intend to go to England alone."

"Certainly not," she said. "I will have my son with me as well as his nursemaid and my maid."

"I suppose I must change my plans and escort you," Nicholas said with a sigh of resignation.

"I fail to see why," said Diana, surprised. "I can get home perfectly well on my own, thank you."

"I can't allow that."

"Cousin Nicholas, I am a grown woman. There is no reason for you to cut your holiday short to dance attendance on me. I would *much* prefer to travel on my own."

"I do not wish to be rude," Nicholas said to the count and Mrs. Benningham, "but I should like to have a word with my cousin in private, if I may."

Mrs. Benningham, apparently sensing a gathering storm as she looked from one face to another, hastily took the count's arm and led him away.

"My dear count," she said cheerily. "Do show me more of these *fascinating* ruins."

He regarded her sardonically and glanced back to see Diana and Arnside about to engage in what he assumed was a lover's quarrel.

Perhaps he would visit the charming Lady Diana in England. Soon.

His thoughts were interrupted when Mrs. Benningham demanded his attention. He turned to her impatiently.

"Let us go in there," she said, apparently selecting a doorway at random. "It's bound to be cooler than the street. All of this sun is bad for my complexion."

"Yes," he said, gazing thoughtfully at her partially exposed bosom. "You wouldn't want to get . . . them . . . sunburned."

She gave a gasp of indignation and preceded him into a low-roofed dwelling partially filled with large earthenware jars.

"Madam," he said coldly, extricating himself when she would have taken his arm again. "I have no interest in engaging upon a flirtation with a female who consorts with the raff and scaff of the city."

"Indeed? That is not a very nice way to refer to *your* friends," she said sweetly. Her eyes were on fire with indignation.

Her looks were so improved by this emotion that he wondered if he had been too hasty in dismissing her as unworthy of his notice.

Then she screamed and threw herself against him. Instinctively, his arms closed tightly around her.

"What is it?" he asked, his face inches from hers.

"A snake," she gasped.

"How *very* trite, Mrs. Benningham," he said sardonically as he released her with unflattering haste. "Surely you can do better than that."

"I *did* see it! It was right—"

She screamed again and jumped behind the count as the snake slithered into the light coming from the doorway. With great presence of mind, the count bashed its head with his walking stick.

"I think I'm going to be sick," Caroline said faintly, leaving him alone with the corpse.

The count stared in fascinated revulsion as the snake slowly uncoiled on the broken tile floor.

Meanwhile, Arnside and Diana continued their argument in the blazing sun.

"Don't be ridiculous," Arnside was saying. "You cannot undertake such a long journey with only two female servants to protect you and your child. I was going to leave soon, anyway. I insist upon escorting you."

"You *insist!*" cried Diana in outrage. "How dare you! I refuse to be obligated to a gentleman who obviously despises me."

"I do *not* despise you."

*A blatant lie,* Diana thought.

"I do not need your good opinion, my lord. In fact, the sooner I rid myself of all my husband's overbearing relations, the better!"

She would have flounced off, but just then she saw Caroline approach with a strained expression on her face.

"Caroline, what happened?" asked Diana in concern as she put a protective arm around her friend's shaking shoulders. "Are you all right?"

"I think so," said Caroline, swallowing hard. "There was a snake. The count smashed its head with his walking stick."

"My poor dear," Diana said sympathetically, picking up her parasol from the ground. "We will go to the villa at once."

"Yes, please," said Caroline gratefully.

"Look on the bright side," Diana said as she led her friend away. "Did you know that snakes were supposed to be a symbol of good luck in Pompeii?"

"Oh, *do* shut up," Caroline said crossly.

# Four

Lord Arnside had been decorated by Wellington himself for valor on the field of battle. However, when he was ushered into the clutches of the dowager Lady Dunwood, he wanted to turn tail and run.

For a moment he recalled his childhood fear that she might eat him up.

When she was feeling affectionate, his Aunt Edith had a way of petting one with her fleshy, slightly moist hands that reminded him of the witch in the fairy tale who felt young Hansel's arm every day to see if he was plump enough yet for roasting.

"My dear boy!" she exclaimed, giving her nephew a playful tap on the arm that nearly staggered him.

Nicholas winced and told himself that as head of his family it was his duty to pay his respects to his widowed aunt, even though she treated him like a precocious ten-year-old when she wasn't making unreasonable demands on his time and his purse. Besides, he felt duty bound to make sure that Lady Diana and her son had arrived in England safely after they left Naples.

Lady Dunwood was entertaining two stout matrons, whom she introduced to him as Mrs. Ormsley and Lady Appleton, so at his aunt's invitation he reluctantly seated himself at the tea table with them and resigned himself to being shown off to Aunt Edith's friends as if he were a trained dog.

"How was your voyage, Nicholas?" his aunt asked majestically. "It must be so interesting to travel." Before he could answer, she added in a stage whisper for her friends' benefit, "Dear Nicholas has just returned from the continent."

After the ladies' expressions of polite interest had subsided, his aunt continued her one-sided conversation.

"Did you prosper in your errand, Nicholas? Did you manage to rescue dear Jane's son from that atmosphere of depravity? I have no opinion of artists."

"I found Bernard in good health, Aunt," Nicholas said mildly. Much as he disapproved of Bernard's choice of vocation, he had no intention of discussing the matter in front of nosy strangers.

"Poor Jane," Edith said with a sigh. "I feel for her most sincerely. It is a sad thing when one's children will not heed one's advice."

Nicholas braced himself. He knew that no matter what topic was introduced, his aunt eventually would turn the conversation to her favorite subject, that of ungrateful children. He had mentally dubbed this phenomenon Aunt Edith's Sharper Than a Serpent's Tooth speech.

"I begged my poor boy not to marry that shameless little jezebel," Edith continued bitterly, "but he wouldn't listen to his mother. If he had, he would be alive today."

"You've been so brave," said Mrs. Ormsley, pressing Edith's hand.

"No one knows what my poor boy suffered at the hands of that woman," said Edith, rendering Nicholas acutely uncomfortable. "My dears, if you knew the half of it! You can imagine my horror when I discovered that she not only practically *haunted* Vauxhall after her marriage, but she wore the most scandalous gowns. The *sheerest* fabric, my dears, and *dampened* into the bargain. She may as well have gone naked."

"Shameless," said Lady Appleton, her eyes bright with gleeful indignation.

The ladies' enjoyment was put to an abrupt end when Lady Diana herself entered the room. She was wearing a demure but excessively becoming violet muslin gown in concession to her status as a widow in half-mourning.

The awkward silence made it obvious that she had been the subject under discussion. She colored faintly.

"I beg your pardon," she said, addressing her mother-in-law. "I didn't know you had guests. Good afternoon, Lady Appleton. Mrs. Ormsley. I hope you had a pleasant crossing, Cousin Nicholas?"

He stood and took her hand.

"I did, thank you. I hope I find you well."

Her smile held something of wariness in it, and he was sorry for it. She probably was afraid he meant to give his aunt a sordid account of their meeting in Naples, which he certainly did not.

Diana turned to the others, who were rather loudly discussing the confections provided by the cook in a clumsy attempt to hide their backbiting.

"If you will excuse me, ladies," Diana said politely, about to retreat. It was plain she didn't expect an invitation to join them. "I apologize for the intrusion."

Just then the butler announced a visitor.

"Lord Banks, my lady," he said, tactfully making his announcement in such a way that he didn't commit himself as to which lady he considered his mistress.

"Robert," breathed Diana, her face radiant. When the handsome, red-haired giant entered the room, she rushed into his arms and he bent to kiss her cheek.

"Thank God you're here, Diana," he exclaimed. "My dear, I am so sorry I didn't meet your ship in Dover! Your letter had gone astray, and it only reached us in London yesterday. How did you and Stephen manage all alone? Will you ever forgive me?"

He broke off, apparently daunted by the sight of Edith, her friends and Nicholas regarding him with varying expressions of curiosity and disapproval. He raised his eyebrows.

"Lord Banks," Diana said for the benefit of her mother-in-law's guests, "is my brother-in-law. Robert, you have met my mother-in-law, Lady Dunwood. And these are our neighbors, Mrs. Ormsley and Lady Appleton. And Rupert's cousin, Lord Arnside.

"Robert, you worry too much about me," she said, turning back to her brother-in-law before the others barely had time to murmur a greeting. "Of course I managed on my own. I simply hired a carriage and came to Kent. You must tell me how Elizabeth goes on. She must be near her confinement. When you did not meet the ship, I naturally assumed—"

"No, not yet," he said, his anxiety showing for a moment.

"I am sure you will excuse us," Diana said without taking her eyes from Robert's face. "I would not *dream* of boring you with our family news."

Since the ladies were nearly hanging out of their chairs in their effort to overhear her conversation with Lord Banks, her bland statement was greeted with frowns of disappointment.

"You cannot know how glad I am to see you," Lady Diana went on vivaciously, taking Lord Banks's arm. "We must visit Stephen in the nursery."

Their voices faded as they left the room.

"Family business, indeed!" Edith scoffed. "They say he was quite madly in love with her, but she jilted him to marry poor Rupert. Lord Banks had not come into the title by then, of course, nor was he expected to. If he had, things might have been much different, more's the pity."

"They certainly appear to be on friendly terms now," Lady Appleton pointed out with a sly look.

"I wonder the minx can hold her head up for shame," Edith said venomously. "Did you see the way she *looked* at him?"

Nicholas had, indeed. He knew that if she ever looked at *him* that way, he would probably fall over a chair.

"Lord Banks married her elder sister, you know," Mrs. Ormsley said with a nasty little laugh. "A placid, soft-spoken creature. Pretty enough, but a mere nothing next to your son's wife. He's kept her buried in the country, breeding, ever since. Of course he only married her out of pique."

"I will never think of her as other than a murderess," Edith said vehemently to no one in particular.

Bitter experience told Nicholas that she was about to embark upon her usual melodramatic accusations against her daughter-in-law, and any attempt to change the subject would be futile.

He excused himself politely, pleading fatigue after his long journey. He passed the hallway leading to the nurseries in the east wing and grimaced, wondering if instead of visiting Lady Diana's son, she and her brother-in-law were trysting in a corner somewhere. He told himself sternly that it was none of his business.


Actually, at that moment Lord Banks was trying to convince Diana to return with him to London, where his family was residing at present, so his wife would be close to the fashionable accoucheur who'd delivered their firstborn.

"Please come," he said. "It would make Elizabeth so happy. Your mother will be with us for the confinement, and I am counting on you to keep me from wringing her neck."

"Robert!"

"She bullies my poor Elizabeth, and I won't have it," he said, his voice softening as it always did at the mention of his wife. "We need you, Diana."

"Don't, please. It is so tempting."

"Well, then—"

"No. I must stay to protect Stephen's rights. Rupert's uncle, Raymond Milton, is here."

"Is he?" Robert asked with a marked lack of enthusiasm.

"Yes. You did not see him because he is usually sleeping off his excesses at this hour," she said in disgust. "I cannot like the liberties he is taking with Stephen's inheritance. He keeps buying *horses,* and stocking the cellars with wine. I'm afraid if I take Stephen away, there will be no one to stop him from running through Stephen's entire fortune."

"But were there not two trustees?" Robert asked, his brows knit. "I seem to recall that Rupert also appointed his cousin—"

"Lord Arnside," Diana said grimly. "I am afraid that I can expect no help from that quarter."

Indeed, she had thought of asking Cousin Nicholas to intervene in Stephen's affairs, but after what happened in Naples he would hardly be inclined to take her word against that of her late husband's uncle.

Robert looked troubled.

"I wish I could do something to aid you, but—"

"I know," she said, placing her hand on Robert's arm in a gesture of reassurance. "You are not a trustee and there is nothing you can do. Perhaps I am worried about nothing."

"Diana—"

"Let us see Stephen," she said, forcing cheerfulness into her voice. "He is right through this door."

Diana dismissed the nursemaid who bobbed a curtsy upon their entrance into a lavishly furnished playroom.

Stephen regarded his large uncle with a startled look on his solemn little face. The child was leaning against the window seat and almost lost his precarious balance. Diana looked at him anxiously. He had started walking later than most children, and she had to clench her fists to keep from rushing to his aid every time it looked as if he might take a tumble.

"What a fine fellow you've become," said Robert heartily, seizing Stephen and jogging him playfully as he tossed him in his arms. The child burst into tears of fright. Diana gently removed him from Robert's arms and soothed him.

She knew Robert was properly chagrined. A devoted father, he prided himself on his way with children. Instead of responding to his roughhousing with squeals of laughter, Diana's small blond son fixed him with terrified blue eyes and pouting, trembling lips.

"My poor little man," Diana crooned as she gently swept a wispy strand of hair from her son's eyes. "Robert, I am at wit's end. Although he will come to me and sit on my lap and seems comforted by my presence, he hardly ever smiles. And he will not go willingly to anyone but me."

"Is he well?"

"He appears to be in good health. He is just so solemn."

"All the more reason to bring him and come home with me," Robert urged. "We'll soon have him in prime twig. Our Edward is only a year older. Perhaps he needs the company of another child."

"I dare not," said Diana wistfully.

"But why?"

Diana hesitated.

"I haven't told anyone else this," she said carefully, "but I am afraid my mother-in-law and Rupert's uncle will try to set aside Stephen's claim to Rupert's estate if I do not remain here to keep an eye on them."

"How is that possible?" asked Robert, puzzled. "Of course, Rupert's son will inherit . . ."

He broke off when he noted the look in Diana's eyes.

"When Stephen was born," she said, transferring her gaze to the floor, "she tried to convince Rupert that he was really fathered by one of Rupert's friends who had been a little too gallant in his attentions. Rupert refused to believe her."

"So I should hope! You *were* a madcap, love, but the idea that you would play Rupert false is preposterous!"

"Thank you, Robert," said Diana, touched by his outrage. "Sometimes it seems as if everyone is willing to believe the worst of me."

"Please come to London with me," he said. "We may not be perfect, but we love you."

"*Such* a clanker, dearest," she said, her eyes twinkling. "As if you didn't break my heart to marry Elizabeth."

"Nonsense! You were never in love with me in your life! You were the silliest chit, Diana. When I think of the way you nearly sabotaged my courtship of Elizabeth, I could box your ears."

"For your information, my lord," she said with spirit, "I shudder to think of the misery we both might have endured if you had returned my childish infatuation."

"True. I am much happier with my Elizabeth, and you will find someone else someday, Diana."

"Thank you," she said in humorous dismay. "What a delightful prospect—another mother-in-law!"

"Look, my dear. If there is anything I can do—"

"There is nothing," she said firmly, stepping to the doorway of an adjoining room and beckoning a nursemaid to whom she surrendered her nearly slumbering son with a final kiss on his head. "There, my precious. Go with Becky now, and have a lovely sleep."

"Will you stay to dine and spend the night?" she asked, guiding her brother-in-law toward the stairs.

"No, Diana. If I cannot convince you to accompany me, I must return to Elizabeth. I would not put it past your loving mother-in-law to poison me. That woman is a dragon."

"You are in no danger," she said bitterly. "If she poisons anyone, it will be me."

Robert stopped and solemnly took Diana's hand in his.

"I hate the thought of leaving you here. If you ever need me," he said earnestly, "just send word and I will come at once to fetch you."

"That is very kind, Robert," she said, touched.

"You *are* loved, you know," he told her. "Very much. Never forget it."

"Oh, Robert," she said, her eyes misting slightly. "Sometimes I feel so alone."

He gave her a brotherly hug, and Diana was still in his arms when Lord Arnside stepped into the hall from one of the guest bedchambers. He stopped dead when he saw them with their arms around one another.

"Pardon me," he said, smiling mechanically as he stepped around them.

Diana blushed scarlet.

"That odious man!" she fumed to Robert when he was out of sight. "By nightfall the entire household will think I am having a mad affair with you. No doubt he **will** go straightaway to darling Edith and tell her the whole!"

An hour later, Nicholas was sitting in the drawing room with his aunt, sipping sherry and waiting for the butler to announce dinner. Diana was late as usual, Edith pointed out.

"Probably primping for her precious brother-in-law," she grumbled.

"He has already left the house," Nicholas said. He had been

watching from a window when Lord Banks's closed carriage swept down the drive.

"Good riddance," Edith said. "I am glad she's late coming down to dinner because there is something I particularly wanted to discuss with you. I think the time has come for us to plan your marriage to Penelope Chalmers. The girl is nearly sixteen."

"Too young for marriage, surely," Nicholas said, taken aback.

"You know it was your father's wish that you marry Penelope. The girl herself expects it."

"She does? I have only met her a few times, and that when she was still a child," he said, remembering a tiny, shy young lady in stringy braids and an ill-fitting schoolgirl's uniform of navy blue bombazine. "She hasn't even been presented yet, has she?"

"Of course not," Edith exclaimed, obviously astonished by his naiveté. "There will be time enough for her to make her bow in society after she is safely married to you."

"I don't know much about schoolgirls, but is it not customary for them to have a season or two on the town before they settle down to marriage and children?"

"With her fortune, you might find yourself cut out altogether if she does," Edith warned him. "Her parents are dead, and her guardian knows the marriage was her father's wish, so there will be no difficulty in arranging things to suit yourself. And you will never have to blush for the manners of such a docile, well-bred girl."

"Aunt Edith, I was very young when my father and hers decided on the match. Penelope was a mere infant."

"You'll never tell me you mean to cry off!" Edith exclaimed in shocked disapproval. "She's my goddaughter!"

"No, of course not," he said, "but I do think it would be better for us to meet before any formal announcement is sent to the newspapers. I cannot like all this haste to rush the girl to the altar. We may not suit, after all."

"Not suit? Penelope's dowry is forty thousand pounds!" Edith fairly shrieked. "Would you deny your father's wish?"

"Of course not," he said, afraid he might have unwittingly touched off her Sharper Than a Serpent's Tooth speech. "But I can't think of anything worse than to be bound for the rest of my life to a lady who isn't suited to me."

"Nicholas, surely you aren't one of these sentimental young men who expect to find passion in marriage," she said in a tone of strong disapproval. "My son's marriage was a love match, at least on *his* part, and see how badly that turned out. The girl was *most* unsuitable. The daughter of an *actress!* And a hoyden into the bargain. To think he left her that *huge* jointure, as well as the town house! I'll never get over it."

Nicholas knew that losing the town house to Lady Diana had been a bitter blow for his aunt, who had counted on having the use of it for her lifetime. Everyone in the family knew that after Edith learned the Awful Truth about her son's will she became so acrimonious that she and her widowed daughter-in-law took residence in opposite wings of the manor, and they frequently threw the servants into varying states of confusion and despair by issuing a great many contradictory orders.

"Penelope is ideally suited to be the chatelaine of your estate in Surrey," Edith said, unexpectedly returning to the subject of Nicholas's marriage. "She has been brought up most carefully. I interviewed her teachers at her school in Bath thoroughly on your behalf, and I am very pleased with her progress. Her education is nearly complete."

"I still think sixteen is too young to marry," Nicholas said, although the prospect of marrying a docile, well-bred young lady was most appealing. Let other men look for fireworks in their marriages; after his turbulent years at war, he was ready for a little serenity in his life. "Perhaps if all goes well we may plan the wedding for next autumn."

"It would be better next spring. That would still give us several months to order brideclothes and—"

"Next fall, Aunt Edith. After the harvest," he said firmly. He had neglected his estate long enough, and he had long months ahead of him in learning the business of caring for the property. *"If* the girl and I agree we will suit."

"All right, my dear boy," Edith said, looking dissatisfied. "It will be as you wish."

Lady Diana and Raymond Milton arrived for dinner at the same moment, and Nicholas could see from Lady Diana's expression that she was less than comfortable in the older gentleman's company.

Mr. Milton, a clergyman who had resigned from his post in order to, as he put it, take the reins of his great-nephew's affairs into his hands, squeezed Lady Diana's arm in a most insinuating manner. She gave him an indignant stare and hastily took a stance as far away from him as possible.

"There you are, Nick, old man," said Mr. Milton heartily, shaking hands with Nicholas. "I am sorry I was not here to welcome you. I trust the servants have made you comfortable."

Nicholas raised his eyebrows at this familiarity. He hardly knew the man. Mr. Milton obviously had installed himself as lord of the manor, and Nicholas could hardly complain. Rupert had named Nicholas and his father's brother jointly as trustees for young Stephen, and Nicholas, who was still in the army at the time of his cousin's death, had been relieved to relinquish all responsibility for the boy and his inheritance into Mr. Milton's hands.

"We'll have some capital fishing, if you're agreeable," he added, as if humoring a ten-year-old. With a sigh, Nicholas reflected that Mr. Milton and the dowager had much in common.

Nicholas nodded politely as Mr. Milton and his aunt chattered on about commonplaces. Lady Diana, he noticed, confined herself to monosyllables and watched him warily, probably in fear that he would tell his aunt about Naples or that odd little scene he'd witnessed between her and Lord Banks.

She needn't have worried. Nicholas was busy thinking about his prospective marriage. If all went well with the spring planting, he could visit the girl in Bath then, dull as he always had found the rubbishing place. That would give them time to get acquainted before the wedding.

However, the following April he found that the Honorable

Miss Penelope Chalmers had a mind of her own, and the enterprising young lady had no intention of residing tamely in Bath until her affianced husband found the leisure to claim her.

# Five

*London*
*April, 1817*

"Just as I suspected," exclaimed Rosamunde Smeltzley accusingly as she was ushered into her daughter's parlor.

"Mother!" gasped Diana, letting her needlework drop to the floor. "Oh, I have missed you so much!"

Diana ran across the room and into her mother's arms.

"There, now, love," said Rosamunde. "I am delighted you have missed me, but that is no reason to crush my gown."

Diana stood back and blinked a little at the magnificence of the formal emerald green satin garment in question. Diana's mother had the same golden hair as her daughter—although its original color had been restored a bit by artificial means—and the same regal figure. Her eyes were just as blue as her daughter's, although a trifle more shrewd.

"Delightful," said Diana admiringly. "Mother, your dress is divine. Did you come to see me on the way to a party? I am much obliged to you."

"No, my dear. We are going to the opera and we haven't much time."

"But, Mama, you know I don't go out. I only came to London to—"

"—Get away from your odious mother-in-law, of course, my dear, but that is no reason to mope about in this *dispiriting* manner. When you wrote to tell me you were coming to London for a few days, I knew how it would be if I did not come along to give you a little push."

"I am just out of mourning, you know."

"Indeed?" said Rosamunde, lifting one delicate, artfully darkened brow. "If you say so, darling, but one couldn't tell it by your appearance."

"What can you mean?" asked Diana, looking down at her blue dress.

"That gown is at least two years out of date, child," said Rosamunde severely. *"No one* wears sleeves like that anymore. It is all very sad to lose one's husband, but one cannot let oneself go to *seed* simply because one is a widow. It is positively disloyal to Rupert's memory. You know how proud he was of your beauty. And, after all, he has been gone these two years, you know."

"But, Mama—"

"You must change at once or we shall be late for the opera. I have invited other guests, and it would be quite shockingly rude for me to keep them waiting."

"Yes, Mama," said Diana, suddenly delighted by the prospect of going out. "Oh, I am so happy to be with you again!"

"And I am happy to be with you," Rosamunde said absently. "On second thought, I will come up with you. I had better have a look at your wardrobe myself to see if you have anything suitable."

Diana bit her lip, torn between amusement and resentment of her mother's tactlessness.

An hour later, heads turned when Diana, resplendent in pink gauze and diamonds, entered the theater in her magnificent mother's wake.

"Ah, the ravishing Lady Diana has decided to come out of hiding," said Lord Arnside's host, who'd been one of London's most notorious rakes before he became a sober married man. "Perhaps the season won't be so dreary after all. But I'd forgotten. Weren't you related to the divine Diana's late husband?"

"Yes."

"I'll wager he died with a smile on his face," said the gleeful gentleman, digging Nicholas in the ribs.

If his companion had not made such inroads into an excellent bottle of port after dinner, he would not have missed Nicholas's icy stare.

Lady Diana's progress to her mother and stepfather's box was slow because of all the gentlemen who detained her for a greeting. Nicholas, for reasons he chose not to identify, could have recited the names of every one of the admirers who exchanged a word with her.

Diana remained seated in her mother's box during the interval, exchanging greetings with all her old cavaliers who came to pay their respects.

Her smile froze on her lips when she found Lord Arnside standing solemnly before her. It quite spoiled all her pleasure to have one of Rupert's disapproving relatives come around to make her feel as if she didn't have a perfect right to be here. If he *dared* cut her mother or stepfather, he would rue the day that he was born!

"Good evening, Lord Arnside," Diana said cautiously while his companion exchanged pleasantries with her mother.

"Lady Diana," Nicholas said, bowing over her hand. "You appear to be enjoying yourself."

His words were innocuous, but she didn't miss the faint disapproval in his voice. Typical. She knew from bitter experience that none of the top-lofty Riverses would single her out in public unless it was to offer criticism.

Well, she had to endure quite enough of that sort of thing from her mother-in-law!

"Rupert died more than two years ago, my lord," she said quietly, "and except for one unfortunate incident you witnessed a year ago, this is the first time I have been to an evening entertainment since his death."

"I did not mean to imply——" he began, looking chagrined.

"I am quite certain you *did,*" Diana persisted, although she kept her voice discreetly lowered. "I would be a simpleton not to know that you disapprove of me, Lord Arnside. I can only say you are the fustiest creature in existence if you can find fault with my attending the opera with my mother and step-father."

"Quite," he agreed, giving her a solemn bow. He probably would have moved on after that if Diana's mother had not taken a hand in the matter.

"Diana, my love," said Rosamunde, her eyes sparkling. "I see you are renewing your acquaintance with Lord Arnside. How delightful to see you, my lord."

"Charmed, ma'am," he said, bowing over her hand. "As usual, I find you in great beauty, Mrs. Smeltzley." He shook hands with Diana's stepfather. "If you will excuse me, I must return to my party."

"My dear," whispered Rosamunde slyly when he was gone. "How clever of you. I could not have chosen better myself."

"Whatever are you thinking of, Mama?" exclaimed Diana, startled.

"Keep your voice down, darling. Lord Arnside, of course. He's not the catch Rupert was, but I'm told he has a very pretty property in—"

"Mother, the man *loathes* me, just like all of Rupert's relations," Diana argued.

"Gammon. He couldn't take his eyes off of you. His attention was on this box from the moment we entered it. He's definitely interested."

"Well, I'm not!"

"If you knew how many caps had been set for him, you would be highly flattered, for he has the most charming manners—"

"I, for one, see nothing so marvelous about his manners," said Diana. "Furthermore, Mama, I'll have you know he is betrothed to a connection of my mother-in-law's with a fortune of forty thousand pounds, and they are to be married in the autumn. Edith has been cackling over it for months."

"That gives us six months in which to work," said the incorrigible Rosamunde, "and if you can't bring a man around your thumb in that length of time, you are no daughter of mine."

The performance began before Diana could do justice to her feelings, and she was obliged to stifle her indignation until they were at her town house.

"Don't fuss at your daughter, my love," said Mr. John Smeltzley as he lounged in the wing chair by the fireplace and sipped a glass of port.

Rosamunde frowned.

"I am not fussing, Mr. Smeltzley," she said. "I am merely pointing out to Diana that she is too young at one-and-twenty to resign herself to being a widow for the rest of her days."

"I agree with you completely, my dear," said Mr. Smeltzley, "but it would not be wonderful if she was so attached to her husband that she would resist replacing him so soon."

"Gammon," Rosamunde scoffed.

Her spouse let out a long, theatrical sigh. "I suppose this means that before I am even cold in my grave you'll be leading some other fortunate fellow down the aisle," he said mournfully.

"Certainly not," said Rosamunde, softening a little. "The cases are not the same. You are the only man to whom I wish to be married."

"Only because you can tour the capitals of Europe whenever you choose, making regular withdrawals from my bankers, and still be assured of a welcome when you return."

Diana flushed in embarrassment, although her stepfather uttered this cynical observation with a teasing smile on his face.

Rosamunde rose and dropped a light kiss on his receding hairline, a gesture so spontaneous that Diana's mouth nearly dropped open in surprise. In all of her life, Diana could not remember once seeing her mother kiss her father like this. Tears of resentment on that unappreciated gentleman's behalf briefly stung Diana's eyes. He had elevated Rosamunde to the peerage by making her a countess; she had relinquished this title to marry plain Mr. Smeltzley, a wealthy Cit, with indecent haste after he died.

"You have quite *ruined* me for all other men, and you know it, my love," Rosamunde said.

"Well, from what you've said of your first, that ain't exactly praising me to the skies!" was Mr. Smeltzley's tactless reply. He glanced at Diana apologetically as soon as the insensitive words were out of his mouth.

"Your pardon, Diana," he said. "It was a stupid remark."

"*Very* stupid. My father was a wonderful man and an excellent father," Diana said with steel in her voice.

This was dangerous territory indeed. Diana had tried so hard to accept her mother's obvious infatuation with her new husband, but she had loved her father dearly and had been shocked when her mother flew in the face of convention and remarried barely seven months after his death.

"Of course he was, darling," said Rosamunde, stepping into the breach. "Charles was loyal to me although I tried his patience abominably, and he gave me two wonderful children. It was my fault that we didn't deal well together. I realize that now. I hope you don't begrudge me my great happiness with Mr. Smeltzley."

"Of course not, Mama," Diana said, conscience-stricken. If anyone deserved to be happy in this life, it was Rosamunde. "I am very pleased for you."

"I know you are," Rosamunde said. "That is why I am so anxious for you to marry again. I want you to find the same happiness."

"Oh, Mama," Diana said in despair. She knew Rosamunde would not rest until she found her a new husband, even though it was the last thing Diana wanted.

At that moment they heard a knock on the outside door, and the butler, entering the room immediately afterward, cleared his throat ominously.

"Jasper?" Diana prompted.

The butler looked hesitantly at the Smeltzleys.

"I have no secrets from my mother and her husband," Diana told him.

"Very well, my lady. Miss Penelope Chalmers is demanding admittance at the front door, and she insists, my lady, that

Lady Dunwood must pay her fare, for she appears to be destitute."

"I will come at once," Diana said.

"Yes, my lady, if you please," the butler said, looking grateful.

Diana and her parents arrived at the scene of the melee to find a bedraggled young lady involved in a brangle with an alarmingly large and menacing man who was loudly demanding his fare immediately, or he would throw her bandboxes into the street.

"See here, my good man," said Mr. Smeltzley, gallantly coming to the lady's rescue. "What seems to be the trouble?"

"This here female, Your Honor, hired me to bring her to this house," the coachman explained indignantly, "and now she says she doesn't have the blunt to pay the fare. She said her godmother would pay for her, but this here butler says her godmother ain't here. So who is going to pay my fare, I'd like to know!"

"That is easily remedied," said Mr. Smeltzley. "How much does the young lady owe?"

At these magic words, the coachman became quite courteous and was even so obliging as to carry the young lady's bandboxes into the hall for her.

Lady Dunwood's uninvited guest was ushered into the parlor by Diana and Rosamunde, both of whom were quite astonished that the girl had arrived so late in the evening and without a chaperon.

"You probably do not remember me," she said to Diana, looking unsure of her welcome, "but I attended your wedding to Lord Dunwood."

"Of course I remember you, Miss Chalmers," Diana said, giving her a friendly smile. "How can I help you, my dear?"

Miss Chalmers had coppery curls and lovely green eyes beneath the dirt of her travel. Her shoulders were slumped with weariness.

"Please don't make me go back to Bath," she begged. "It's *horrid!* All the girls left at school are babies because all of my particular friends are making their come-outs *this* season, and I can't *bear* it if I have to wait until *next* season, when I'll already be married—"

"There, there," Diana said, patting the young lady's shoulder. "Don't cry. First you shall get out of those dusty clothes and have a nice cup of tea. Then we will decide what is to be done."

"You won't make me go back to Bath?" the girl asked anxiously.

"I have no authority to make you do anything, my dear," Diana said. She pulled the bell rope. When a footman answered, she directed him to send for her maid and bid her to wait upon Miss Chalmers. When the girl left the room with Bessie, Diana turned to her mother.

"What a remarkable coincidence," Diana said, amused. "Miss Chalmers is the young lady who is betrothed to Lord Arnside. He thinks she is residing patiently in Bath, waiting for him and my mother-in-law to settle her fate between them. She's an orphan, poor girl, with no family of her own to take her part."

Diana was sick to death of hearing Edith boast about her cleverness in procuring a demure, unspoiled bride of unexceptionable breeding and manners for her nephew, and she thought it unconscionable that they would rush the innocent young lady into marriage straight from the schoolroom for the sake of her precious forty thousand pounds.

The masterful Lord Arnside would be in for a rude shock when he discovered that his aunt's protégée was hardly the stereotypical shy Bath miss he had been led to expect.

It served him right for thinking he could ride roughshod over the girl, Diana thought with satisfaction.

"Oh, my dear," Rosamunde wailed mournfully. "What a *waste!*"

"Nonsense," said Diana, who knew exactly how her mother's mind worked. "I think Miss Chalmers is very pretty."

"Yes, for which we can only be thankful," Rosamunde said, "because it will make our task easier. We will simply find someone more suitable for her, which will leave the field open for you to have Lord Arnside."

"Mother, I beg of you to abandon this ridiculous scheme! It will not do, I assure you."

"Yes, it will, love," Rosamunde insisted. "We will be doing him a great favor, for that girl would lead him *such* a dance! Believe me, I know. I was just such a one when I married your father, and you know how miserable I made him. Only very *old* gentlemen have the patience to mold spirited young girls to their liking."

"Speaking of tiresome spouses, my dear," Mr. Smeltzley interjected mildly. "This has been most instructive, but I am very tired and must arise early tomorrow."

"Your stupid business, I suppose," Rosamunde said with a sigh.

"Yes, my love," he agreed, smiling at her. "The stupid business that allows you to dress so delightfully requires some attention on my part, I fear. Your arm, Rosamunde."

A slow smile spread over Rosamunde's face in answer to his, and she took his arm.

"Good night, my dear," Rosamunde said airily to her daughter. "Sleep well, and don't let that silly girl walk all over you. I know what a soft touch you are for small, helpless creatures."

"I am gratified by your confidence," Diana said as she hugged her mother and then, with less enthusiasm, her stepfather. "Thank you both for a lovely evening."

As the sun rose the next morning, so did the spirits of the lively Miss Penelope Chalmers.

"So you see," said that young lady, embarking upon her second piece of ham as Diana poured her another cup of tea, "I quite *had* to run away from school. I hoped Godmama would invite me to stay with her for the season, but it was no such thing. She wrote me the most odious letter telling me I was much too young to make my debut. She said she would sponsor me next year, after I am married. But all of my friends are at least as young as I am, so she is quite *wrong,* do you see, Diana?"

It hadn't taken them long to be on first-name terms. Diana

found her thoughts lingering pleasantly upon what fun it would be to take Penelope around to all the shops and how amusing it would be to see how the *ton* accepted her protégée.

Diana had made her own debut at sixteen and quite agreed it was the most poor-spirited thing imaginable to be forced to wait until one was married to a man *years* older than oneself to enjoy the pleasures of the city.

"Do you mean to say," asked Diana, caution asserting itself briefly, "that you didn't tell *anyone* you were leaving school?"

"Of course not! I didn't want anyone to stop me. I expected my godmama to be here, and I was confident that once she saw that I am quite grown-up, and not an immature schoolgirl at all, she would *want* to present me. But I dare say it has worked out for the best, because it would be even better if *you* would present me instead. You wouldn't mind, would you, Diana?"

This artless question was asked with such a note of uncertainty that Diana's heart turned over.

"Nothing would give me greater pleasure," Diana said regretfully, "but it would hardly be the thing, because I am no relation to you at all."

Penelope's face fell.

"However," added Diana, "I think the best scheme would be to write to your godmother and ask her to join us here. Then we can make plans for your debut. Surely, since you're already here, she won't refuse to present you."

Especially if Diana was willing to bear the cost, she added shrewdly to herself.

"Oh, Diana, thank you," Penelope exclaimed, impulsively throwing her arms around her benefactress.


Diana's carefully worded letter and Penelope's pleading one reached the dowager within the week, and she left for London immediately.

This was, despite the martyred tone of her return letter to the two ladies, no real sacrifice, since she sorely had missed the convenience of having a home in London at her disposal.

She was eager to install herself in Mount Street before her despised daughter-in-law could rescind the invitation.

Unfortunately, she tarried long enough to send Lord Arnside an impassioned, though cryptic, missive announcing that his future bride had somehow fallen under the influence of the Fatal Widow, who was about to corrupt his innocent blossom with her deadly charm and lead her into all sorts of shocking scrapes that would, Edith predicted, cause him much embarrassment in the eyes of his peers.

Nicholas, who received the announcement of these alarming tidings the day after he arrived at his estate in Surrey from London, had expected to spend the rest of the spring involved with his acres and was extremely annoyed by this disruption of his plans.

While he was not gullible enough to believe the half of his aunt's obscure assertions of Diana's perfidy in somehow luring Miss Chalmers to London in order to accomplish her ruin, he did agree that it was his responsibility to investigate the matter.

He shuddered to think of the mischief that awaited an unfledged chit in London with no other steadying influences than his extremely foolish aunt and his cousin's widow, who had been known to keep some very fast company in the early years of her marriage.

To his servants' surprise, a rather grim-faced Lord Arnside ordered his town clothes, which had only just been put away, packed immediately, and arrived at Diana's town house just in time for the hastily organized ball that would introduce his fiancée to society.

# Six

Lord Arnside's impeccable appearance in evening dress on that mild spring night gave no hint of his muddied and thoroughly exasperated arrival at his own town house after his betrothed's debut ball was in full swing.

As it was, he didn't arrive until Diana and his Aunt Edith, with the ebullient Penelope between them, had stopped receiving.

Diana caught her breath when she saw him pause for a moment in the doorway and scan the company with those dark, penetrating eyes. She had never seen him look so magnificent, so she was absurdly flattered when he walked straight to her side.

"Lord Arnside," she said, flashing her very best social smile when he released her hand. "What a wonderful surprise! After the invitations went out, we discovered you had left London. We sent another to you in Surrey, but we were afraid you wouldn't receive it in time to—"

"Never mind trying to turn me up sweet," he whispered under his breath in a tone that made a lie of the smile on his handsome face.

"I beg your pardon?" she said, wrinkling her brow.

"My aunt wrote to me as soon as she learned Penelope was in your house. I came from Surrey immediately, of course."

"Ah. Now I know why I am suspected of treachery," Diana said, smiling brightly. Like most ladies of her class, Diana was adept at putting on a social facade in a room full of people when what she really wished to do was box her companion's ears.

He had the grace to look sheepish.

"Well, her account was colorful, to say the least," he admitted. "It also was somewhat obscure, but I got the impression—"

"Never mind," she said hastily. "I don't think I want to hear it. Penelope is with that group by the French windows."

She took his arm and would have led him to his fiancée had he not exerted force to keep her in place. She looked up at him in surprise.

"Don't think you can dismiss me so easily," he said, as if he were addressing an obstinate child. "I am quite willing to hear your side of the affair. In fact, that's why I came."

"That, and to save Penelope from my evil clutches!"

"Now see here," he said impatiently. "I've tolerated quite enough of that fustian rubbish from my aunt. I came here in perfect civility to hear a round tale from you, my girl, and I want it now. In private."

Her chin lifted.

"Surely you aren't suggesting that I leave Penelope alone in the ballroom with no chaperon to watch her, my lord. Your aunt is in the salon drinking tea with her intimates."

"We'll have to talk here, then," he said, glancing in the direction of her gaze. "Which one is she? They all look alike in those insipid white dresses."

"My lord!" she exclaimed, shocked.

"Well, I haven't seen the girl in—I suppose she's the one with the gingery hair."

"Gingery *indeed,*" said Diana indignantly on behalf of her protégée, "when you can see that her hair is the most ravishing shade of—"

"On the whole she is much improved," he said exactly as if, Diana thought furiously, he were discussing a new acquisition to his stables.

Before she could give Arnside the set-down he so richly

deserved, several guests moved close enough to hear their conversation.

"You are to be congratulated, ma'am," Lord Arnside said, reassuming his polite social mask. "Quite a squeeze."

"So kind," she murmured.

Arnside glanced over to where Penelope was thoroughly enjoying being in the center of a court of scarlet uniforms. Diana had no difficulty interpreting the carefully bland look on his face.

"I don't blame you for being worried," Diana said with mock sympathy. "They look *so* dashing, and I'll wager not one of them is older than two-and-twenty. There is always the danger that a young lady of sixteen about to be shackled to a gentleman of your advanced years might decide to bestow her hand and her precious forty thousand pounds elsewhere."

"Oh, very good!" Lord Arnside said, his eyes glittering with amusement. "I am only six-and-twenty, Cousin. Hardly in my dotage."

"You astonish me, my lord!" Diana exclaimed. "I would have taken you for a *much* older man. One usually doesn't become fusty and opinionated until one is at *least* forty!"

Lord Arnside, Diana felt sure, would have retorted with something positively crushing if he had not seen his aunt approach him, wreathed in smiles.

With great presence of mind, he seized Diana by the waist and swept her into the waltz that was in progress.

"My lord!" Diana said breathlessly.

"Don't think I'm dancing with you because I want to." His voice was gruff. "I am just in no humor to deal with my aunt at present."

Because of her unusual height, their faces were very close. This was a new experience and not an unpleasant one for Nicholas, who was accustomed to dancing with smaller women and bending his neck uncomfortably to talk to them. Their steps matched perfectly.

"Very well," she said, her eyes grave. "Proceed."

"I beg your pardon?" he asked, returning her gaze.

"You had something you wished to say to me," she reminded him. "About Penelope, perhaps?"

"Oh, yes. Penelope." Gad. He had completely lost his train of thought when he looked into her eyes. Nicholas pulled himself together. "I thought it had been decided that Penelope would make her debut next season."

"Naturally, it would be expedient for you to have her safely married before she has an opportunity to meet any other gentlemen," Diana said dryly. "I don't suppose it would occur to you to consult Penelope's wishes."

"You make me sound like an unprincipled fortune hunter," he said, offended.

"Well, pardon me if I've misjudged you," Diana said, her voice dripping with sarcasm, "but I should think even a person of minimal sensitivity would see something a little high-handed about sentencing that poor girl to languish in Bath when all her friends are making their debuts this season."

"Are they?" he asked naively.

"Of *course* they are! The girl is sixteen years old!"

"Well, how should I know?" he demanded. "I don't know anything about girls."

"That is perfectly obvious," Diana said sweetly. "By the way, my lord, if you wish to avoid attracting the kind of notice which I know a pattern card of virtue such as yourself would deplore, I suggest that you loosen your hold on my waist."

"The orchestra is making such a shocking din, I can hardly hear you," he complained as he complied with her request. "Where did you find such excruciatingly awful musicians?"

"They were the best I could hire on such short notice."

Nicholas saw his aunt walk purposefully toward Penelope, whose innocent flirtation with the officers had become rather noisy. He abruptly took Diana's elbow and led her, protesting all the way, through the French doors and into the gardens.

He released her when they were alone in the semidarkness. The gardens were illuminated by prettily decorated lanterns on poles, and he could see other couples strolling romantically among the shrubbery.

"Aunt Edith can jolly well keep an eye on the girl while we have our conversation in peace," he said before Diana could give voice to her indignation.

"Very clever, my lord," she snapped. "The spectacle of you dragging me out to the gardens with that *murderous* look in your eye should keep the gossips occupied for the rest of the evening."

"Never mind that," he said impatiently. "We have more important things to discuss. You probably mean well, but I can't think of a more unsuitable chaperon for a young girl than you."

"You are referring to my shocking reputation, of course," she said with dangerously glittering eyes. "Look at that ballroom, my lord. You will find it occupied by all of the very highest sticklers and young people from families of the very *first* consequence. *They* don't find my company so repulsive that they cannot accept my hospitality."

"Yes. I never saw such a dull parcel of old tabbies in my life. You are to be congratulated, but—"

"You are never going to let me forget what happened in Naples, are you? I was wrong! I admitted it! As for my other crimes, I was only seventeen when I indulged in the pranks my mother-in-law never tires of prosing on and on about!"

"I never believe the half of what Aunt Edith—"

"And I am *not* having an affair with my brother-in-law!"

Nicholas blinked in astonishment at her defiant glare.

"Whatever are you talking about?" he asked mildly.

"I know what you thought when you saw Robert and me that day. I suppose your aunt was delighted when you told her—"

"I told her *nothing!*" he protested.

Diana was too furious to heed him.

"For your information, my lord, Robert has been as a brother to me these past several years, and only a person with a perfectly *foul* mind would—"

"That is enough!" he roared. He lowered his voice, biting off every syllable. "I was not throwing your shocking reputation in your face, so you may stop giving me a bear garden jaw."

"What did you mean, then?" she asked suspiciously.

"Only that you are much too young to take responsibility for a girl of Penelope's age. You and I both know that my aunt will not exert herself in the least for the girl, much as she likes to meddle in other people's affairs. And, apart from her laziness, I never have considered her understanding more than moderate. I still have no idea of how Penelope came to London. I don't see how you persuaded her guardian to countenance such a thing.

"Unless, of course," he added maliciously, "you *did* kidnap her."

"Is that what my mother-in-law said in her letter?" Diana's eyes gleamed with mischief.

"It was strongly implied."

"What nonsense! She ran away from school, of course. Any young woman of spirit would have done so."

"Good God," Nicholas said, shocked. "Alone?"

"Yes. She expected to find her godmother in London, and she hoped to persuade her to present her this season. What could I do? Throw her out on the street? Send her back to Bath? It would have been too cruel!"

Nicholas was stunned. So much for the biddable, well-behaved young lady Aunt Edith insisted would make him a perfect wife.

"Does her guardian even know she is in London?" he asked.

"Certainly. I informed him immediately and suggested that he make arrangements for her debut. He sent me an extremely uncivil letter saying that he has no intention of wasting his ward's money on a come-out when she is already in the way of being married."

"Does that mean Penelope's presentation is being franked by *you?*" he exclaimed, mortified.

"That hardly signifies," Diana said with a shrug. "I can

well afford it, and it has been rather pleasant to go to parties again after being so long in mourning."

"But this ball!"

"I would have done some entertaining anyway this season. Pray don't regard it."

"I don't suppose it occurred to my aunt that it is more her responsibility than yours to pay for Penelope's keep?"

"I assume that question was purely rhetorical, my lord?"

"Yes," Nicholas said with a sigh. "Aunt Edith is the most clutch-fisted person of my acquaintance."

"Well, she may have met her match in Penelope's guardian. Anyway, he said he will not expend a single penny for such extravagance, and he recommended that I send her back to school. He agreed, however, that she might stay in London provided I assume all financial responsibility for her, and her godmother continues to be her official sponsor."

"Generous of him," Nicholas said sardonically. "Send me a Dutch reckoning, then, and I will reimburse you for your expenses."

"I certainly will not! Really, Cousin Nicholas. There is no reason to cut up stiff over it. I wish I hadn't told you."

"You have been put to a shocking amount of inconvenience by having the girl foisted upon you," he said. "If I could take her off your hands, I would do so, but I can hardly house her under my roof. She would be well and truly compromised by such an arrangement."

"How vastly unfortunate," Diana murmured.

"Yes," he agreed as his imagination conjured up a hideous vision of his comfortable bachelor household disrupted by the antics of a lively schoolgirl and the meddling of his foolish aunt.

"However," he continued, "I think it would be best to make other arrangements for Penelope. With your permission, I will investigate the possibility of finding a respectable relative of either her own or mine to house her."

"All right, my lord," she said in a subdued voice.

"Is there something else?" he asked, lifting his eyebrows. He perceived that she did not look satisfied.

"I hope . . ." she began, then stopped, as if uncertain how to proceed.

"Such reticence is strangely unlike you," he said, amused.

"Very well, Cousin," she said indignantly. "I merely wanted to suggest that you go back into the ballroom and dance with your fiancée. Tell her how charming she looks. Try to behave as if she is a lovely young woman instead of a marker in a shrewd business transaction that will leave you in possession of her forty thousand pounds."

"I thank you, my lady, but I hardly need instruction from you on how to conduct a courtship," he said, annoyed that she apparently considered him an aging roué determined to take advantage of an inexperienced young girl.

"As you please, my lord," she said, "but I would remind you that Penelope is your future wife, not a badly disciplined horse. No one thinks yours is a love match, but there is no reason to make the girl feel like a chattel."

Then she turned her back on him and stalked back into the ballroom, unscrupulously depriving Nicholas of the last word. It was just as well, because for a moment he was speechless with indignation.

Of course he had intended to greet his future bride as soon as he had talked with Diana. He was, in fact, on his way to her side when he was accosted by his aunt.

"Nicholas!" she exclaimed dramatically as she clutched his arm.

"What is the matter, Aunt Edith?" he asked wearily.

"That *woman,* of course!"

Nicholas steeled himself to receive yet another impassioned catalog of Diana's iniquities only to find it was Diana's mother, and not Diana herself, who had offended the dowager this time.

"*Flaunting* herself as if she belonged here," she hissed, recounting her dismay upon discovering the wife of a Cit among the guests at her goddaughter's come-out ball. "What must people think?"

Nicholas, seeing that Diana was standing just behind his

aunt, tried in vain to silence her. But the damage had been done.

"They may think anything they choose, ma'am," Diana said quietly.

Edith turned, speechless for once. Several guests were staring openly.

"Further," Diana continued, "I will have you know, ma'am, that my mother will always be welcome at any gathering held in my home. Any of my guests who object to her presence may go straight to . . . shall we say, Kent?"

Edith flounced away with her cheeks burning, and Lady Diana watched her departure with ill-concealed satisfaction.

"I believe you were going to take Penelope a glass of lemonade," she said, turning to Nicholas with a challenge in her fine eyes.

"Very true, ma'am," he said. He fetched a glass of lemonade and sought out his fiancée.

He found her enjoying the attentions of a group of young men noisily clamoring for her hand in the next dance. The men grew silent and made way for him as he walked up to Penelope and handed her the lemonade.

"Thank you, my lord, for I am quite parched," Penelope said, recognizing him at once. She smiled shyly at him as the other claimants for her favor melted away.

She was happily conscious of envious feminine looks being cast in her direction.

Now, Penelope thought expectantly, he would ask her to dance and she would impress him with her grace and skill. He would tell her that she had grown into a beauty and he was proud of her.

Instead, he good-naturedly told her to drink up her lemonade like a good girl, deposited the empty glass on a table, and towed her to a chair.

Penelope felt deflated, but Nicholas didn't notice. His eyes were on Diana, who was enjoying a lively conversation with a wealthy earl who gossips claimed was in the market for a second wife.

"I beg your pardon?" he asked politely when Penelope addressed a remark to him.

"I asked if you wanted to dance with me," she said.

"Not now, my dear," he said very kindly. "We must decide what to do about you."

"*Do* about me, my lord? What do you mean?"

"We must find a better situation for you. You cannot continue to take advantage of Lady Diana's hospitality."

"Is that all?" she said, her blow clearing. "It is of no consequence, because Diana said she likes having me here."

"She was being polite," he said.

"No, she wasn't—"

"She was," he said, sounding exasperated. "Did you seriously believe that an attractive widow would choose to spend her first season out of mourning playing propriety for a debutante?"

"Yes, I did," said Penelope in a small, mortified voice.

Until now it had not occurred to Penelope that she might be imposing on her kind hostess. Diana had seemed delighted to have Penelope as her guest, but perhaps she *was* pretending in order to be polite. Penelope felt tears sting her eyes at the prospect of leaving the only person who had made her feel wanted since her parents died.

"Penelope, my dear, what is wrong?" asked Lord Arnside, his dark eyes puzzled. "It will be all right. You shall have your season under the aegis of a proper chaperon, I promise you. Is there anyone among your female relations who—"

"I don't think so," Penelope said. "They don't seem to like me much, although Aunt Helen once sent me a book for my birthday, and Cousin Claire used to visit me when I was a child and bring me chocolates."

"There you are, then. I'll call on both of those ladies without delay. Do you know their direction?"

"Cousin Claire is in India with her husband, who is an officer in the army, and Aunt Helen died two years ago."

"Oh, well. We shall find someone to answer the purpose," he said optimistically.

"Are you certain you wouldn't like to dance with me?" she asked wistfully.

"No, I thank you, my dear," he said kindly. "If I may give you a hint, it isn't quite the thing to ask a gentleman to dance, you know."

"I thought since we were to be married it might be permissible," she ventured.

He must have sensed her disappointment, because he smiled and offered her his hand.

She brightened and went happily with him to dance the country dance that was just forming. He was an excellent dancer, but Penelope got the impression that he didn't enjoy it much. When the dance was over, he led her to a chair and exchanged stilted commonplaces with her until the precise moment he could leave without giving offense.

"It is late," he said, rising. He took Penelope's hand and kissed it. "I must go, my dear, for I have much to do tomorrow. I will see you again soon."

"Goodbye, my lord," she said gravely.

He smiled and flicked her cheek carelessly with his forefinger.

"I suppose you know you have grown excessively pretty since I saw you last," he said.

"Thank you, my lord," she said, smiling hopefully.

When he had gone, Diana walked up to Penelope and put a maternal arm around her.

"Tired, Penelope?"

"A little," she said, forcing a smile to her lips.

"Well, are you enjoying your debut ball, my dear?"

"Oh, yes," Penelope said gravely. "I honestly didn't mean to impose on you."

"Impose on me? What nonsense is this?" she asked, surprised. Then her brow cleared. "You've been talking to Lord Arnside, and he has told you that you are under a crushing obligation to me! Don't let him cast you into the mopes. I enjoyed having the ball very much. What else did he say to put your nose out of joint?"

"He said I had grown excessively pretty since he saw me last," said Penelope, sounding wistful.

"There, you see?" Diana said, sounding pleased. She put her hand on Penelope's shoulder. "I know he seems a bit stiff at times, but he'll come about. And he'll make you an excellent husband once he realizes you are no longer a little girl. Surely seeing you tonight has opened his eyes."

Yes, thought Penelope. And it opened hers as well.

Her interlude of freedom would endure only until her affianced husband could find a jailer more to his liking. Until then, she vowed, she would enjoy the season to the fullest, even if she had to spend all the rest of her days in disgrace.

# Seven

"But, Mama! You've only just returned from Paris," Diana said in dismay when Rosamunde visited her the afternoon after the ball and informed her she was on the point of setting out on another journey.

"I know, darling, and if I'd known dear Elizabeth meant to go to the continent so soon after my return, I would have stayed to meet her. Thank you, my love."

Rosamunde accepted a cup of tea and began to sip it with such an innocent expression on her face that Diana laughed.

"How *wicked* of you, Mama! You know very well Elizabeth and Robert are going on their honeymoon. You and Mr. Smeltzley will be very much in the way."

"Can you not bring yourself to call him Papa, my dear?" asked Rosamunde in heartrending accents, shamelessly evading the issue.

"Certainly not," Diana said crisply, "nor does he expect it. You won't get me off the track that easily. I think it the outside of enough that you have invited yourself to play gooseberry for Elizabeth and Robert."

"Nonsense. They have been married for years and years! If they wanted a wedding trip, why did they not take it four years ago?"

"Because the war made it impossible for *anyone* to go to the continent, as well you know, Mama. They *cannot* want you along."

"For your information, Elizabeth was quite delighted with the scheme when I told her—"

"And next you will tell me Robert is in transports," Diana said dryly. The mischievous twinkle in Rosamunde's eyes confirmed Diana's worst suspicions. "So *that's* it. You're doing this to annoy Robert! Of all the *spiteful*— "

"Don't be silly. How can you accuse me of setting out to encroach upon a romantic idyll when they are taking little Edward and Baby Susan along as well as Robert's sister, her husband and their three perfectly beastly sons?"

"Well, that does make quite a crush," Diana admitted.

"Why don't you go with us?" Rosamunde asked impulsively. "Of course you are vaporish, being so recently out of mourning. And Edith Milton's company would cast anyone into the mopes. Elizabeth would be so thrilled—"

"No, Mama. Don't tempt me. Of course I would love to go, but have you forgotten Penelope? She has nowhere else to go at present, and you couldn't be heartless enough to suggest that I send her back to Bath."

"Well, surely your mother-in-law can take charge of the chit," Rosamunde said indignantly. "I must say, I don't know why you should give up all your pleasure for a girl who is no relation to you—"

Diana silenced her mother with a gesture.

"There you are, Penelope," Diana said. "Come in, my dear."

Penelope entered the room with an uncertain look on her face. Her eyes were suspiciously bright and she swallowed painfully, as if her throat had a lump in it. Obviously, she had heard Rosamunde's careless words.

"I have the most wretched tongue," Rosamunde said ruefully. "Please forgive me, dear child."

"You are right, of course," Penelope said, sitting down near Diana. "If you wish to be rid of me, Diana, I will go."

"Nothing of the sort," Diana said. "My mother has been trying to persuade me to go to the continent with her, but I have explained that I could not abandon you to my mother-in-law's care. Furthermore, I have no desire to subject Stephen to such racketing about, and I would not go without him."

"Are you going to *Paris,* ma'am?" Penelope asked Rosamunde with reverence in her voice.

"Yes, and Brussels and Madrid and Rome and—I have the most brilliant idea! Why don't *you* go with us, Penelope? Then Diana needn't stay behind, and it would be *good* for Stephen to get to know his cousins—"

"Mother! Of all the improper notions! We could not take Penelope out of the country! It would be tantamount to kidnapping! Her guardian would never allow it, and her godmother and her fiancé would make the most *appalling* fuss. I'm sorry, darling," Diana said, patting Penelope's hand.

Penelope looked so wistful that Diana could quite cheerfully have strangled her mother at that moment. But before anything else could be said about the matter, Edith entered the room, obviously unaware it was in use, and rather stiffly accepted a halfhearted invitation to join the party since it would have been awkward to retreat.

They were casting about in vain for a topic of conversation when they were interrupted by Diana's butler.

"Lady Banks, my lady," intoned Jasper, standing aside to admit a tiny, fashionably dressed young matron with glowing chestnut curls and a mischievous twinkle in her blue eyes along with two small children.

Elizabeth wasn't a beauty like her mother and sister. Childbearing had slightly thickened her formerly ethereal figure, and her features, while pleasant, lacked the classical perfection of Rosamunde's and Diana's. But on the strength of her charm and kindness she was universally described as a very pretty, agreeable young woman.

"Elizabeth!" exclaimed Diana when her sister stepped into her fond embrace. "And Edward and Susan!" She bent to hug her one-year-old niece and three-year-old nephew.

"Good afternoon, love," said Elizabeth, returning Diana's embrace. "How delightful you look. Is that a new gown?"

"Yes. Mother insisted that I replenish my wardrobe," Diana said, laughing. "She said I was a disgrace to her."

"That you were, dearest," Rosamunde said, hugging Elizabeth in her turn.

"How is Stephen?" Elizabeth asked.

"Very well, thank you. I will have nurse bring him down," Diana said, pulling the bell rope.

A few minutes later, the ruler of the nursery brought two-year-old Stephen to visit with his cousins. Lord Dunwood was precise to a pin in his spotless little blue suit, frilled shirt and soft kid slippers. He looked daunted by the sight of so many adults.

Edward, who was precocious for his age, walked over to his cousin and offered to shake hands like a little man as his mother looked on proudly. Stephen stared at him with frightened eyes. Edward gave a little sniff of contempt and went to join his mother on the sofa.

"I don't want to play with stupid old Stephen," he announced.

"Edward!" exclaimed Elizabeth, mortified. She met her sister's eyes guiltily.

Stephen, instinctively reacting to the uncomfortable atmosphere in the room, began sniveling softly. Diana held him on her lap and soothed him.

"Diana, I am so sorry," Elizabeth said, her face pink with embarrassment. Penelope looked at Diana with an apprehensive look on her face.

"It's all right, Elizabeth," Diana said in a constrained voice after a moment.

Edward, knowing he was in disgrace, sat close to his grandmother Rosamunde for comfort and looked at his mother with repentant eyes.

"Children are always honest," Edith said with thinly veiled satisfaction. "You can hardly blame the boy for speaking the truth."

"I think it's time we took our leave," said Rosamunde, giving Edith a look that should have burned her to cinders. "Goodbye, Diana darling. Shall I bring you a beaded reticule from Paris? Or a lace mantilla from Spain?"

"Either would be lovely, Mama," said Diana, smiling valiantly.

When she hugged Elizabeth and kissed her cheek, Diana whispered, "You are not to punish Edward, mind!"

"We shall see what his father has to say about that," said Elizabeth ominously, glaring with uncharacteristic ferocity at her cherished firstborn.

After Diana had kissed the children, Elizabeth and Rosamunde found themselves on the sidewalk and heaved a sigh of relief.

"Lord, the atmosphere in that house!" Rosamunde said furiously. "I could kill that bitch!"

"Mama! The children!" With a reproachful look at her mother, Elizabeth looked down quickly to see if Edward, who had learned to talk early and eagerly added to his vocabulary at every opportunity, was listening.

He was, of course. His bright, intelligent, little blue eyes were thoughtful. Elizabeth sighed.

"Not that I don't agree with you about Diana's precious mother-in-law," Elizabeth said. "Oh, I was ready to sink! And that horrible woman positively enjoyed it! Did you see the look on Diana's face? I could cry."

"Well, I hope you won't," her mother said hastily. "If there's anything I can't abide, it's a watering pot!"

"It's plain to see that Edith Milton does not dote on her only grandchild," Elizabeth said, her voice stiff with disapproval.

"Obviously," Rosamunde said dryly. "She is forever telling Diana that if Stephen is backward it is Diana's fault because she abandoned him as a baby while she went to Greece with Rupert."

"Oh! How *unprincipled* of her, when she must know that Diana suffered *agonies* of remorse over leaving her child for so long. Everyone knows Diana went to Greece because Rupert insisted!"

"Everyone but his mother, it seems. She believes that Rupert would have lived to a hoary old age if he had remained in England."

"How uncomfortable it must be to live in that house," said Elizabeth with an eloquent shudder.

"You mark my words," Rosamunde said bitterly. "No matter how uncomfortable it becomes, Edith Milton won't have the decency to leave so long as she may continue to enjoy a good London address during the season at no expense to herself. She wanted Diana to pack Stephen off to Kent with his nurse because, if you please, it is too disruptive to have a child in the household when there is so much entertaining to be done in connection with Miss Chalmers's debut."

"How *dare* she call Stephen disruptive!" exclaimed the child's loyal aunt. "That is the most shocking lie! I have never in my life seen such a quiet, meek little boy."

"Yes," Rosamunde said sadly. "It is most dispiriting."

After Elizabeth and Rosamunde left, Diana gave Stephen a quick hug and then set him down on the floor. Diana's heart turned over at the trusting way he looked up at her. He was her whole world.

"My precious," Diana crooned lovingly. "You look so sweet in your new suit. You may have some milk and cakes, and then you may be comfortable."

She gave him the promised treats over his grandmother's objections that they probably would make him restive. As if Stephen were *ever* anything but good as gold.

When Penelope and Edith left on an excursion, Diana took her son to the playroom. It was there that Lord Arnside found them when he came to call.

"Good afternoon, Cousin Nicholas," Lady Diana said, looking self-conscious. She had been on the floor rolling a ball toward her son, and her narrow skirt made it a trifle difficult for her to rise with any semblance of grace. Arnside took her hand and pulled her to her feet, saving her from an undignified struggle.

"What is wrong?" Nicholas asked, startled by the sad expression on her face. Her eyes were suspiciously swollen and there was the suggestion of a tear drying on her smooth cheek.

"Nothing at all," she said, managing to smile. She turned

to her son. "Here is Cousin Nicholas come to visit us, darling."

"Good afternoon, Cousin," Nicholas said politely as young Stephen just stared at him. He was a thin, solemn child with wispy blond hair and his mother's big blue eyes. Nicholas smiled at Diana. "I see I should not have come up to you unannounced. I beg your pardon. Jasper was occupied elsewhere, and one of the footmen showed me up here—"

"It is of no consequence. I would rather not send Stephen back to the nursery just yet," she began hesitantly, indicating the ball on the floor.

"No. Of course not," said Nicholas, smiling at Stephen in a friendly manner. "I never have approved of the social convention that dictates one's children must be kept out of sight when visitors are present."

She looked at him in surprise.

"Cousin Nicholas," she asked, "do you *like* children?"

"What a peculiar idea you must have of me," he replied quizzically. "Of course I like children. It would be an odd thing to contemplate matrimony if I did not."

"Very true," Diana said, as if fascinated by this insight into his character.

"I did have something rather particular to discuss with you, but I suppose it will keep," he said pleasantly. "Penelope isn't somewhere about, is she?"

"No. She went with her godmother to call on some acquaintances."

"I see. Well, then. Don't let me interrupt your game."

"It isn't a *game*, precisely," she said. "I just roll the ball to him. You may join us, if you wish."

"Maybe I'll just watch for a little while to get the idea," he said, curious to see how Lady Diana would play with her son. He had assumed that she was one of those society mothers who leave the care of their children to a competent staff of nursemaids, but it appeared that Lady Diana took a more active role in her child's upbringing. Otherwise, she would hardly be lolling about on the floor with her son when there was no audience to impress with her maternal devotion.

"All right, then," Diana said, taking a deep breath. "Here we go."

She lowered herself to sit on the floor, which wasn't easy because of her narrow skirt, and she rolled the ball very gently to Stephen. The child gravely watched it approach, then took himself out of the way when it was about to touch him. He watched the ball roll to a stop, then looked at his mother questioningly.

Diana gave a moan of frustration.

"Stephen, darling. You are supposed to catch the ball and roll it back to me," she said. The child merely looked confused.

"It's no use," she said, turning helplessly to Nicholas. "He does not understand."

"No," he agreed. "I don't think he does. Forgive me, but is it so important?"

"Of *course* it is important," she said, as she scooted on her bottom to her child and took him into her arms. "My poor darling, what have I *done* to you?"

To Nicholas's dismay, a tear coursed down her cheek. Stephen, as if sensing his mother's distress, began to pat her head, spoiling the elegant arrangement of her golden curls.

"Lady Diana, whatever is the matter?" Nicholas asked.

"I am being silly," she said, wiping her eye with the back of her hand and setting her son on the floor beside her. "Mother tells me it is of no consequence, but he's so *quiet*. He rarely smiles, and he *never* laughs. And he doesn't make noise or get into scrapes like other little boys. He doesn't even get *dirty!* I have the most lowering thought that the nursemaids despise him. What can be done with him? Do you suppose he's . . ."

The word she was about to utter apparently was so frightening that she left the sentence hang, but Nicholas had no difficulty in deciphering her meaning.

"No," he said thoughtfully as he regarded the child, who returned his look with frank curiosity. "I don't think he is mentally deficient, or anything of that nature. His eyes are clear and intelligent."

"He was such a fat, happy baby," Diana sniffed. "I can't

understand it. It's all my fault for leaving him when he was a baby—"

"Now, who could have put such a ridiculous idea into your head?" he asked wryly. "My aunt, of course. It's all nonsense. He'll be a normal, clattering boy before you know it."

"How would you know?" Diana asked, looking hopeful.

"I just know," he said. "Let's try something else."

He approached the child slowly and held out his hand as if there were all the time in the world for the child to respond. Stephen, curiosity plain in his eyes, put his own into it. Arnside lowered himself to the floor, heedless of his spotless nankeen pantaloons, and Stephen allowed himself to be settled in the gentleman's lap.

"You handle him so well," Diana marveled. "Stephen usually won't go to men. In fact, he cries whenever my brother-in-law approaches. Robert *will* toss him in the air in the belief that all little boys like to be jostled, and it always reduces poor Stephen to tears."

"He probably doesn't see many men in the common way except for the servants," Nicholas said, careful to keep his voice calm and make no sudden movements. "There, now. He seems quite content. You might give the ball a little push this way."

Diana took the ball into her hands and was about to launch it when Nicholas laughed out loud.

"My good girl, do try to look a little less as if the survival of the world depends on this," he said.

Diana smiled ruefully.

"That's better," he said, patting Stephen on the head when the boy looked up into his face.

She rolled the ball, and Nicholas caught it to send it spinning back to her. She caught it and sent it back.

They continued in this manner for several minutes before Stephen, who had been watching carefully, put out a hand and attempted to stop the ball himself.

"Good boy," Nicholas said approvingly. The child smiled, and Nicholas looked to Diana in triumph.

With a mischievous grin, Diana sent the ball spinning out

of control so Nicholas was constrained to scoot after it with Stephen clasped under one arm like a piglet going to market.

"Well, my lady," Nicholas said with lifted eyebrows. "Two can play at that game."

Before long they were batting the ball back and forth at each other recklessly, but broke off at an unfamiliar sound. Stephen was making a peculiar gurgling noise.

"Oh, Nicholas! I think he's laughing," Diana cried joyfully.

"It's a start, anyway," Nicholas said, grinning at the child. "Well, the poor little fellow hasn't heard much laughter with that old Tartar of a nurse minding him. She's the same one that Rupert had as a child, unless I miss my guess, and she scared me witless when I came to visit."

Diana regarded him in dismay.

"Are you saying she is an improper person to be in charge of him?" she asked anxiously. "Rupert and his mother were so insistent that we retain her for Stephen that I—"

"No, of course not," he said. "I wouldn't be surprised if she dotes on the boy in her own gruff way. But she's not exactly full of mirth."

"My poor child," Diana said, looking at her son with concern in her eyes.

"You worry too much," Nicholas said, trying not to smile. "I was an only child, just like Stephen, and I had a stern nurse, too. I was just as quiet as he is, and no one has accused me of being queer in my attic."

"Are you saying that just to make me feel better?" Diana asked, obviously wanting to believe.

"Certainly not. My mother died when I was born, and my father was never one for infants, so I was very quiet as a child. But that changed when I was sent to school and had to hold my own with the other boys."

"You could not possibly have been *this* quiet."

"I rather think I was," he said, returning Stephen's solemn regard with a little smile on his face. "I utterly disgraced myself when my cousin Horace came to visit. I was a little older than Stephen. Horace took one look at me, knew me for a paltry fellow, and knocked me down. I cried loudly enough to raise the dead, and I was in my father's black books for days because Horace is younger than I, and of course he was much smaller—"

Nicholas had been looking at Stephen, who was all but asleep in his lap, but he broke off when he happened to glance at Diana to see whether she was entertained or bored by this narrative.

"My good girl," he said softly. "Kindly take that expression off your face."

"What do you mean?" she asked, her beautiful eyes melting with compassion for that poor, lonely, misunderstood little boy.

"You know very well what I mean," he said a little harshly. How embarrassing. He had meant it to be an amusing story, but the tenderhearted Diana had unerringly detected his long-buried feelings of shame and betrayal. "I only told you all that ancient history so you would be less anxious about the boy. Shall I carry him to bed? He's asleep now."

"If you please, Cousin," she said, leading him to Stephen's room, where a nursemaid was putting away linen under the supervision of the head nurse. The elder woman rushed to meet them, muttering complaints that the child would not close his eyes all night if he was to have a nap so late in the afternoon. Nicholas ignored her and laid the child on his narrow bed.

Diana self-consciously tried to pull her disheveled hair into some semblance of order as they went downstairs and into the drawing room. When they were seated on opposite sides of the room, she turned to Nicholas.

"I forgot until this moment that you wanted to discuss something with me," she said.

"Yes," he said ruefully. "I am embarrassed to admit that, although I rather unhandsomely insisted that my fiancée be removed from your home without delay, I must ask you to keep her a while longer."

"I should be glad to do so," Diana said with a twinkle in her eyes. "Could it be that it was not quite so simple to find someone to take her as you had imagined?"

"You may well say so," he said grimly. "Not one of my

female relatives is willing to undertake the task of chaperoning Penelope this season. And Penelope's own relatives are quite adamant in their refusal to do so. It seems Penelope was quite headstrong as a child, and although none of them have seen her for many years, they are convinced that living with her would be very uncomfortable."

"How very unfair, when she is the most delightful girl!"

"I am relieved that you think so. Even so, it is most generous of you to house Penelope when it means you must house Aunt Edith as well. I am at a loss to understand why you continue to do so."

"Well, I feel very sorry for her," Diana admitted. "I had a *splendid* come-out when I was her age, and I enjoyed it so much. It seems a pity that such a pretty girl should have to do without. And one would think it would be unnecessary, considering that her fortune is quite handsome."

"True. But, as you found out for yourself, her guardian is an elderly bachelor who lives in the country and takes very little interest in the girl. He is almost as clutch-fisted with her fortune as he is with his own, and he's the one who holds the purse strings. I'll visit him next week to see if I can make him see reason. If not, I insist upon reimbursing you for your expenses until I can make other arrangements for her."

"It would hardly be proper for you to support Penelope before your marriage!"

"Possibly not," he agreed, "but I cannot imagine why *you* should be expected to do so."

"We have been over this ground before, Cousin," Diana said firmly. "And I've already told you that the paltry expense of housing Penelope doesn't signify in the least."

"And *I've* told *you*— "

The conversation was interrupted by Edith and Penelope, who had just come in from their outing in the park, so this topic had to be abandoned.

Diana felt very self-conscious about her tangled hair and wrinkled gown under her mother-in-law's steely eye. Edith's eyes left their slow inspection of Diana to rest suggestively on Lord Arnside's crumpled neckcloth. Her gaze narrowed, and both of her victims flushed guiltily, even though they were innocent of wrongdoing. Edith gave Penelope a penetrating look, obviously eager to see what the girl made of their disordered state.

Despite Edith's evident suspicions of improper behavior between her daughter-in-law and nephew, the gentleman's fiancée herself apparently saw no particular significance in their untidiness. Penelope was too intent upon giving Diana an account of whom she had seen in the park.

"I met a friend of yours," Penelope said. "She is coming to call tomorrow."

"How nice! Who is she?"

"A Mrs. Benningham. She was wearing the most *ravishing*—have I said something wrong?"

"No. Certainly not," said Diana, quailing a little under the disapproval in Lord Arnside's eyes. "That is, we are very busy tomorrow, so I am not certain—"

"I should think," Edith said haughtily, "that even *you* would draw the line at considering *that creature* a fit acquaintance for a young girl. We all know how disastrous her friendship has been for *you,* Diana."

"Perhaps," Diana replied, matching her tone, "but when Rupert died, Caroline Benningham was the only one of my many, many London friends who took the time to write to me during my year of mourning. And when my year of half-mourning began, she invited me to go to Italy with her because she was afraid I was lonely."

"Bent on mischief, probably," Edith sniffed.

Diana flushed slightly and glanced at Lord Arnside, but, mercifully, Penelope had claimed his attention and he hadn't heard Edith's remark.

The party broke up on this uncomfortable note. Lord Arnside took his leave to see if his eloquence would move the flinty heart of Penelope's guardian, and Edith went to her boudoir for a short nap to recruit her strength for dinner. That left Diana and Penelope alone to plan their *toilettes,* for they were going to a *ton* party that night.

"Is Mrs. Benningham an improper person for me to know?" Penelope asked innocently. "She was so droll."

"Caroline is a good friend of mine," Diana said carefully, "but the high sticklers consider her fast, so I suppose she would be considered an undesirable companion for a girl just finding her feet in society."

"Such *stuff*," said Penelope. "If she's a friend of yours, I don't care *who* says she's an unfit person for me to know."

"I am much obliged to you, my dear," Diana said, uncertain how to explain that although Caroline was her friend, she didn't think her a desirable intimate for her protégée.

Diana had been strongly attracted to Penelope from the first because the girl reminded her so much of herself at that age. Penelope was ripe for any adventure, and, although her manners were all one could wish in company, it wouldn't take much to lead her into a scrape.

She shuddered to think what would happen if the outrageous Caroline Benningham decided to take the impressionable Penelope Chalmers under her wing.

# Eight

Lord Arnside returned to London from his visit to Penelope's guardian at well past nine o'clock, but he was so eager to share his news with the ladies in Mount Street that he didn't think they would mind receiving a visitor at such an advanced hour.

He found, to his surprise, that Lady Diana's town coach was drawn up at the door, and Diana herself was about to step inside. She didn't look pleased to see him.

"Cousin Nicholas," she gasped when he greeted her.

"I did not mean to startle you," he said apologetically. "Are Penelope and Aunt Edith in the coach?"

"No," she said, watching him warily.

"Are they in the house, then?"

"No. They're not. Penelope is . . . visiting friends. Lady Dunwood is attending a card party."

She broke off as Nicholas removed the black garment from her hands.

"A domino," he said, his eyes taking in the magnificence of her white spangled ball gown and the mask dangling from her fingers by its strings. "Are you going to a masquerade?"

Nicholas became aware that a man was sitting inside the coach. He looked questioningly at Diana, surprised she hadn't introduced her companion to him right away. Lady Diana, Nicholas reminded himself firmly, had a perfect right to go anywhere she wished with whomever she pleased as long as she was discreet. Her plans for the evening were none of his business. His feelings of annoyance and disappointment were *entirely* inappropriate.

She took a deep breath. "Lord Arnside, this is—"

The man inside didn't say a word, although Arnside saw him shift position in the glare of the carriage lights.

"Come down, Gaskin," Diana said with a sign of resignation.

"Yes, Your Ladyship," said the man, descending from the coach with alacrity. He was a tall, gangling creature whom Diana apparently had tried without much success to turn into the image of a gentleman. A black domino draped his lanky frame. The poor man seemed embarrassed.

"I know your schemes are none of my concern, Lady Diana," Nicholas said after a short, pregnant silence, "but it occurs to me that I might be of some assistance to you."

Diana hesitated. Then she seemed to come to some decision.

"Now that Lord Arnside is here, I won't need your assistance, Gaskin," she said. "You may give him the domino and mask. Mind you, I will be most displeased if you say a *word* about this—"

"No fear, Your Ladyship," Gaskin said in relief as he stepped down. Nicholas recognized his face now; he was one of Diana's footmen.

"I have the most lively sense of foreboding about this," Nicholas said conversationally. "How may I help you, Cousin?"

"There is no time to be lost," she said, giving him a nudge that was far from gentle.

He assisted her into the coach, followed her inside and signaled the footman to shut the door. When the coach was in motion, Nicholas turned to Diana.

"Where are we going?" he asked, sprawling comfortably on the seat across from her.

"It's Penelope," she said, making a clean breast of it. "She went to a public masquerade. At least, that's what I think happened. I was going to look for her."

Nicholas stared at her in silence for a moment.

"She will be ruined."

"Not if we're quick enough," Diana said. "She is such an innocent that I'm sure she had no idea it would be so improper—"

"She must have had some idea the scheme would not meet with your approval, or I would doubt she would have found it necessary to sneak from the house. Or did she?"

"Of course she did," Diana said, stung. "Do you think I would have allowed her to do such a thing? She said she was going with Lieutenant Ramsey, his sister and his aunt, a most respectable elderly lady, to a musicale. I should have *known!*"

"Should you? Why are you so certain she did not go to the musicale?"

"I had two dominoes, this black one and a red one. The red one is missing. I wouldn't have noticed, except that my maid asked me tonight what had become of it. She was putting some of my shawls away and saw it was not with the other."

"That does sound incriminating," he said.

"There is a public masquerade tonight," Diana said. "I should have known this would happen after I overheard the lieutenant telling her about a masquerade he attended. He is afflicted with the most painful case of calf-love I've ever seen. She could talk him into anything, and I *know* she talked him into taking her to this masquerade."

"I am perfectly willing to rescue her," he said, "but she probably won't be grateful."

"No. I hoped I could find her and bring her back before it came to your ears. Try not to think badly of her. Remember, she's so young—"

"All the more reason she should have been left at school instead of being thrust into society before she was mature enough to avoid getting into one scrape after another."

Diana looked indignant, but he interrupted her before she could give voice to her emotions.

"Don't bother telling me what a high-handed, insensitive beast you think I am," he said. "You've already made that perfectly clear."

"I must say, you are taking this rather well," Diana conceded.

"Praise indeed!" he said sardonically.

Masks in place, they arrived at the hall after the masquerade was in full swing.

Once inside, Diana screamed when a hairy hand reached out and grabbed her arm. Nicholas competently dealt with the hairy hand and pulled Diana closer to his side.

"How vexatious it must be to be irresistible," he murmured.

She glared at him.

"There is a girl in a red domino," she said hopefully.

"No. Too tall," he said. "That one by the window looks about right."

They made their way to the girl by the window only to be disappointed. The lady's escort was inclined to take offense at their inspection of his companion, and they beat a hasty retreat.

"My relations won't thank you, my lady, if you manage to get me killed in a brawl," he whispered.

"Hypocrite," Diana said, giving him a shrewd look. "You are *enjoying* this."

"It is rather a change from my usual pursuits."

A masked, dark-haired woman suddenly took Diana's arm. Nicholas hastily put himself between them.

"Good God! It's Lord Arnside," Caroline hissed. "Why on earth did you bring *him,* Diana?"

"Where do *you* fit into this coil?" asked Nicholas. He recognized Mrs. Benningham's voice at once.

"I assume you are here to find Miss Chalmers. I have her safe in a private room, and I was about to take her home to you once I found someone to call my coach."

"Thank heavens!" Diana said in relief. "Caroline, you are an *angel!*"

"She is just through that door on the right," she said, brushing aside Diana's gratitude. "Try not to scold her too much, my lord. She was as sorry as she could be when I explained how wrong it was for her to be here. Some rough customer tried to drag her into the garden by her hair, and that precious lieutenant of hers was so foxed he would have let him."

"She must have been frightened half to death!" Diana exclaimed.

"I should think so! She set up a screech you could hear all over the place."

Nicholas began striding purposefully in the direction of Penelope's hiding place. Diana would have followed if she had not been accosted by a man in a black domino who twitched her mask off and held it behind him when she tried to snatch it back.

"What a pleasant surprise," he said in his deep, melodious, slightly accented voice. Count Zarcone. Of all the rotten luck! "The beautiful Lady Diana."

"Oh, no! . . . I mean, good evening, Count," she stammered. Nicholas turned back and put his arm around her shoulders as if to stake some sort of claim.

"Ah, and Arnside as well," the count said smoothly. "This *is* a small world." He eyed Diana speculatively, and then Nicholas. "I understand I am to congratulate you."

"I beg your pardon?" Nicholas asked.

"You are to be married, are you not? Your cousin mentioned it. He came to London with me, by the way."

"Our betrothal is common knowledge among the members of our families, although it has not yet been formally announced," Nicholas said, not liking the way the count was leering at Diana. "It is always a very great pleasure to see you, Count. Now if you will excuse us——"

"Ah, is that the delightful Mrs. Benningham?" the count said, catching sight of that lady. "I am surrounded by *old* friends." Caroline gave him a challenging look.

The count immediately turned his attention back to Diana.

"Am I to understand that Lord Arnside's fiancée is your guest in Mount Street?" he asked, his eyes glittering. "What a piquant situation. While Lord Arnside and his bride are occupied with one another, I must do my best to see that you are properly entertained. You may be sure you will see me in Mount Street very soon."

"How very kind," Diana said, her eyes narrowed. She stared pointedly at the mask in his hand, and he returned it to her with a flourish. "I am afraid Penelope and I have a great many engagements, so I doubt that you will find us often at home."

"Well, never mind," said the count, apparently amused by this gentle snub. "I am a patient man."

The count then offered his arm to Caroline and walked off with her.

"Cousin Nicholas—" Diana began.

"One crisis at a time, if you please," he said with a sigh.

She followed him to the private room Mrs. Benningham had indicated and saw Penelope standing alone by the window. Diana brushed by Nicholas and threw her arms around Penelope as if to protect her from him.

"I will thank you both to stop looking at me as if I am going to beat her," Nicholas said. "Come along now."

Actually, he *had* intended to impress upon Penelope just how improper her behavior had been. But her tear-stained face convinced him that she already had suffered for her offense.

Once they were inside the carriage, Penelope cowered next to Diana, who patted her shoulder in consolation.

"It was *horrid!*" she said tearfully.

"Not romantic at all, in fact, but rather sordid," Nicholas agreed. "Someday *I* will take you to a masquerade if you behave yourself, but in a respectable house, not in a public hall. Here. Take my handkerchief and dry your eyes like a good girl. I refuse to go all the way to Mount Street in the company of a watering pot."

"Y-yes, my lord," Penelope said.

"My name is Nicholas," he said kindly. "When you say 'my lord' in that awed voice, you make me feel like your grandfather."

"Yes, Nicholas," she said with the suggestion of a watery chuckle in her voice.

Diana alighted from the coach. Then she stood stock still, almost causing Penelope to collide with her as Nicholas handed the girl down.

"What is it?" Nicholas asked, steadying Penelope.

"Your Aunt Edith," Diana said in dismay. "I had forgotten all about her."

"*Please* do not tell her what I have done!" Penelope pleaded. "She will never let me hear the end of it. She is always telling me what a paragon you are, Nicholas, and that I must be very, very good if I am to deserve the honor of being your wife."

"Of course we will not tell her," he said, annoyed that either lady could think he would be so base as to tattle to Aunt Edith. "I will say I am escorting you both home from the musicale."

"That would answer," Diana said slowly. "She left the house before Penelope did, so for all she knows, I may have decided to accompany her and her friends. You encountered us there, and you offered to escort us home—"

"Yes, and we shall hope she does not ask what has become of the good lieutenant."

As it happened, Lady Dunwood already had gone to bed, and Penelope, who was exhausted from her little adventure, immediately followed her example.

Nicholas rose to take his leave, but a glance at Diana's face arrested him.

"What is it?" he asked.

"I was wondering how to meddle in your affairs without being told to mind my own business," she said frankly.

"Am I about to be favored with more unsolicited advice on how to conduct a courtship?" he asked with a sigh of resignation.

"When you put it that way, it *does* sound horrid," she admitted. "Dear heavens. When I was Penelope's age I vowed I would never become one of those *managing* females who try to promote love matches between people who are quite old enough to make their own decisions."

"I take it you are about to abandon this admirable resolve," he said, sitting down again.

"I fear I am."

"Very well," he said resignedly. "What is it, then?"

"Penelope. Please do not be angry with her."

"I am not angry with her."

"But you think she was very foolish tonight."

"Yes. Would you not agree?"

"Of course I would," said Diana. "But even though she was not very wise to embark upon such a silly adventure, she is neither stupid nor frivolous."

"Only immature."

"Not even that," she said, her beautiful eyes pleading with him for understanding. "Nicholas, she will make you a charming wife once she becomes accustomed to the excitement of being presented to society and of being betrothed."

"Rather rushing things, are you not? I have not officially offered for the girl yet, you know."

"But you will."

"I suppose so," he said slowly. "It was my father's wish, and it is more than time that I was married. She is a very agreeable young lady, although I trust she will curb this alarming tendency to run off with cavalry officers after we are wed. You must admit it makes one wonder if she is at all anxious to become my wife."

"On the contrary. I doubt that Penelope has even considered the possibility that you will not marry. She can hardly wait for the engagement to become official so she can begin choosing her bride-clothes."

Diana laughed at his look of astonishment.

"What do you expect?" she asked. "Landing one of the leading prizes on the marriage mart when one's first season has barely begun is quite a triumph. It has added immeasurably to her consequence in the eyes of the other debutantes, particularly when one considers the number of caps that have been set for you."

"Spare my blushes, if you please, Cousin," he said. "It makes me queasy when you talk about Penelope and her friends competing for husbands in that cold-blooded fashion."

"Is it any less calculating for a gentleman to be willing to marry a young lady he hardly knows for the sake of her fortune, I wonder?"

"I should have known you would start carping on Penelope's precious forty thousand pounds," he said with a sigh of exasperation. "Although I am willing to honor the wishes of my late father and her guardian if the girl should prove congenial, I have no intention of taking advantage of her. I always intended to get to know her first, then see if we would suit before I offered for her officially. I'll have no unwilling bride, no matter how large her dowry."

"Very noble," Diana said. "I see I have misjudged you."

He glanced at her quickly, certain this must be sarcasm. "More impertinence, Cousin?" he asked, quirking an eyebrow at her.

"No. I thought—"

"I know what you thought," he said curtly. "You thought I wanted to keep the girl confined in Bath so she would have no opportunity to form an attachment to anyone else. Then I would marry her out of hand and keep her buried in the country, breeding, while I set about squandering her fortune."

"I am afraid I did think that," she admitted. "And so did Penelope, I should imagine."

"What I do not understand," Nicholas said, perplexed, "is why the girl would submit so tamely to such cavalier treatment. She does not appear to lack for spirit."

"Cavalier treatment? You mean becoming engaged to a gentleman of the first stare, and a war hero besides? Much as I hate to feed your vanity, Cousin, you are accounted to be a very handsome man by those who happen to be susceptible to great, dark, brooding eyes, and—"

"That will *do,* Diana," he said sternly. An uncomfortable thought occurred to him. "Good God! The poor girl has not convinced herself that she is in love with me, has she?"

"I should not be at all surprised," Diana said with a chuckle. "Do not look so horrified. It is very natural under the circumstances."

"But she doesn't even know me!"

"She knows you as well as I knew Rupert when we were married," Diana said with a reminiscent gleam in her eye. "I was only sixteen when Rupert offered for me, and my mother was so thrilled you would have thought he had offered for *her.*"

"You were no older than Penelope!" he exclaimed.

"Actually, I was a few months younger."

Nicholas digested this in silence for a moment. For years within his family, he had heard his cousin's bride styled as an unprincipled vixen who had successfully laid a snare for the susceptible Rupert with her dangerous wiles. Nicholas began to wonder if, on the contrary, it wasn't his cousin who took advantage of young Diana's innocence.

"Listen to me ramble on about my moment of glory," Diana said with a self-deprecating smile. "When I was Penelope's age, I also promised myself that I would not prose on and on about my former triumphs when I was past my prime."

"Yes," he scoffed. "You must be all of twenty now."

"One-and-twenty, I am afraid," she said with a twinkle in her eye. "And a *mother!*"

"As old as all that," he mused. "So you were betrothed in your first season, much to the amazement and envy of all your friends."

"My parents were so proud of me," Diana said, smiling reminiscently. "I had the prettiest gown and a lavish wedding. You know this, for you were there. I thought I was the most fortunate girl in existence."

Her smile faded.

"Have you ever been in a girls' school?" she asked.

"No, I thank God."

"You may well say so. I hated every moment of it. When the headmistress took us into Bath, we had to walk in rows through town with our eyes straight ahead. Boys on the street would make fun of our ugly uniforms. I can't bear the sight of dark blue bombazine to this day. The headmistress was so parsimonious that in winter we could see our breath in the bedchambers. And meals made no concession to a growing girl's appetite. I was always hungry."

"It sounds inhuman," he said, taken aback. "No wonder Penelope ran away. I am surprised *you* did not run away."

"So am I, frankly," Diana admitted. "Then I turned sixteen and made my come-out. Suddenly I had lovely dresses to wear, wonderful food to eat, invitations to all the best parties, and admiration. It went to my head. Rupert was mad to marry me, but once we were married, I found out that he did not approve of my friends. His mother did not approve of *me*. He grew cold and impatient . . ."

She broke off and looked down at her hands.

"Be patient with her, Nicholas," she said quietly. "She will have to settle down and be a sensible wife soon enough."

Nicholas had a mental picture of Diana as an innocent young bride, hurt and confused by her formerly doting husband's sudden coldness.

"I will," he promised. "I intend to spend the next few months getting acquainted with Penelope. If all goes well, we may announce our betrothal in the summer and be married in the autumn. If she decides she would rather not marry me, I will honor her wishes. A girl with her looks and fortune would have no difficulty marrying elsewhere, as you never tire of reminding me." He smiled at her look of chagrin. "Does that satisfy you?"

"Yes," she said, looking relieved.

An awkward silence developed.

"I have not thanked you for coming so handsomely to the rescue," Diana said at last.

"It was my pleasure," he said. "And I have yet to discharge the errand that brought me to Mount Street tonight. I talked with Penelope's guardian, and he agreed, very reluctantly, to pay you a stipend for Penelope's expenses while you have her with you. So your tender conscience need not suffer at the prospect of *my* paying for Penelope's keep."

"How wonderful," Diana said admiringly. "I do not know how you did it."

"Perhaps I will engage my cousin Bernard to paint Penelope's portrait," he said thoughtfully. "Bernard is staying with the count, and I'd like to get him away from that unwholesome influence as often as possible."

*"Now* who is meddling?" she asked teasingly.

"Well, you must admit that painting her portrait should keep them both out of mischief."

"I think it's a charming idea."

"Until tomorrow, then."

# Nine

Penelope had thought it would be amusing to have her portrait painted, but instead it was a dead bore. And so was the artist.

She had expected Mr. Rivers to be slender and aesthetic and given to impassioned utterances in French like Mr. Bonnet, the drawing master at school.

Some of the more adventuresome girls had kissed Mr. Bonnet behind the door, but Penelope was not of their number. She had just turned thirteen when Mr. Bonnet was asked to leave the institution after the headmistress found out just what sort of gratuitous instruction he had given some of his more advanced pupils.

Not that Penelope wanted Mr. Rivers to kiss her.

He was a prosaic, businesslike man in his early twenties, and nothing could have been less romantic than his tidy, competently cut clothes, neatly trimmed sand-colored hair and intelligent hazel eyes. He didn't seem in the least impressed by her appearance in the elaborate ball gown she had selected for her portrait.

When she attempted to school her features into the much practiced attitude of sophisticated world-weariness she wished the finished portrait to convey to posterity, he offended her mightily by laughing aloud.

"No need to pout," he said cheerfully, unforgivably interpreting the world-weariness as sulkiness. "It won't be all that bad, I promise you. Just a trifle tedious."

Then he proceeded to tell her to sit up straight, but to turn her face just the least bit toward the window, and to keep her chin lifted, and not to let her hands flop like dead fish in her lap, and to sit at the very edge of the chair because her nether limbs were so short her feet did not touch the floor.

Within a half hour her cramped muscles were begging for release. The room was insufferably hot, but when she asked if she might have the curtains drawn before she roasted alive in the sunlight streaming through the window, he told her he needed the light for his work.

"You need not bother to entertain me," he said kindly when she attempted to make polite conversation with him. "In fact, I'd rather you did not for this first sitting. It breaks my concentration. Lift your chin a bit. That's the way."

When she sighed pointedly after forty minutes, he begged her to have patience.

"This first sitting is very important," he said, "especially when dealing with a subject such as yourself."

"Is it?" she asked, obscurely flattered.

"Yes. It is often so when one is taking a likeness of very young persons or of pets," he said, sinking himself beneath reproach in Penelope's eyes. "Being so young, your features are unformed, and it isn't easy to capture them."

"I suppose you would rather I were old and wrinkled," she grumbled, thinking this was poor compensation for her discomfort.

"Certainly not," he said, smiling at her as if she had said something extremely childish. "You are a very pretty girl, if I may say so. In a few years your face will have more countenance. Perhaps Nick will ask me to make your portrait again someday, if I am not in India by then."

"India!" Penelope exclaimed, forgetting her grievance in her excitement. "Are you going to India?"

"Miss Chalmers, I beg of you," he said, frowning.

"I'm sorry," she said, conscience-stricken as she resumed her pose. "I always have wanted to go to India. It must be *wonderful* to travel. I have never been anywhere except for

Surrey and Bath and now London, of course. Nicholas said you have studied in Italy. Was it very pleasant?"

"Sometimes," he said in a dampening tone. "I suppose that will do for today. My concentration is ruined, I am afraid."

"Have I ruined it?" she asked, at once contrite.

"It is all right. You have done as well as could be expected," he said kindly, irritating Penelope very much by making her feel like a badly behaved lapdog. "May I come tomorrow at the same time? The light is just right at this time of day."

"I suppose so," Penelope said ungraciously.

"Have I said something to offend you, Miss Chalmers?" he asked, looking surprised.

"No. Of course not," she said. "Did you go to many parties in Italy?" she asked as she walked down to the front door with him.

"None that you would be interested in," he said after a slight hesitation.

"Were the women very beautiful?"

"Some of them," he said, as they arrived at the front door and Jasper opened it for him. "Good day, Miss Chalmers. I shall see you tomorrow."

*Well! What a disagreeable, secretive man,* Penelope thought as she watched him walk down the path to the street.

When she went into the parlor to join her hostess, Diana rang for tea and began to question Penelope about the sitting.

"Was it very tiresome, my dear?" she asked sympathetically.

"Very," Penelope grumbled. "My face is not very interesting, you see."

"Surely he did not say so," Diana said, surprised.

"Being so young, my features are unformed," Penelope explained. "He often has difficulty capturing the likenesses of very young persons and lapdogs."

"Oh, dear. It does not sound as if that went well at all," Diana said, trying not to laugh at Penelope's indignation. She suspected that young Mr. Rivers was just as forthright as his cousin. As if her thought had summoned him, Jasper informed Diana that Lord Arnside had arrived.

"Show him in, if you please, Jasper," Diana said.

"Good afternoon, Cousin Diana. Penelope, my dear," Nicholas said. "Can I interest you in a carriage ride in the park?"

"I should like it of all things, Nicholas," Penelope said gratefully. "It was so hot and stuffy in that room that I long for some fresh air."

"Oh. The sitting. How did you get on with Cousin Bernard?"

"I haven't any idea," she said stiffly. "You would have to ask *him*."

"I shall do that," he said, lifting one eyebrow. "Will you join us, Cousin Diana?"

"Oh, Diana, *please* go with us," Penelope pleaded. "If you do not, we shall be obligated to invite my godmother along."

Diana surmised that Edith's criticism of Penelope's favorite new ball gown as too dashing for a chit her age had not gone down well. Since Edith's evil genius had prompted her to imply that Penelope's error of taste could be attributed to Diana's unfortunate influence, Edith was in neither lady's good graces at the moment.

Nicholas seemed just as anxious to avoid Edith's company as Diana and Penelope were. Diana did not think this surprising, considering that every time Nicholas called at the house, his aunt plagued him to settle matters with Penelope's guardian and make their engagement official before some other man captured Penelope's tender heart and her forty thousand pounds.

Therefore, when Diana announced her willingness to go for a ride with them, heroically sacrificing her plans for the afternoon, which included a visit to her favorite modiste, it took little persuasion from the ladies to convince Nicholas and themselves that a headache Edith complained of two days ago was a sufficient excuse to preclude asking her to join them.

As bad luck would have it, the first person they encountered in the park was Count Zarcone on horseback accompanied by his protégé, Bernard Rivers.

"Ah, well met, Arnside," the count said, leering at Diana. "How fortunate I am to encounter you. Your servant, Lady Diana. And who is this charming young lady?"

"Count Zarcone, may I present Miss Penelope Chalmers?" Nicholas said. He looked far from pleased at this development and he glared at Bernard as if he thought his cousin should somehow have prevented this unfortunate meeting. Bernard smiled and shrugged as if to mollify his cousin.

Then he caught sight of Diana and nearly fell off his horse. Diana felt her cheeks flame scarlet, both at being ogled by the count and at being recognized by Bernard. She should have known that his artist's eye would unerringly identify her as the supposed Italian working girl he sketched a year ago in Naples at a party that no lady of quality could attend without being ruined in the eyes of civilized society.

"A very great pleasure," said the count, smiling at Penelope with such an admiring look in his eye that, in her innocence, she appeared to be quite flattered.

"How are you, Bernard?" Nicholas asked, eyes narrowed at his cousin's sudden ineptitude in the saddle. Like Diana, he had probably hoped that Bernard would not connect her with that unfortunate Italian girl.

"Quite well, Nick," he said, his face carefully blank.

"My dear Lady Diana," the count protested when Diana politely declined his offer to take her to the opera. "It will be quite an unexceptionable party. I shall invite your mother-in-law and the charming Miss Chalmers and Lord Arnside as well."

"You are very kind," Diana said firmly, "but I am afraid that we must decline."

Lord Arnside intervened when it appeared that the count was unwilling to take no for an answer. "We had better be on our way," he said. He put the carriage in motion so abruptly that the count was interrupted in the middle of an elaborate compliment.

He looked a little foolish when he turned to see Caroline's amused eye upon him.

"Poor Antonio," Mrs. Benningham said, obviously delighted by his discomfiture. "Your conquests have made you a trifle clumsy, my *old* friend."

A stifled noise from Bernard's direction earned him a glare

from his benefactor. Bernard gave him a self-effacing little smile and rode off, apparently in the belief that the count wished to converse with the lady in private.

"I was unaware that we had progressed to the stage of using Christian names, my dear Mrs. Benningham," he said sweetly.

"That was meant to wound me, I suppose," Caroline said with a sigh. "I *knew* I would regret flirting with you. I assure you I flirt with *all* presentable gentlemen. Do not think you are special."

"Of course," he said with a smirk.

"I thought you would be amusing," she continued, "but now I see your reputed charm and elegance of person is nothing but a take-in."

"You dare snub *me?*" he asked in astonishment.

"My, you *are* quick! You may as well stop pursuing Lady Diana, by the way. She was disgusted by your behavior in Naples, and I rather doubt that anything you say will persuade her to receive you."

His eyes kindled.

"I will have Lady Diana before the month is out," he vowed.

Caroline stared at him.

"Will you, indeed?" she asked. "Perhaps you would be good enough to define your meaning of the verb 'to have' in that context."

"It means exactly what you think it means, my *dear* Mrs. Benningham."

"How inexpressibly crude. If you intend 'to have' Diana, you had better be prepared to marry her, *if* she will have you, which I doubt she will. Diana is virtuous to the point of saint-hood, and dissipated rakes have never been to her taste. Nor is Diana without male protection. She has an extremely mus-cular brother-in-law who probably would be delighted to—"

"That shows how much your opinion is worth," he scoffed. "Did you not see what happened between her and Arnside in Naples? A child would know she is his mistress, but now that he is about to be married—"

"You poor fool," she said. "My dear count, I owe you an

apology, for I have wronged you. I do believe you *are* going to afford me amusement by making a great fool of yourself."

He gritted his teeth in annoyance as she turned her mare and left him.


"You knew, then?" Caroline said, blinking in surprise when Diana took the news that Count Zarcone intended "to have" her with matter-of-fact calm.

"The gentleman had more finesse than to put it in so many words, but I gathered he was determined to make me the object of his gallantry," Diana said indifferently. "He will soon tire of the game and find another lady to inflict his attentions upon."

Caroline was alarmed to see that Diana was not taking her warning seriously.

"I shudder to think what he might do," Caroline said.

"I do not think he can do anything. But it is particularly vexatious to have him pursuing me just now when it is so important to present a proper appearance to the world for Penelope's sake."

"Very true. Penelope is a darling girl, of course, but do you not miss dancing until dawn in company that is not *quite* the thing?"

"Not very much," Diana said, laughing. "Do you?"

"No. I am grateful, by the way, for your aid in making me respectable again. One might pardon you for refusing to countenance one whose reputation is as tarnished as mine when you have a debutante to present to society and a son to rear creditably."

"Nonsense, Caroline. I refuse to feed your outrageous vanity by suggesting you were ever quite *that* depraved."

"So you say now, but it was a most uncomfortable moment yesterday when old Lady Larchwood took one look at me and started to take her leave."

"You may thank my meddlesome mother-in-law," Diana pointed out with a reminiscent smile. "When she took Lady Larchwood aside and told her she wouldn't blame her at all for giving me a set-down, I knew it would be all right. Of course, Lady Larchwood stayed in order to spite her. She has detested Edith for years."

"Penelope certainly made a hit with the old ladies."

"I am very proud of her. And you acquitted yourself admirably as well, I might add. Poor Caroline. It was a very dull party, I am afraid."

"Not at all," said Caroline. "I enjoyed myself prodigiously."

Diana looked at her friend askance, obviously suspecting sarcasm. But Caroline assured her that she was fascinated by old Lady Larchwood's droll description of her eldest son's adventures in India.

Young Lord Larchwood was, to his mother's dismay, rendering his ancestral home hideous with his trophies, most of which utilized the earthly remains of various large and hairy animals in imaginative ways.

"In fact," Caroline declared, "you might say the luncheon party was a turning point in my life."

"Liar!" Diana said as mischief danced in her eyes.

"No, not at all. I am much obliged to Lady Larchwood, for I was quite depressed at the prospect of becoming middle-aged and colorless as my fortieth birthday approaches. Now I shall do famously."

"What folly are you contemplating, Caroline? I have learned to mistrust that particular look in your eye."

"And well you should, my dear, for I am about to become an eccentric. What else can a lady of comfortable fortune do with the rest of her life?"

"You might marry one of the scores of earnest gentlemen who have cast themselves at your feet over the years in a hopeless desire to reform your wicked ways," Diana suggested.

"No. I have had enough of marriage. After being so taken in by Giles, I am not about to let myself in for *that* again. My scheme is much better. I shall go to India. Or perhaps Egypt. Then I shall return and redecorate my house with elephants' feet and death masks and those curious cane throne chairs Lady Larchwood dislikes so much."

"You are insane," Diana said with an uncertain laugh.

"Not at all. On cold evenings I shall wrap myself up in shawls and turbans by the fire and hold forth about my adventures. I shall serve wine in elephant tusks. It is quite respectable, you know, to be a lady explorer."

"*You?* A lady explorer? The way you sunburn?" Diana scoffed.

"I can always captivate a maharaja or a sheikh if things get too dull," Caroline said thoughtfully. "I must see my dressmaker immediately. I fancy something severely mannish and dashing in drab green linen with the sheerest of cambric blouses belted at the waist with leather. It would become me, would it not?"

Diana's eyes grew wide with dismay.

"You are *serious* about this!" she exclaimed.

"Of course I am. My only other recourse would be cats. Scores of them all over the house. I can't abide the creatures, quite apart from the fact that they make me sneeze."

"But, Caroline, it could be dangerous!"

"So it might. On the other hand, it probably would be dangerous to remain in London, for the last time your precious count saw me, he looked ready to commit murder. I can't imagine why."

"I can, if you provoked him half as much as you are provoking me right now," Diana said grimly. "But never mind. I trust you won't be going on your explorations quite yet. Maybe I can talk you out of your mad plan."

"No. You shall have the pleasure of my company for the rest of the season; then I shall go. Town is so boring in the summer, you know, and I quite detest the country. Although, if you are going to Brighton, I might be persuaded to go along."

"You quite detest the country, but you are going to India or Egypt?" Diana asked quizzically.

"Or perhaps Africa. That would be distinctive, would it not? I don't see how you can compare going on a grand adventure with being buried alive in the country. Of course I don't go any more often than I must, but I saw not a single elephant or maharaja in Lancashire on my last interminable visit to my relations."

"Very true," Diana said gravely.

"I say, Diana. Perhaps you should come along."

"To India or Africa? Not on your life! If I weren't frightened to death at the prospect of being eaten by tigers, I have my son to think about."

"But you haven't considered! He would grow tanned and muscular and, of course, speak whatever exotic language they speak like a native. And he would fall in love with a native princess, and you will insist that her father provide you with rubies the size of pigeons' eggs for her dowry—"

"No, I thank you. My son is going to be reared at his estate in Kent and marry a proper English girl. The prospect of becoming a mother-in-law is daunting enough the way it is."

"Oh, well. If you're going to be a dull dog," Caroline said with a lurking twinkle in her eye. "I must leave you now. I just wanted to warn you about the count and his base intentions. He is so deranged with jealous passion he imagines you are Arnside's mistress. What a filthy mind he must have."

"Quite," Diana said, choking a little. "Thank you for the warning. I shall take care not to go anywhere unattended by less than six stalwart protectors."

"Hmmm. That *does* sound like fun," Caroline said with an arch smile. She took her leave and almost collided with Lord Arnside on the doorstep. He was wearing riding dress, and she could see a boy holding the reins of a magnificent dappled gray on the street.

"Good morning, Lord Arnside," she said. "This is rather early for you."

"You are rather unfashionably early yourself," he said pleasantly. "Are the ladies receiving?"

"Diana is. I did not see Miss Chalmers. Have you come to take your fiancée riding, by any chance?"

Nicholas mistrusted the tone of her voice. Something apparently amused her, and he was dashed if he could see what it was.

"Is there any reason why I should not, ma'am?" he asked guardedly.

"No. No reason at all," she said, her eyes twinkling. "I hope

you will have a pleasant ride." Then she laughed again and
favored him with a jaunty wave as she walked down the street.

When he helped his intended to mount her spiritless mare,
Nicholas knew why Caroline had been amused.

Penelope flinched every time a carriage or another horse
got within five yards of her. Her horse was incapable of ex-
erting itself beyond a sedate canter, which was fine with its
rider.

"What is her name?" Nicholas asked Penelope as he firmly
restrained his restive horse from outdistancing her mount.

"She already had a name when I received her. Diana had
her brought down from her stables in Kent for me. Was that
not kind? Her name is Molasses."

"How appropriate," he said dryly.

Penelope looked up at him apologetically. "I won't be miffed
if you want to go ahead of me once we get to the park, although I hope you will help us get through the traffic. Molasses is not used to it."

Nicholas looked at the placid little mare and burst into
laughter.

"True," he said. "It would be a shocking thing if she fell
asleep on the street."

Penelope was inclined to be indignant on behalf of her steed.

"She's not quite *that* bad, Nicholas!"

Once they got into the park, Nicholas was chagrined by the
number of his acquaintances who pointed them out to their
companions and laughed uproariously. Molasses felt no more
ambitious in the park than she did in the street, and it was
hard work to keep Nicholas's spirited stallion slowed to her
plodding pace.

It was with some relief that he greeted Penelope's friends.
The young ladies were accompanied by a court of officers
pleased to encounter a veteran of Waterloo. They would have
demanded that Nicholas tell them stories of his adventures in
combat if he hadn't put a stop to the business at once by saying
the ladies certainly would not wish to hear about bloodshed
on such a beautiful spring day. Actually, he suspected the ladies
would have liked nothing better, but they could hardly say so.

Waterloo was for him still too fresh and painful to serve as a topic of idle chatter to amuse a parcel of young aristocrats. After it was over, he hadn't felt heroic. He just felt heartsore and weary. These smooth-faced lads in their smart uniforms would learn the awful truth about the glory of battle soon enough if England went to war again.

Molasses apparently did not require much exercise and was content to stand still while Penelope discussed prospective rout parties and balls and Venetian breakfasts to her heart's content. Nicholas excused himself politely in order to exchange a word or two with his cronies. He told Penelope he would return soon to collect her.

Captain James Burnside was on the catch for an heiress, and Miss Chalmers was made to order for his purposes. He was certain that such a romantic young lady could be persuaded to repudiate an arranged marriage in order to elope with him. It was not difficult for him to join the usual court of red-coated rattles that formed around every pretty debutante and pursue her in earnest right under Lord Arnside's aristocratic nose.

Her fiancé, in fact, was so sure of her that he had left her with a gaggle of extremely silly chits who, James found, were easily persuaded to go on their merry way and leave Miss Chalmers in his company. The girl blushed prettily at finding herself alone with him.

Given the young lady's inexperience, James knew he would have to accomplish his goal in easy stages. For the present, he would be satisfied to lure her to a clandestine meeting.

"But, Captain Burnside, I *couldn't,*" she exclaimed when he made this alarming proposal.

"They do not mount a guard over you, do they?"

"No. Of course not. But it would be most improper for me to meet you."

"Yes, it would. Forgive me, my dear. I should not have spoken."

"I am an engaged woman, you know," she told the captain.

"I hoped you would take pity on a lowly soldier who adores you," he said, sounding dejected.

"You must not say such things!"

His quarry looked around quickly to make sure no one else was near. *Good.* A girl convinced of her attachment to her fiancé would have refused to listen to James instead of looking around to make sure there were no witnesses.

"You are right," he said with a heartrending sigh. "It can only give me pain. But I cannot help myself."

The young lady whose self-esteem had been undermined by a kindly fiancé who treated her as if she were the merest child, a portrait painter who approached her with the same enthusiasm he reserved for fidgeting lapdogs, and a godmother who thought her too immature to choose her own gowns was thrilled by such blatant admiration.

Captain Burnside was an excessively handsome man blessed with golden hair and bright blue eyes that seemed to melt when he was moved. They were melting all over Penelope right now.

"I don't want you to be unhappy," she said, "so maybe we should be careful not to meet again. It makes me very sad to think I am giving you pain."

"No, not at all," he hastily assured her. "It would be even more painful for me not to see you."

"I must go," she said, spotting Nicholas riding toward her. "Here comes Nicholas to collect me. Have a pleasant day, Captain."

"Do not give me a thought, I beg," he said. "I shall become accustomed to my disappointment."

He then rode off in an impetuous manner as if he could not trust himself to say more.

"I did not mean to frighten your friend off," Nicholas said pleasantly.

"He did not wish to meet you—I mean, he had another engagement," said Penelope, feeling rather guilty. The unworthy thought crossed her mind that a more satisfactory fiancé might show *some* sign of curiosity, if not outright jealousy, at the sight of his betrothed in the solitary company of another man.

"My poor girl, you look fagged to death," Nicholas said, apparently not recognizing the melancholy demeanor of a young lady who somehow had found the strength to crush an admirer's most ardent hope. "I will take you home."

# Ten

As it turned out, Nicholas and Penelope returned to the house too late for Penelope to share the rather substantial breakfast it was her custom to enjoy. When Diana offered to have a tray prepared for her, Penelope refused it rather than keep Mr. Rivers, who had arrived some twenty-five minutes earlier, waiting any longer.

Conscience-stricken, Penelope realized she had forgotten the appointment she'd made with the artist for a sitting that morning.

She repented her stoicism almost immediately. She was hungry. The air was like an oven, the sunlight hurt her eyes, and the fumes from the paints and chemicals made her dizzy. Frowning in concentration, Bernard kept her sitting in that uncomfortable position for almost two hours. When he told her for the fiftieth time to stop fidgeting and hold her chin up, her control snapped.

"I am *not* fidgeting," she said, gritting her teeth. "And if I hold my chin up any higher, my neck will break."

Bernard put down his brush and stared at her.

"What are you looking at?" she asked belligerently.

"What is wrong, Miss Chalmers?" He stepped out from behind his easel.

"Nothing," she said. "Nothing at all. When will you be finished?"

"I have made a lot of progress today," he said after a moment of silence. "If you sit like this for me every day, I could finish it in a few weeks. Would you rather sit every other day instead? It will take longer, but perhaps it is asking too much to expect such a young lady to—"

"It is *miserable* sitting here day after day with the sun beating down on me until my head aches," she said angrily, "and all you do is make insulting remarks about my age and lapdogs and tell me to stop fidgeting!"

"Lapdogs?" he asked, looking mystified. This obtuseness irritated Penelope so much that she leaped up to stalk in outraged dignity from his presence, but to her dismay she was so lightheaded from the stuffiness in the room that she had to hold onto the chair for support. Mr. Rivers rushed to her assistance.

"You are ill!" he exclaimed as he put an arm around her waist to support her. "Why did you not tell me?"

"I am *not* ill," she gasped. "It is insufferably hot in this room."

"I will help you to that sofa. I had no idea you were in delicate health. You look so sturdy."

The last thing a young lady with pretensions to fashion wants to be told is that she looks sturdy.

She tried to push him away, but she was no match for his strength. When she closed her eyes on another wave of dizziness, Mr. Rivers lifted her into his arms and carried her over to the sofa. When he laid her down, she sat up so quickly her head swam. He put his arm around her.

"No! I am quite all right now," she said, fighting tears of humiliation. "It is just the heat."

"This is all my fault," he said, looking conscience-stricken. "Rest a minute. I will call someone."

"I suppose, young man, there is some reasonable explanation for this extraordinary spectacle?" asked the dowager Lady Dunwood from the open doorway.

The icy tone of her voice made it clear just how the scene appeared to her.

When Mr. Rivers released her rather abruptly, Penelope sagged against the back of the sofa and took deep breaths to keep from being sick.

"I was just coming for help," Mr. Rivers told the dowager, looking down at Penelope with a worried expression.

"So I see," Edith said, raising one haughty eyebrow.

Diana looked into the room at that moment and took in the situation at a glance.

"Penelope, my dear. Are you ill?" she said, rushing to her at once. She turned to Mr. Rivers. "What happened?"

"She became dizzy while she was sitting for me," he said.

"I am not surprised. It is much too hot in this room." Diana touched Penelope's cheek with a gentle hand. "My poor dear. You are not going to faint, are you?"

"No, of course not," Penelope said, hoping it was true. "I just felt a little dizzy. I missed my breakfast—"

"So you did. Well, you shall lie down in your room, and I will have a tray sent up directly."

Diana helped Penelope stand and took her away, leaving Bernard and his aunt together.

Edith walked over to where the portrait was standing on an easel and gave it a critical look.

"I do not see that you have made much progress for as long as you have been working on this," she said belligerently.

"What are you implying, ma'am? That I have attempted to take advantage of Miss Chalmers? It is not true."

"I am acquainted with your circumstances, Bernard," she said deliberately. "It is only prudent for you to seek a young lady of means, but in aiming for Miss Chalmers you have looked too high. Be so good as to leave this house at once."

She cast a fastidious eye over his paints, brushes and the unfinished painting.

"And be sure to take this appalling mess with you," she added.

Bernard made her an ironic little bow. The dowager always succeeded in making him feel like the poor relation he was. He stalked from the house and ran his cousin to ground at Tattersalls, where Nicholas was looking at a chestnut pair.

"Well met, Bernard," Nicholas said as he approached. "What do you think of these chestnuts? They may be just the thing to draw my curricle."

"I don't care anything about horses, Nick. You know that," he said impatiently.

"Were you looking for me, then?"

"Yes. Something has happened."

"What is it?"

"We can't talk here," Bernard said.

"Can it wait until I have decided about the horses?"

"No."

Bernard walked a little distance away and gestured for Nicholas to join him. Nicholas shrugged apologetically at the groom holding the horses and went to join his cousin.

"This had better be important, Bernard," he said.

"It is. Aunt Edith appears to think I have been forcing my attentions on Miss Chalmers."

"I see. And have you?" Nicholas asked, looking amused.

"Dash it, Nick! Of course I haven't. It's not a laughing matter."

"All right," Nicholas said, schooling his features. "Why should Aunt Edith think you have suddenly conceived a passion for Penelope?"

"Well, Miss Chalmers was sitting for me as usual and she suddenly became dizzy. I tried to make her lie down while I went for help. Then Aunt Edith walked in."

"It must have looked suspicious," Nicholas said. "Are you sure you aren't trying to cut me out?"

"I wouldn't lay a hand on your fiancée after all you've done for me," Bernard said hotly, irritated by the amusement in his cousin's voice. "If you were any other man, I would call you out for that insinuation!"

"Would you, indeed?" Nicholas asked. "If so, it would be the first time anyone succeeded in provoking you to a duel. It's a shocking waste of an excellent eye."

"I am not a coward, and you know it. I have better things to do than go around putting holes in people for the fun of it."

"How very optimistic of you." Nicholas was a deadly man with pistols or swords, and every sportsman in London knew it.

"Dash it, Nick—" Bernard began furiously.

"All right, all right," Nicholas said, holding one hand up in surrender. "I will have a talk with Aunt Edith."

"She means to forbid me the house," he warned. "I suppose I will not be able to finish the portrait even if Miss Chalmers would agree to continue to sit for me."

"It's not Aunt Edith's house. It's Lady Diana's until her son comes of age, according to the terms of Rupert's will. Why shouldn't Penelope continue to sit for you?"

"I don't think she likes me. The room is too hot and stuffy, her neck hurts from posing, and she keeps babbling about lapdogs."

"Lapdogs? What about them?"

"I haven't any idea," Bernard said. "You would have to ask the lady."

Nicholas decided he definitely would have a talk with his fiancée. An hour later, he arrived at Mount Street to be told that Edith had left the house, Penelope was not receiving, and Lady Diana was with her son in the nursery. He asked if Diana could spare him a few minutes.

"Good afternoon, Cousin Diana," Nicholas said when he had been ushered up to the nursery. When the pleasantries of greeting were over, he absentmindedly seated himself in the nearest chair, which was so short it compelled him to sit with his knees stuck out at uncomfortable angles. This was not an auspicious beginning to an interview about a delicate matter.

Diana laughed. So did Stephen. Nicholas noticed that Stephen's laugh was a perfect imitation of his mother's.

"I am sorry. This is the only adult chair," Diana said, indicating her own. She stood, holding the book in one hand and balancing Stephen on her hip.

"He is too heavy for you," Nicholas said as he took the child from her arms. Stephen immediately gave Nicholas's neckcloth a healthy pull and destroyed its crisp folds.

"Stephen, my man will have my head for this," Nicholas said in mock despair. "And you were so afraid, Cousin, that your son wasn't normal."

"Oh, Stephen," Diana cried at the same time. "Don't pull Cousin Nicholas's neckcloth!"

"Why?" the child asked, his blue eyes twinkling as he gave the neckcloth another tug.

Diana sighed, but her lips twitched.

"It is his favorite word now," she said ruefully. "I am so sorry, Nicholas."

"Why?" Stephen asked.

"See what I mean? We were just reading a book," she said, "but it's time for Stephen to have his nap now."

"Why?"

Diana shook her head.

"Naughty boy," she said fondly. She summoned a nursemaid and delivered the child into her hands.

"We will go to the drawing room, Cousin Nicholas," she said. "I assume you came to discuss what happened today."

"I did," he said grimly.

"Who told you, Mr. Rivers or your aunt?"

"Bernard."

"And you are suspicious," she guessed.

"Not at all," he replied, surprised. "Should I be?"

"Certainly not. I talked with Penelope. I don't know what your aunt thinks happened between them, but I am persuaded it was nothing to make such a piece of work about. Penelope missed breakfast, and it was so stuffy in the room she almost fainted. Perhaps Mr. Rivers had been making her sit too long, but I am certain he committed no other impropriety. Your aunt has a . . . colorful imagination."

"I suspect that the phrase on your lips before you thought better of it was 'filthy mind.' "

"Precisely," Diana said, seating herself on a chair in the drawing room. "I think too much has been made of the incident already. Edith and I had the most dreadful row because she insisted that she would deny him the house if Mr. Rivers has the effrontery to show himself, and I told her in the most shockingly brassy way that this is not her house, but mine, and I will decide who may be admitted."

"Shocking indeed, not that I blame you. I am afraid Aunt

tell them I do not want a chaperon, they might think I want you to . . . flirt with me."

"And we both know that is preposterous," he said harshly.

"Of course. You think I am a lapdog!"

"Miss Chalmers," Bernard said carefully. "I will not be responsible for my actions if you make one more reference to a lapdog without telling me what the *hell* you mean by it!"

Penelope clapped her hands over her ears, and he gave a derisive little laugh.

"You," she said fervently, "are the most despicable person—"

"You must have told them some wild tale of my behavior if they've suddenly decided I cannot be trusted in the same room with you," he snapped, knowing when he said it that it was unfair to take his frustration out on Penelope. He couldn't seem to help himself.

"I didn't! Honest!"

"Nick would have been perfectly within his rights to challenge me to a duel," Bernard said, still smarting from his cousin's amusement at the thought that Bernard might be remotely attractive to a young lady of Penelope's birth and fortune. "You'd love provoking him to fight his own cousin over you, wouldn't you? *That* would make quite a page in your diary!"

"I would not!" replied Penelope, glaring at him.

"You would so!"

"I would *not!*"

This argument might have deteriorated further had not Diana not looked into the room to see what was keeping them.

"Enough!" Diana said, calling the embarrassed combatants to order. "Come drink your tea."

# Eleven

Diana had been joking when she told Caroline she would not stir from the house without six stalwart protectors. She was no fledgling debutante but a respectable widow and a mother. No one would *dare* trifle with her.

Or so she thought until she was walking to her carriage from her favorite milliner's establishment one day and a pleasant male voice at her ear bade her halt.

"I have a pistol under my coat, my lady," the fellow told her. "If you don't make a fuss, you won't be harmed."

She turned in surprise to see quite a respectable looking man dressed in a brown suit. He took her arm and started to pull her toward a closed carriage waiting nearby.

"Do not make a sound," he warned.

Deciding he could not very well shoot her on the street, Diana screamed at the top of her lungs.

The young man threw her over his shoulder and carried her, kicking and screaming, toward the carriage.

"My wife," he explained to a middle-aged gentleman who looked as if he might take Diana's part. The other passersby merely looked away and pushed on, obviously not wanting to get involved. Unfortunately, it was too early for her fashionable acquaintances who might be depended upon to recognize her to be abroad. She had sent her maid across the street to the apothecary's shop, so she was quite alone.

With some difficulty, the man got her into the carriage and

signaled the driver to drive on. Diana righted herself on the seat and glared at the man sitting across from her.

"Who are you?" she asked furiously.

"That is not important," he said.

She tried to wrench open the door of the coach, but the man pulled her back.

"We are going too fast for you to jump out safely, my lady," he said. "There is no need for you to panic. You will not be harmed, I promise you."

"This is an outrage! I demand that you release me at once!"

"I cannot do so, even if I wished to. The coachman has his orders."

*"Whose* orders?"

"I regret that I am not permitted to say more."

To Diana's fury, he refused to answer any other questions. In a short time they arrived at their destination and she saw she was in front of a perfectly presentable town house, although she did not recognize the street.

"You will not be harmed, ma'am, I promise you," her abductor said as he helped her down. She tried to run away, but his hand closed on her elbow and he compelled her to enter the house. She struggled, but as bad luck would have it, there were no witnesses who might have aided her.

"What do you want?" she asked, really frightened now. "Ransom?"

"All in good time, my lady," he said.

A proper-looking gray-haired butler approached. Diana blinked in astonishment. He looked so . . . normal.

"If you will follow me, my lady," he said majestically.

"I most certainly will not!"

She turned and saw that the man in brown was blocking the door. He gave her an apologetic smile and a shrug.

"Good afternoon, Lady Diana," said Count Zarcone, entering the hall from another room. "Please come in. I mean you no harm."

"No harm? How *dare* you, sir?" she said indignantly. "I have just been kidnapped on a public street and mauled in the *most* ungentlemanly fashion."

The count glared at the man in brown.

"She started screaming," he said defensively.

"I told you she was to be treated with the greatest respect," the count said, his eyes cold. "I will deal with you later. Go.

"I apologize, my lady," the count said to Diana after the man's departure. "He will be punished. Will you take refreshment? Everything is prepared."

"I beg your pardon?" she asked in disbelief. "Prepared for *what?*"

"For us," he said with a bland smile. "If you will come with me."

He turned his back, plainly expecting her to follow him. She turned toward the door to gauge her chances of escape, but the butler was standing in front of it. Two burly footmen silently entered the room and flanked the butler.

She reluctantly followed the count.

"I do not understand," she complained when they were seated at a small table.

"I will explain," he said, "after we have eaten. Will you pour?"

She looked at him speculatively and picked up the heavy silver teapot. She hefted it in her hand to gauge its weight. She thought about hurling it at him, but she met the amused look in his eyes and poured the tea into cups instead. The count was dressed in the English style and looked perfectly civilized, although he couldn't conceal the predatory look in his eyes. She didn't trust him, but she didn't trust her aim from across the table, either. She forced herself to remain calm in the hope of catching him by surprise and making her escape. Instinctively she knew that losing her head would be a mistake.

"This is absolutely ridiculous," she said in what she hoped was a disdainful tone. "Milk?"

"If you please," he said, obviously enjoying himself. "I am happy to see that you are going to be sensible about this."

"I am going to have tea because I have a feeling I am going to need my strength," she said grimly. "You will taste everything before I do, so I can be sure the food isn't drugged. We shall see whether I am going to be 'sensible about this' after you explain why I have been subjected to this outrage."

His eyes kindled.

"I can see we are about to begin a very pleasant and entertaining association," he said.

"You are quite mistaken," she said coldly. "I should like one of those sandwiches, if you please."

The count handed the plate to her, but instead of taking it she looked at him with raised eyebrows. He took a sandwich and bit into it. She watched him chew and swallow it, and then she accepted one.

"Delicious," she said after eating it. "You must have your cook send my cook the recipe."

"It would be a very great pleasure, my lady," he said politely. *Good.* Apparently he thought she was resigned to playing the game with him.

Diana prolonged the meal as long as possible. She had three cups of tea and several helpings of everything else. She kept up a flow of inconsequential chatter about the opera and recently published books. She asked polite questions about his childhood in Naples. All the while, she scanned the room for likely weapons.

"Enough," he said at last. The wolfish look in his eye terrified her, but she forced herself to maintain the semblance of calm.

He rang, and a servant cleared away the tea things. When the servant was gone, he smiled at her.

"Now, my dear," he said, "I will answer all of your questions."

"I am not your 'dear,' if you please," Diana said. "I demand to know why you have brought me here."

"It would not have been necessary if you had not denied yourself when I called in Mount Street," he said in a tone that was maddeningly reasonable, "or if you had accepted my invitations to the theater."

"I do not wish to know you. A gentleman would have honored my wishes."

"I am not a monster, my lady," he said. "You received an

inaccurate impression of me when we met under such unusual circumstances in Naples."

"Well! Having me kidnapped is an excessively original way of correcting that unfavorable impression!" she responded indignantly. "I demand that you return me to my home at once! I am a respectable Englishwoman, sir! And a mother!"

"This was not the impression you gave when you gained entry to my house in Naples under false pretenses," the count said archly. "It takes an extremely adventuresome lady to do such a thing, one who commands my entire admiration. Let us be frank. I am perfectly aware that Lord Arnside is your lover, and you resist embarking upon a friendship with me out of some misguided sense of loyalty to him. But he is to be married to another, so why should we not enjoy ourselves?"

"That is a lie," Diana insisted. "Lord Arnside is my cousin by marriage and the fiancé of my houseguest, nothing more."

"Of course he is," Count Zarcone said with a knowing smile that made Diana want to slap him. "However, there is the matter of a certain delightful painting that has graced my bedchamber all these months since our meeting in Naples."

He walked to a corner of the room and pulled a piece of fabric from a large canvas. Diana looked at the painting and gasped.

"How? . . . Where?" was all she could say.

He watched her reaction with every appearance of enjoyment.

"I am not an unreasonable man," he said blandly. "If we manage to come to an agreement, I might be persuaded to part with this painting. Otherwise, I will arrange to have it exhibited publicly. The artist who rendered it has such obvious talent that it would be a great pity not to share it with the world, do you not agree?"

That unleashed Diana's tongue.

"And you claim you are not a monster! First you have me assaulted—"

"That was a mistake. I already have told you so," he pointed out.

"—Then you have me abducted," Diana continued as if

there had been no interruption, "and now you are attempting to blackmail me."

"Certainly not! I would never stoop to anything so crude."

"Well, you are trying to frighten me, then. That is just as bad."

He pulled her into his arms and attempted to silence her protestations with a passionate kiss. She slapped him so hard she feared her wrist was sprained, and ran for the fireplace.

"Do not come near me," she said, holding a poker aloft.

He burst into delighted laughter.

"All right," he said, holding both hands up in surrender. "I will not touch you. Put that down and come here."

"I prefer to stay where I am."

"You may bring the poker if it makes you feel more comfortable," he said in a tone that suggested he was humoring a willful child.

"I do not trust you," she said.

He approached her slowly, deliberately prolonging the suspense in order to unnerve her.

"I admire a woman of courage and passion," he said.

"Keep your distance!" she shrieked when he tried to pull the poker from her grasp. She slashed at him with it, but he dodged the erratically swinging poker easily.

"Stay *back*," she snarled, brandishing the poker. The sound of furious knocking on the door distracted her for a moment, giving the count the opportunity to take the poker from her hands and drop it to the floor.

She screamed as he pulled her into his arms again.

"No one will come to your aid, my lady. My servants know their place."

Diana stomped hard on his instep. When he let go of her with a cry of surprise and pain, she retrieved the poker. They were circling warily when Caroline and a slightly disheveled Lord Arnside burst into the room. Nicholas was wearing that exhilarated-little-boy look of a man who has been in a fight and won. Two footmen, one sporting a torn sleeve and the other a darkening eye, were in pursuit.

Nicholas gave a roar of sheer rage and charged the count.

Diana dropped the poker and ran thankfully into Caroline's arms. Nicholas grabbed the count by the throat and would have planted him a facer if Caroline had not intervened. Several more footmen ran into the room.

"That is *enough*, Lord Arnside," Caroline said. "Let him go. The footmen are ready to jump you, you fool!"

"Get out of here, idiots," the count shouted at his footmen.

"You have gone too far this time," Nicholas growled as he shoved the count hard against the wall. "Name your friends!"

"No, Nicholas! Don't!" Diana shouted, forcing herself between the men.

"Someone must avenge this insult—" Nicholas said.

"It will give me great pleasure to meet you, my lord," the count said with a sneer. *"Very* great pleasure." He put his hands possessively on Diana's shoulders. She jumped as if stung, and Nicholas made another lunge for the count.

"No! I will not have it! Are you both *insane?"* Diana's voice broke on a note of hysteria, and Caroline pulled her away from them.

"For heaven's sake," Caroline snapped at Nicholas as she put a supporting arm around Diana's waist. "Let him be and help me get her home. It's *over!"*

"Diana," Nicholas asked, looking deadly, "did he hurt you?"

"Of course I did not hurt her," the count said angrily. "I am not a barbarian!"

"Only because you did not get a chance," Diana said.

Nicholas picked up the poker. "So I see," he said dryly. "Perhaps Lady Diana did not require our assistance after all."

"Don't be odious. I want to go home," Diana told him. Her voice sounded pathetic to her own ears.

"My seconds will call on yours," the count said grimly.

Diana broke loose from Caroline's protective arm. "He is not going to meet you," she said. "I forbid it!"

"We will discuss this another time," Nicholas told the count. He took Diana's arm and led her away.

Caroline, meanwhile, had discovered the painting. After a

moment of shocked silence, she put the cover on it and picked it up.

"It has been a privilege," she said softly, "to observe your masterful technique with women."

"Damn you," Count Zarcone said, outraged that Caroline had witnessed his humiliation. He always had been irresistible to women after the customary token resistance that added spice to the game. He did not think Lady Diana, despite her unusually spirited defense, would have been any different. He fancied she had even enjoyed their play until Lord Arnside and the vexatious Caroline Benningham chose to interfere.

"Mrs. Benningham!" Arnside bellowed from the hall. "Are you coming?"

"Have a pleasant afternoon, Count," Caroline said scornfully. She balanced the heavy painting on one hip and stalked out.

The look in her eyes made Count Zarcone feel truly ashamed for the first time in his selfish existence.


Nicholas, Caroline and Diana arrived in Mount Street to find an agitated Penelope being comforted by a good-looking officer in a scarlet coat.

"Oh, Diana," Penelope cried, interrupting her companion in the middle of a consoling platitude. "I was so frightened."

"I am all right, love," Diana said soothingly. "I think I will go up to my room for a little while. Will you have Nurse bring Stephen to me?"

"Yes, Diana," Penelope said.

"Caroline, thank you," Diana said, taking her friend's hands in hers.

"I did nothing except send for Arnside after Bessie ran home and told us you had been kidnapped."

"I do not care to think what might have happened if you had not," Diana said. She bit her lip and looked up at Nicholas. "I am in your debt once again, Cousin. You are not to meet him, do you hear me?"

"Yes, Diana," he said, biting down hard on his frustration.

When Diana left the room, Nicholas turned to Penelope's companion and gave him such a malevolent stare that the gentleman hurriedly took his leave.

"Who was that coxcomb?" Nicholas demanded when Penelope returned to the room. "And what was he doing here?"

"He came to call after you and Caroline went to find Diana," Penelope said, quailing a little. "I was so worried that Captain Burnside offered to stay with me until you returned."

"Don't you know we must keep this business quiet?"

"It won't be easy with you shouting it at the top of your lungs," Caroline interrupted caustically. "If there is a servant in the house who does not know everything there is to know, it is no thanks to you!"

"Captain Burnside will not tell anyone, Nicholas," Penelope said tearfully.

"How do you know that?"

"Because I asked him not to," she said, avoiding his eye.

"He will tell everyone in his regiment! How could you have been such a little *fool,* Penelope?"

Penelope burst into tears and ran to her room.

Caroline and Nicholas faced each other.

"If you think I'm going to let you bully me, too, you're out of your mind," she said. "What possessed you to rage at Diana like a demented bull in the coach? You acted as if it were *her* fault that depraved monster snatched her."

"I didn't mean it," he said. "I was angry."

"One would think *you* were the injured party!"

Nicholas buried his face in his hands for a moment. "You are right," he said. "God, I'd like to take that damned count by the throat and—"

"It probably would make you feel better to get yourself killed, or to kill the count so you would be forced to flee the country," Caroline said dispassionately, "but I'm just an ignorant female, so I fail to see what good you think that would do Diana. Remember Diana, my lord? The *victim?*"

With that, she stamped out of the room.

Nicholas sat alone in the room for a quarter of an hour.

Jasper came into the room once, but Nicholas chased him away.

Edith joined him briefly.

"I knew it! My son's wife has bewitched you with all the rest," Edith said when he cautioned her not to breathe a word about the incident to her friends.

"She has *not* bewitched me," Nicholas said, although he feared it was true. "It could be damaging to her reputation if the tattlemongers catch wind of this affair."

"It would be no more than she deserves. She led him on, of course. No gentleman goes to such lengths without encouragement."

His reply was so crushing that she went to her room to sulk.

Servants cautiously peered into the room at intervals, but no one dared to speak to him.

"Nicholas," Diana said hesitantly, coming into the room some time later.

"I am sorry, Diana," he said at once. "I have been making a bloody fool of myself."

Her defenses shattered. He looked so dejected.

"It's all right," she said, just as if *he* were the one who needed comfort.

"It is *not* all right."

His head was slightly bowed, exposing the nape of his neck. With an effort, she restrained herself from caressing his thick, dark hair. Somehow, he reminded her of Stephen just then.

"Do you want to talk about it?" she asked, guessing he was angry with himself for shouting at Penelope. The poor child had fled to her room in tears.

"No."

"Then, at the risk of being inhospitable, I think you should go home," she said, trying for a light tone. "Penelope and Edith are afraid to come out of their rooms for fear you will eat them alive. And you've frightened my poor servants half to death."

"I was in such a blind rage I wanted to kill him," he said. "I *still* want to kill him. The thought of that degenerate filth touching you or any other decent woman makes me want to—"

"You promised me you would not meet him!"

"I won't. That would make it even worse. Then the whole world would think you are my mistress."

"It's over. He won't approach me again," she said soothingly.

"I'll go now," he said, standing up. "I'll call tomorrow, if I may. I owe Penelope, at least, an apology."

"Of course you may," she said, accompanying him to the front door.

Nicholas sent his carriage on without him and walked home slowly.

That night he couldn't sleep.

Tomorrow he must force himself to make amends to his fiancée for his cavalier treatment. He wouldn't blame her if she repudiated their engagement.

He refused to acknowledge the forlorn hope that flickered briefly before he snuffed it out.

# Twelve

A lesser woman might have retired to her bed with her vinai-grette clutched in her trembling hand at the prospect of all her carefully laid plans gone awry, but Edith had never been a lesser woman.

Her favorite nephew was about to succumb to the wiles of the designing hussy who had ruined Rupert, and Edith was going to save him for his own good, and for the good of her innocent goddaughter.

Some might say her method was unprincipled, but Edith, who was rarely given to introspection, merely congratulated herself upon her presence of mind.

She sat at her writing desk and drafted the fatal document. Then she stole down to the hall where the family's letters awaited the post.

Once back in her room, she smiled with sour satisfaction. Nicholas was going to have to marry Penelope now. Edith had left him no choice.

A week later, Nicholas was glancing idly at the London papers over breakfast when an item on the social pages caught his eye and made his spine go rigid.

He read it over in disbelief.

It was a terrible mistake. It had to be. And when he found out who was responsible for it, he would . . .

Nicholas brought himself up short.

What exactly *would* he do?

Once more he read the announcement of his betrothal to Miss Penelope Chalmers.

After all, his intention to marry Penelope was common knowledge in his family circle. He had avoided a formal engagement until he could be certain that the girl was not being constrained against her will. It had not occurred to him that *he* might be the one to have second thoughts about such an advantageous marriage.

Now he was well and truly trapped. He could never subject the innocent girl to the humiliation of having her engagement repudiated once it had been puffed off in the papers.

Not for a moment did he suspect Penelope herself of this treachery.

His Aunt Edith was the culprit, of course. She had been pushing him to make the engagement official because Penelope had been attracting too much attention from the dashing officers stationed near London for her peace of mind.

The devil of it was, Nicholas could not expose his aunt's perfidy without embarrassing Penelope, and he had no wish to hurt that pretty child, particularly since he himself had led her to believe he would marry her. He was willing to bet his new matched grays that Penelope had no idea the engagement announcement was a fraud.

He had a number of errands to perform first, and then he must see his aunt and Penelope. But when he was ushered into Dunwood House, the only occupant of the parlor was Diana, and he could tell she was furious.

"Well," she said, her eyes fairly shooting sparks. "I suppose you are pleased with yourself."

"Not especially," he said, trying to keep his own temper in check.

"I should think not. How *could* you do such a thing! And without a *word* to Penelope! What happened to your altruistic resolve to allow the poor girl to become properly acquainted with you before the engagement becomes final? Afraid of the competition?"

He was just as furious as she was.

"My affairs are none of your business, Diana," he said crisply, "but, for your information, I had nothing to do with this."

"And you expect me to believe that!"

"You may believe whatever you choose. For now, I should like to speak with my aunt in private."

Diana's eyes grew wide.

"Edith," she breathed. "I might have known. But Penelope thinks—"

"I can imagine what she thinks," Nicholas said ruefully. "The poor girl. Some engagement. I didn't ask for her hand in form, although her guardian's approval is a settled thing and has been for years. I didn't even ask her to marry me in so many words before the announcement appeared in the papers. She probably thinks I'm an arrogant boor."

"Not that," said Diana, "but two of her friends have called on us already, agog to see what you gave her for a betrothal present, and although you may sneer at such fripperies—"

"Of course I'm not sneering," he said wryly. "Penelope was probably embarrassed at having no token to produce from her betrothed husband. I can remedy that problem, at all events."

He produced a small gift box from the breast pocket of his waistcoat.

"I visited Rundell & Bridges this morning," he said.

"You will go through with it then," Diana said carefully.

"Of course. Have I any alternative?"

"No. I suppose not. It is just so awkward."

"Yes. And I intend to discuss that at length with Aunt Edith," he said grimly. "Where is she?"

The resulting interview with Lady Dunwood was short, to the point and extremely acrimonious. Edith endured Nicholas's clipped strictures with fortitude, angering him very much by making it clear she was unrepentant. She was willing to endure his ingratitude, she told him virtuously, for the satisfaction of seeing her dear ones happy.

She rounded off the discussion neatly with her Sharper Than a Serpent's Tooth speech.

The next interview was even more difficult for Nicholas in a different way.

When Penelope joined him in the parlor, her face was pink and young and vulnerable. She smiled shyly at him. He launched into his rehearsed explanation for the "misunderstanding."

"Penelope, I am covered with shame," he told her. "I penned the announcement last week, intending to visit your guardian in form to ask permission to pay my addresses to you this week and then ask you to marry me upon my return. My idiot of a secretary must have seen it on my desk and posted it."

It wasn't very plausible, but he could tell by the relaxation of her features that she accepted it.

"Will you marry me, Penelope?" he asked ruefully. "I shall look like the devil's own fool if you will not."

"Yes," she said, smiling tentatively at him. She looked a little apprehensive, but Nicholas supposed that must be natural under the circumstances.

He kissed her hand, then her cheek. He presented his gift.

"Oh, Nicholas!" she exclaimed as she took the emerald and diamond earrings from the box. "How very beautiful!"

They were a little sophisticated for a damsel in her first season, but Penelope was thrilled. She had a jewel box full of demure pearls and amethysts. His gift represented her first adult jewelry.

"I am glad you like them," he said. "Would you care to go for a drive in the park with me?"

She would like nothing better, she assured him.

Nicholas drove too fast, and Penelope was always queasy at the end of their excursions. But she was only human, and she hoped the two ladies who had laughed up their sleeves at her for not having a betrothal gift to show them earlier in the day would be in the park to witness her triumph.

Now she felt well and truly betrothed. Her natural surprise and disappointment at learning about her own engagement from reading the newspapers was forgotten.

When she was beside Nicholas in his curricle, she stole a

glance at him from under her lashes. He was looking straight ahead, and his gaze was abstracted.

Once they arrived in the park, it wasn't long before her usual circle of friends gathered around them to offer their congratulations and wishes for her happiness.

Penelope obviously enjoyed being at the center of an admiring crowd. When her friends asked her about her wedding plans and how many gowns would form her trousseau, she gave every appearance of a young lady enthusiastically looking forward to the day when she would become a viscountess.

Well, Nicholas told himself firmly, he knew it was not likely to be a love match when it was first proposed to him. He still was determined to spend as much time with Penelope as possible, but at that moment he wished they had been on horseback so he could leave Penelope with the gaggle of silly chits while he exchanged greetings with his friends. He could hardly leave Penelope alone in the curricle while he sought entertainment elsewhere, however.

Still, riding was not exactly a high treat when one was escorting a lady with a nag as lethargic as the exasperating Molasses.

"Wouldn't you like a different horse?" he asked when her friends moved on. "A younger one with a bit more spirit?"

Penelope only looked alarmed.

"No," he said glumly. "I suppose not."

He would have been surprised to learn that a certain dashing cavalry officer was as discouraged by Arnside's excursion with his fiancée as he was.

For Captain Burnside, Lord Arnside's persistence in remaining at his future bride's side during every waking moment was fraught with sinister implications. It was becoming more and more difficult for the captain to have a private conversation with Penelope.

The announcement in the papers filled him with alarm. He had to marry her soon or he would be in the basket. It was not going to be easy to snatch the prize from under Lord Arnside's nose, particularly now that the engagement was official, but he would manage. Everything depended upon it.

Nicholas and his fiancée had just done their third turn around the park when Penelope gasped and laid a hand on her escort's arm.

"What's the matter? Shall I slow 'em down?" Nicholas asked in alarm. He had soon learned of his betrothed's unendearing tendency to get sick in carriages that were traveling too fast.

"Mr. Rivers! I promised him I would meet him in Mount Street for a sitting at two o'clock today!"

"You are ten minutes late already," Nicholas said, glancing at his timepiece and trying to look regretful. "We shall leave right now."

By the time they arrived in Mount Street, Penelope was a half hour late. They found Bernard having refreshments with Diana and Edith.

"There you are, my dear," Diana said, smiling. "We have been feeding Mr. Rivers to keep him against your return."

"I am so sorry, Mr. Rivers," Penelope said. "I lost track of the time—"

"It is perfectly all right," the artist said politely. He looked a trifle strained.

"I will change immediately—"

"No, have some tea, Miss Chalmers," he insisted. "I would prefer that you eat something. There is no hurry, unless you have another engagement."

She glared at him and sat down. He was treating her like a baby again.

"It has been four weeks," she told Mr. Rivers. "Is it *ever* going to be finished?"

"Soon," he said noncommittally as he helped himself to another scone.

"Penelope, dear," Diana said. "You must have one of these sandwiches."

Penelope's hostile look made Diana blink with surprise.

"Cousin," Mr. Rivers said to Nicholas after he had finished his scone, "may I have a word with you before I go upstairs?"

"Certainly, Bernard," Nicholas said. "Will the ladies excuse us?"

"Of course," Diana said politely. "You may use the library."

The men were silent until Nicholas closed the library door.

"I will get right to the point, Nick," Bernard said. "I'm homeless."

Nicholas grinned.

"Good for you," he said. "I must admit it was a trifle awkward having my cousin living as a dependent in Count Zarcone's house."

"It was uncomfortable for me as well, especially lately when he ordered me to carry peace offerings from him to Lady Diana and I refused. But my pockets are to let at present. I spent all of my blunt on supplies because I expected to have free lodging in England while the count is here."

"That problem is easily remedied," Nicholas said. "I would be delighted to have you stay with me. I've plenty of room."

"I am obliged to you," Bernard said, avoiding his cousin's eye. "It isn't an easy thing to ask."

"I know," Nicholas said, clasping him on the shoulder. "You've always been proud as bedamned, unlike all my other Rivers relations, who can't get enough of hanging on my sleeve."

"I'd better go upstairs now," Bernard said, looking a little embarrassed. "Miss Chalmers will be ready for her sitting."

"Yes. We are all anxious to see this masterpiece."

Bernard gave him a weak smile.

"Lady Diana accepted my apology for that other painting at once, even though I would not have blamed her for refusing to let me into her house. She said it was not my fault but hers, since she should not have been at the count's palace in the first place. It made me feel a good deal more comfortable, I can tell you."

"She is a remarkable lady," Nicholas said, thinking it was just like Diana to be sensitive to Bernard's feelings. "By the way, you are to have the painting back."

"I thought surely Lady Diana would have it destroyed," Bernard said, astonished. "I would not blame her."

"Neither would I, but Penelope made a persuasive case for its preservation. She seems to think that, despite the potential embarrassment to Lady Diana, it is unconscionable to destroy an artist's work without his consent. She and Lady Diana have put their heads together and agreed you shall have it back with the stipulation that you will not sell it or exhibit it until several decades have passed, so no one who sees it will remember what she looked like in her youth. Does that seem agreeable to you?"

Bernard was astonished.

"I had not hoped for such consideration from Lady Diana, or such sensitivity from Miss Chalmers," he said slowly, digesting the fact that one so young as Penelope would be wise enough to recognize the link an artist forms with all his work. It made him feel oddly exposed. "Lady Diana's condition seems infinitely reasonable."

"Very good. I have the thing stored in a cupboard at my house. You may have it any time you choose."

"Thank you, Nick. I had better join Miss Chalmers now." He left the room to make his way to the studio. Bernard found Penelope standing before the portrait, which was covered with a heavy cloth bag. Her head was tilted to one side as if she were trying to see through the wrappings. She reminded him of a curious ginger kitten.

"Patience," he said, smiling. "Where is our watchdog?"

"No watchdog today. Diana is having a party tonight and all the servants are busy."

"I see."

"Why are you looking at me that way? Is something wrong?" she asked, blushing.

"No. Nothing at all. May I offer you my felicitations upon your engagement?"

"You may. Thank you, Mr. Rivers," she said in a small voice.

He unwrapped the portrait, careful to shield it from Penelope's eyes, and set it on the easel. Then he methodically laid out his supplies.

"There, now," he said when everything was arranged to his satisfaction. "If you'll take your position . . ."

Bernard worked swiftly, glancing at her now and then with

an absorbed scowl. Suddenly he put down his brush, stood back and sighed.

"It is finished," he said. He looked at her, then at the clock. "Oh, Lord. It's been almost two hours. Forgive me. I lost all track of time."

"May I see it?" she asked.

"Of course."

He stepped back so she could look at the portrait. She stood in her curious kitten pose for a long time.

"Do I really look like that?" she asked, turning at last. Her eyes were shining.

"Yes," he said solemnly. He looked at her so intently that her smile faded and she bit her lip.

"May I call the others?" Her voice was a little breathless. "Perhaps Nicholas is still in the house."

"If you wish."

He stood by silently while Lady Diana, the dowager and Nicholas filed into the room after Penelope to see the wonder.

"It is exquisite," Diana exclaimed. "Nothing could be more charming!"

"Delightful," the dowager said with chilly dignity. "Just the thing for your dining room at Hillwood, Nicholas."

"Yes," Nicholas agreed, looking pleased. "You have done a superb job, Bernard. I am quite literally in your debt. If you will accompany me to my house, I will pay you for the portrait. You may move in at any time, by the way."

"Thank you, Nick," Bernard said absently.

"Penelope, my dear," Diana said. "You look fagged to death. You must lie on your bed for an hour or two, or you will be in no position to enjoy the party tonight."

"I am rather tired," Penelope said. She looked at Bernard, but he could not think of a thing to say to her.

Penelope gave him an uncertain smile and left the room with Lady Diana and the dowager.

"Are you ready?" Nicholas asked Bernard.

"I beg your pardon? Oh, of course. I need to get my things together. I will be with you directly."

Nicholas went over to the portrait and looked at it carefully.

The painted face was radiant, and the copper hair was bathed in light. Nicholas never had seen a portrait so luminous and delicately executed.

"I had no idea you were capable of this, Bernard." There was awe in his voice. "It's stunning."

"It's finished, at any rate," Bernard said, running a hand through his disordered hair.

Nicholas turned and regarded Bernard with some surprise.

"What is wrong, Bernard? Are you not satisfied with it?"

"Yes, of course," Bernard said. "Don't regard me. I am always like this when I finish a painting. In the beginning I have an idea of how it will look when I am finished, then it becomes something quite different. It's . . . disquieting."

Nicholas smiled.

"You make it sound mysterious."

"It is, rather," Bernard said, lapsing into moody silence.

After a moment, he straightened and gathered his wits about him. He put his supplies in the case he always carried, then accompanied Nicholas downstairs to take leave of the ladies.

"I understand from Penelope that you expect to leave London at the end of the season," Lady Diana said conversationally.

"Yes," Bernard said. "I will go home to the country to visit my mother. I expect I will be in India by the end of the year."

"You must delay your trip to India at least until autumn," Nick said heartily, "so you may come to the wedding. Is that not so, my dear?"

"Of course," Penelope said at once.

"We shall see," Bernard said, not meeting her eyes.

# Thirteen

"James, you must not!" exclaimed Penelope as she clutched at the sleeve of Captain Burnside's uniform. The knife blade gleamed wickedly in the moonlight.

"Do not try to stop me," he said. "I don't care to live if you won't marry me."

"You must not say such things!" she cried.

They were in the garden of Diana's town house. Penelope had wanted to refuse when Captain Burnside suggested that they step outside to get some relief from the hot, stuffy ballroom, but she had not wanted to appear missish. Now she wished she had remained inside.

"My darling, listen to me," he said earnestly. "He doesn't love you. You will become an old woman before your time, married to a cold, unfeeling husband like Arnside."

"I *must* marry him," Penelope said, wide-eyed.

Captain Burnside pulled her into his arms.

"There isn't anything I wouldn't dare to make you mine!"

She pushed him away.

"No," she said, trembling. "You will forget me—"

"Never," he said in a defeated tone. "I shall kill myself."

"No!"

"Yes! It would be better this way. A quick death is better than a long life of misery without you."

"You must not!"

"I will. You have my life in your hands, Penelope."

Penelope was absolutely wretched. When she had met Captain Burnside at the beginning of the season, he was a happy, high-spirited officer. She had driven him to this desperation, although she had not meant to. He was so tender and romantic. He adored her. And he needed her.

On the other hand, her affianced husband was always kind, but he hardly behaved like a man in love.

Penelope looked at the captain's pleading face and weakened.

Perhaps Nicholas would not mind so *very* much if she did not marry him.

"All right, James," she said in a small, terrified voice. "I will marry you."

"My angel!" he said ecstatically. "You have made me the happiest of men." He kissed her passionately, and Penelope trembled. When he released her, she felt numb.

"My poor little one," James said tenderly, "I have frightened you with my ardor. Forgive me. I won't do anything you don't like. I promise."

He kissed her hand.

"I must hire a coach," he said. "I will get a message to you when all is ready. It will hurt me to see you dance with him tonight, but I will endure it because I know you will be mine."

He took her back into the ballroom, where they engaged in conversation with some of his fellow officers.

"That fellow again," Nicholas said crossly to Diana, indicating Captain Burnside. "He has been dangling after Penelope for weeks."

Diana frowned.

"He does seem to seek out Penelope's company rather often," she said. "It's only a case of calf-love, of course, but I will have a talk with the man."

"Perhaps I should see him," Arnside suggested. "No offense, my dear, but it's unlikely you will be able to frighten him into propriety if he's determined to make a cake of himself."

"I do not think you should dignify his pretensions," Diana said thoughtfully. "The affair should be treated as the childish attachment it is. We don't want any talk."

"I suppose you're right," he said. "Do you know anything about him?"

"Not much. Good birth. No fortune. His commission was purchased by a rich uncle, but he is not the uncle's heir."

"For someone who attaches no particular significance to the man's attentions, you certainly have had him thoroughly investigated," he said. "Is he a fortune hunter?"

"He might be," she admitted. "He appears to be a rather expensive man."

Nicholas scowled.

"It is time I paid some attention to my fiancée."

He strolled over to his betrothed and took her hand. He didn't bother to greet her companions.

"Penelope, my dear," he said compellingly. "Come dance with me."

"So masterful," sighed one of Penelope's female companions wistfully to her friend. Nicholas winced.

Before Penelope had a chance to respond to his invitation, Nicholas had pulled her into a set that was forming for a country dance.

Lady Diana approached Captain Burnside and put a hand on his arm to get his attention as he watched Penelope with hot, jealous eyes. She was accompanied by a blushing young woman.

"Captain Burnside, you are not dancing," Diana said in her best hostess voice. "May I present Miss Willoughby as a very desirable partner?"

Anne Willoughby was a shy young lady with dusky curls and wide, trusting amber eyes. The captain regarded her with well-bred indifference. She was pretty enough, but James had made a minute study of all the season's debutantes and he knew that although Miss Willoughby was the cousin of a wealthy heiress, the girl herself was as impoverished as he was. Still, he made his bow to the young lady and was accepted for the next dance.

When the dance was over, he wandered over to the refreshment table and procured a glass of champagne. Then he stood against the wall and watched Penelope dance with her fiancé.

Lady Diana approached the captain again. He was relieved to see she did not have another insipid debutante in tow for him to dance with.

"Captain Burnside," she said. "I wonder if I might have a word with you."

The ensuing conversation, although it was conducted in the guise of a gentle warning, was enough to put Captain Burnside on his guard.

Lady Diana was perfectly civil in her request that he stop being so particular in his attentions to Penelope. But he realized he must act before Penelope's jailers took steps to remove Penelope from his influence. It would be fatal to his plans if Penelope was taken to Lady Diana's manor in Kent, where James would have difficulty gaining admittance.

Between dances he contrived to whisper into Penelope's ear.

"Lady Diana suspects," he said tersely. "We must not be seen together for a little while to avoid suspicion. But do not despair. I will come for you soon."

A few minutes later, he took his leave of Lady Diana and the dowager Lady Dunwood.

Penelope watched him depart with troubled eyes. She was relieved to see him go, because his relentless pursuit left her confused and apprehensive. But she knew he was only going so he could plan their elopement. It would make a dreadful scandal. Nicholas would be humiliated. Diana would never speak to her again.

"What have I done?" Penelope whispered.

"I beg your pardon, Miss Chalmers?" asked Mr. Rivers, who had just arrived.

"Oh. I did not see you, Mr. Rivers," she said, trying to smile. Her voice sounded too high-pitched to her own ears.

"You look flushed. Are you all right?" he asked.

She eyed him with disfavor.

"Mr. Rivers, I am *not* delicate!"

"No?" he said, touching the short lace sleeve of her dainty gown. "You *look* delicate."

"That almost sounded like a compliment," she said incredulously.

"Clever girl!" he said with a disarming smile. "Maybe you should sit down for a little while. Shall I procure some lemonade for you?"

"If you please," she said, thankful he didn't suggest a walk in the gardens. Not that *he* would want to marry her. He didn't even like her. The compliment must have been an aberration.

Mr. Rivers led her to a chair and excused himself to fetch the lemonade. However, Nicholas brought her the promised beverage.

"Bernard tells me you are unwell, my dear," Nicholas said, giving her the glass.

"I am all right. Just a little tired."

"Bernard was afraid he had worn you out with the sitting today. He is very sorry. Why don't you dance with him when you are recovered to show him you forgive him?"

"All right, Nicholas," she said, deciding it was useless to point out there was nothing in the least the matter with her. She sipped her lemonade, and he left her as soon as he decently could.

If Nicholas were in love with her, he wouldn't make his relatives dance with her so he wouldn't have to. Clearly, her duty was to elope with Captain Burnside, for she couldn't have his blood on her hands. Diana and Mr. Rivers walked over to her after a few minutes.

"Are you feeling better, Penelope?" Diana asked kindly.

"Yes. I was so parched," she said, although her smile was a trifle forced. She suspected that Mr. Rivers told everybody in the room she was feeling unwell.

"Then perhaps you will dance with poor Mr. Rivers. He doesn't know many people in London because he was in Italy for so long."

Penelope realized that Mr. Rivers was looking a little uncertain. Poor man, she thought. It must be very uncomfortable to be a stranger.

She gave him her hand. He led her into the waltz and held her somewhat stiffly away from him as if he were half afraid to touch her.

"Don't you want to dance with me?" she asked.

"Of course I do," Bernard said, mentally scolding himself for his awkwardness. He relaxed and held her closer, but not too close for decorum. "Better?"

"Yes," she said, blushing slightly.

"I'll probably step all over your feet," he said conversationally. "I've not had much practice."

"I think you're very good," she said.

They were silent for a moment.

"Mr. Rivers?"

"Yes, Miss Chalmers?"

*"Now* will you tell me about Italy?"

Her expectant face was so adorable that he had an overpowering impulse to kiss her. The innocent girl had no idea what she was doing to him.

"All right," he said, smiling crookedly.

Nicholas came out of the card room, where he had gone to exchange greetings with friends. His eyes went straight to Lady Diana, who was standing by the door and accepting the compliments of the guests who were leaving.

"You look very pleased with yourself," he said when the guests had taken their departure.

"I am," she said triumphantly. "I think I handled the business with Captain Burnside quite well. He was perfectly reasonable. In fact, he seemed unaware he had been so particular in his attentions and begged my pardon."

"That's all right, then," Nicholas said.

"So you no longer need fear being jilted."

"I wasn't worried about that," he said, his eyes glinting with amusement. "I just didn't like the idea of the fellow making a cake of himself over my fiancée. Shockingly bad *ton,* you know."

"Quite," Diana agreed.

"Where is Penelope, by the way? Not flirting with any more besotted officers, I trust?"

"No, she's dancing with your cousin," she said. "See?"

"Ah," Arnside said, noting with approval that Bernard was holding Penelope at a proper distance. "I can depend on Bernard to behave himself. Besides, he's not in the petticoat line."

"I'm delighted that he is no longer employed by the count," Diana said benevolently. "Your cousin is a very nice man."

"Yes, and he's earned his reprieve," Nicholas said as the waltz ended. He sighed but went with perfectly good grace to dance with his fiancée.

# Fourteen

A few weeks after Captain James Burnside ceased to haunt Mount Street, Penelope's natural gaiety reasserted itself. Until then she was a nervous shadow of her former self, afraid at any moment that he would claim her.

When he failed to do so, Penelope allowed herself to believe she was safe and entered into the whirl of balls, routs and theater parties with renewed vigor.

Perhaps, she hoped, he had decided against the scheme. For herself, she regretted her rash promise to marry him. The scandal would be dreadful. She never again would be received in polite company. And, besides, it would be a shame for all the beautiful brideclothes she had ordered to go to waste.

Like every young lady of high birth, Penelope wanted a lavish wedding. It occurred to her that if she were truly in love with the handsome captain she would consider irrelevant such mundane considerations as a trousseau that was the envy of all her friends.

Optimistically believing that Captain Burnside had reconsidered his plan to fly with her to the border, she was totally unprepared for his summons when it came.

She was in the lending library perusing a book when an urgent whisper from the next stack of shelves arrested her attention.

"Penelope," whispered the captain.

He was peering at her from behind the leather bindings, and she had a cowardly impulse to run. Instead, she reluctantly approached him, and he walked around the bookcase to face her.

"Lady Diana is with me," she whispered.

"I saw her. Listen, my love. It is arranged for tomorrow night. The coach will be waiting in the next street. You must slip out of the house when everyone is asleep and join me there. I will wait all night if necessary."

"James, I don't think——"

He grasped her wrist. His face was close to hers.

"You must not fail me," he said urgently. "If you do, my death will be on your hands."

Diana came up behind Penelope at that moment and touched her on the shoulder.

Penelope jumped guiltily and saw that the captain, who apparently had seen Diana approach, had disappeared.

"Were you talking to someone, Penelope?" Diana asked.

"No. No one," Penelope said nervously.

Diana frowned.

"Is something wrong, then?"

"No. Nothing at all."

"Good. We must return to the house. Did you find your book?"

"No," Penelope said distractedly. "Someone must have borrowed it."

"What a pity! Well, we must be on our way."

For the rest of the day Penelope answered all questions addressed to her quite at random. She ate very little. And she excused herself from a ball that evening, saying she preferred to stay at home and retire early.

"Isn't Penelope feeling well?" Nicholas asked Diana when Penelope left the parlor on the pretext of a headache during his visit.

"Apparently not," Diana said, looking worried. "If I didn't know better, I would swear . . ." She broke off and became absorbed in selecting a biscuit from the plate.

"You would swear?" prompted Nicholas.

"Nothing," she said.

Edith and Nicholas began talking about the wedding, and

Diana hardly spoke at all. Nicholas left eventually, and Diana sat for a long time in the playroom with Stephen, rocking him and thinking about Penelope's odd behavior.

Diana had seen such behavior before. Penelope acted exactly the way Diana had behaved as an adolescent whenever she was about to do something dreadful. Penelope loved balls. She must be very disturbed if she would voluntarily miss one to go to bed early.

That night Diana got up from her bed several times and looked in on Penelope. Each time she found her sleeping fitfully. Perhaps, Diana told herself, she was just nervous about her wedding. The poor girl had no mother, and she might be dreading the intimacies of marriage. Perhaps Diana could put her mind at rest.

When she tried to discuss these matters with Penelope the following morning, however, Diana saw that she had succeeded only in alarming the poor girl.

Penelope's nervousness became more apparent throughout the day. When Nicholas called to take her riding in the park, she begged off.

"Something is wrong," Nicholas told Diana and Edith in concern after Penelope had gone to her room with another headache. "Perhaps she has been wearing herself to a thread with so many parties."

"Perhaps," Diana said. "She declined an invitation to a ball at Lady Kirkland's last night, so maybe she is tired."

Diana excused herself from the parlor as soon as she decently could because she had an idea what was wrong with Penelope and she didn't want Arnside to know about it. She went up and knocked gently on Penelope's door, hoping the girl would confide in her, but Penelope turned her tearfully away.

A little before three o'clock in the morning, Diana's worst fears were realized. She woke suddenly and, unable to go back to sleep, walked up to the nursery to check on her son. When she went to Penelope's room, she found her bed empty.

A letter addressed to Diana was propped on the pillow. Diana read it and then let it fall from nerveless fingers. Plainly,

Penelope had not intended for it to be read until the following day. It was stained with tears.

*Don't panic,* Diana told herself sternly. She rang for Bessie and swore her to secrecy. Then she summoned Jasper, who joined her looking as majestic as ever, his dignity impaired only by an appearance of having donned his clothes in a hurry.

"Yes, my lady?" he inquired. He was much too well trained to express surprise that Her Ladyship was up and dressed for the street at half past three in the morning.

"Jasper, please send word that my coach must be readied immediately. I am going out."

"Yes, my lady."

"And, Jasper," she said, "if anyone asks where I have gone, you will say it is a family matter and I will return within a day or two. Miss Chalmers will return with me."

"Yes, my lady," he said, his voice perfectly bland even though she knew that his brain must be reeling with conjecture.

"You will know how to depress speculation, Jasper, will you not?" she asked, giving him a straight look.

"You may depend on me, my lady."

"Thank you, Jasper."

She took her coachman and Gaskin, her most loyal and discreet footman, with her in case Penelope's companion should prove difficult. Soon she was on the road to Scotland. It wasn't long before her coach was nearly swept off the road by a black equipage drawn by four magnificent horses. The black coach stopped ahead, blocking her way.

The driver of the coach jumped down from the box and approached. Diana heard the scrape of her coachman's firearm being drawn from its place, and pushed open the door of her carriage.

"No, wait," she said to her coachman, recognizing the crest on the other coach as her eyes adjusted to the moonlight.

Nicholas put down the steps so she could alight.

"What do you know about this business, Diana?" he asked grimly.

"Nicholas, she's eloped with that dreadful Captain Burnside! I never would have believed it of her. We must stop her before—"

"*I* shall stop her," Nicholas said firmly. He looked up at the coachman and Gaskin sitting on the box. "Take your mistress back to Mount Street, and not a word of this business to anyone or I will personally cut out your livers."

This was said in a perfectly civil tone, but the men, hastening to reassure His Lordship, seemed to have no doubt he would carry out the threat in spirit, if not in literal truth.

"Wait! I am going with you!" Diana said as he turned and was about to return to his coach. "You will scare the poor child to death."

Nicholas stopped and looked at her.

"It would serve her right," he said grimly.

"Why are we standing here arguing? We must stop them!"

Nicholas sighed and helped Diana onto the seat beside him, then whipped up the horses.

Light was just clearing through the trees when they came upon a sad-looking equipage and two weary horses stopped by the side of the road.

Captain Burnside looked as if he would like to turn tail and run when Nicholas stepped down from the seat of his coach. Diana, left to her own devices, scrambled down as best she could.

"I don't know how you persuaded my fiancée to run away with you," Nicholas told the captain calmly, "but it will give me the greatest of pleasure to put a bullet through you."

"Never mind that! Where is Penelope?" Diana demanded fiercely after she looked inside the open door of the hired coach and discovered it to be empty. "Speak, you villain!"

"I am here," came a weak voice from the trees beside the road. "I was just . . . sick for a moment."

"My poor dear," Diana said when Penelope tottered wearily from behind the trees. Her face was wan and tear-stained in the dawn light. She went straight to Diana, who enfolded her in her arms and whispered soothingly to her as if she were Stephen's age instead of a worldly sixteen. "It's all right now, darling," Diana crooned.

After a moment, Penelope emerged from Diana's embrace and went to stand, shamefaced, before Nicholas.

"Nicholas, I am so sorry," she said tearfully. "I didn't want to do it. James said he would kill himself if I didn't run away with him."

"It appears Captain Burnside will find himself dead in any case, I'm afraid," Nicholas said with an unpleasant smile on his face.

"No, Nicholas, you must not!" Penelope pleaded as Diana put her hands on her hips in exasperation and glared at him.

"Surely you do not wish to marry him after all," Nicholas said coldly.

"You know I don't. I'm thinking of you."

"Are you afraid he'll kill *me,* Penelope?" he asked in grim amusement. The look in his eye seemed to strike terror in Captain Burnside's breast.

"No, but you'll kill *him,* and then you'll have to flee the country and it will be all my fault!" she said.

Nicholas smiled at her. "You are right, my dear," he said. "I don't wish to flee the country, much as I would enjoy exterminating this vermin."

Captain Burnside gave a hiss of outrage at this insult.

"Stop it," Diana said crossly. "Let that horrible man go so we can take Penelope home!"


Nicholas chafed at the slow pace he had to maintain on the journey back to Mount Street in consideration for the state of Penelope's stomach.

"We'll arrive in London just as people are going about their business," he grumbled. "You'll have to get inside with Penelope before long."

"What I don't understand," Diana said from her seat beside Nicholas on the box, "is how you knew he would do this."

"Pure chance. Captain Burnside rented the coach from a stable owned by one of my former servants. I set the man up in business, and he is very grateful to me. Our friend the captain could not resist boasting to this insignificant little man about his conquest of the rich heiress. The silly gudgeon didn't think the names Lord Arnside and Miss Chalmers would mean anything to a lowly stable master. The man sent me a message, but I was out and didn't come home until well after three o'clock this morning. When I saw your coach on the road, I knew we were on the same errand."

"Don't be harsh with her, Nicholas," Diana begged.

"I won't. She's suffered enough." He gave a crack of laughter. "And so has he. Can you imagine being trapped in a coach all the way to Scotland with a female who becomes nauseated by the motion of a carriage?"

"That is *not* funny, my lord," Diana snapped.

He cocked an amused eyebrow at her. "So it's 'my lord' again, is it? Actually, my dear, you might admit that I'm behaving beautifully about all this. I haven't even repudiated my engagement."

"You would never do such a thing!"

"Of course not. But I assure you that no one would blame me, if word of this night's work gets out."

"It *mustn't!*" Diana said vehemently.

But it did.

Penelope's aborted flight to the border with Captain Burnside was common knowledge almost before Nicholas set the ladies down in Mount Street.

Penelope was prostrated with shame. Several of her more brazen acquaintances presented themselves on Diana's doorstep early in the afternoon in order to wring the shocking details out of Penelope, but Diana had the foresight to have Jasper deny her to visitors.

Edith, roused to fury at the thought that Penelope would dare make a botch of the marriage she had arranged, railed at the poor child for her treachery.

"Heaven knows you don't deserve to marry so fine a gentleman," Edith scolded.

Indeed, the gossip mill reported that Nicholas already had cried off.

"What are we going to do?" Diana asked Nicholas when he came to call on the ladies.

"Well, for one thing, I am not going to cry off," he said, kissing Penelope's hand. "I have something for you, my dear. By good fortune, it arrived from the jeweler's this morning. Flash this at the tabbies the next time you go out. That should silence them."

He reached into his waistcoat pocket and produced an emerald and diamond engagement ring, which he placed on her finger. Then he kissed her cheek.

"Oh, Nicholas! You are so kind to me," she said, her lower lip quivering.

"None of that, my girl," he said bracingly.

"I don't deserve your forgiveness after what I've done."

"It wasn't your fault. That fellow should be horsewhipped for imposing on you. What do you say, Penelope? I wouldn't have to flee the country if I merely horsewhipped him."

In spite of herself, Penelope laughed.

"That's better," Arnside said approvingly. "It's not so bad, my dear. They'll find something else to talk about in a week or two."

"It will be excessively uncomfortable for us until they do," Diana pointed out. "I suggest we retreat."

"Retreat?" Nicholas asked.

"To Kent."

"Do you think that would answer?" Penelope was beginning to look more hopeful.

"I do, indeed," Diana said with a mischievous twinkle in her eye. "You can depend on me to know what is best in this instance. I have had a great deal of experience in living down scandals."

"I would not boast of it," Edith said maliciously.

"I assure you, I am not," Diana told her with a cool look.

"I wouldn't mind going into the country," Penelope said. "It's no fun going to parties, anyway, when everyone is whispering about you."

"It would only be for a week or two," Diana promised her, "until the talk dies down. Nicholas will come with us, of course."

"Will I?" he asked, looking astonished.

"Of course you will! If we go into the country and you don't go with us, it will only give substance to the rumor that you intend to cry off."

"True," he said. "I hadn't thought of that. Very well. I could stand to rusticate for a little while. I will look into Stephen's affairs while I am in Kent. I am one of his trustees, and I have shirked my responsibilities long enough."

"Are you implying that Mr. Raymond Milton is mismanaging my grandson's fortune?" Edith asked coldly.

"I never said so," Nicholas told her. "I only said it was my responsibility to look into it."

Edith glared at Diana, and Diana glared right back at her. Diana knew that Edith never had been convinced that Stephen was Rupert's son. In the dowager's mind, her husband's brother had every right to do as he pleased with the legacy that should have been his. Diana had no doubt that Edith would cheerfully throw her despised sister-in-law out of her own house with only the clothes on her back and Stephen with her, if she could.

# Fifteen

The journey to Kent was accomplished in good time because Penelope only asked to stop twice on the road to allow her queasy stomach to settle.

Diana went straight to the nurseries located in the east wing and installed her sleeping son there. No one saw her for several hours.

Meanwhile, Nicholas drew Mr. Milton aside and told him he wished to examine all the accounts that had to do with the estate. The older man's beefy neck turned red, but he kept up the pretense of joviality.

"You hasty young fellows," he said, wagging an admonishing finger at Nicholas. "Always finding fault where none exists."

"I would remind you that I am Stephen's other trustee, Mr. Milton," Nicholas said patiently.

"You may depend on me to protect my great-nephew's interests."

"I am certain you are right," Nicholas said calmly. "The accounts, if you please."

Edith, who was listening to this conversation with growing displeasure, chose to intervene.

"My daughter-in-law has been filling Nicholas's head with a lot of nonsense, Raymond," she said. "I'd like to know what that hussy knows about managing an estate."

"Naughty minx," said Mr. Milton, assuming a playful tone.

"Mustn't stick her pretty little nose into what doesn't concern her, eh, Arnside?"

He would have accompanied this repellent sentiment with a hearty dig in Nicholas's ribs if Nicholas hadn't stared him down.

"Nevertheless," Nicholas said firmly. "I'll satisfy myself."

Edith was inclined to argue, but Nicholas curtly informed her that the matter at hand was between the two trustees. She flounced from the room in a miff.

Nicholas examined each bill of sale with compressed lips, extracting one for several purebred hunters from among them.

"What is this?" asked Nicholas, tossing it before Mr. Milton.

"My great-nephew is a gentleman, sir. Surely a sporting man such as yourself would agree he needs a first-rate stable."

"Considering he will not be hunting until most of these specimens are in their dotage, I think the question is moot," Nicholas said dryly.

"I know it seems a trifle expensive, my boy, but I have introduced a great many economies to the household."

"I suppose you mean the firing of the bailiff and the steward. I should like to hear more about that, if you please."

Mr. Milton squirmed uncomfortably, confirming Nicholas's suspicion that both these employees had been fired because they had dared to protest the high-handed manner with which he was managing the estate.

"Eh, well, it seems an extravagance to employ two men to manage the estate when I can do so perfectly well. After all, I was born here."

Nicholas's eyebrows rose when he examined another bill.

"I see that my nephew is a proud possessor of a great quantity of vintage wine."

"You can't say *that's* not a good investment. By the time the boy is twenty, it should be prime."

Nicholas suspected that not a single bottle would survive the year. All the signs of high living were on Raymond. He had grown a paunch. His nose was perpetually red. His clothes were expensively made, exactly what a well-breeched country squire would wear. Nicholas knew that Diana was right about his mismanagement of Stephen's fortune. The papers had revealed several dubious investments that might make significant inroads into Stephen's legacy if they failed, as Nicholas had no doubt they would. If by some miracle they proved sound, Nicholas suspected the resulting windfall would line Mr. Milton's pockets rather than Stephen's.

Nicholas had been serving with his regiment when Rupert died, but he should have taken an active role in his young cousin's affairs upon his return from war. If he had done his duty by the child, Nicholas thought guiltily, Mr. Milton would not have felt secure enough in his position to make free with his great-nephew's fortune.

"All of you must be very hungry after your journey," said Mr. Milton, apparently eager to end this uncomfortable interview. "Edith said she would have tea and refreshments laid out. Let us join the ladies."

"All right," Nicholas said, standing. "I expect the rest of it will wait until tomorrow."

Mr. Milton looked resentful.

"I have nothing to hide!" he said.

Nicholas raised his eyebrows.

"Have I said you did?"

Feeling depressed, Nicholas joined the others around the tea table in the parlor. Edith had never been a particularly competent mistress. Nor, because of her utter indifference to domestic affairs, had the servants put themselves to any pains to keep the rooms clean. He couldn't help contrasting the house's general air of neglect with the orderliness of Diana's household on Mount Street.

Nicholas suspected that only during Diana's brief tenure as mistress during her marriage to Rupert had there been any improvement at the estate in Kent. Now with Rupert dead, Edith had reasserted her authority over the household, and her brother-in-law supported her.

The female servants were undisciplined and slatternly. Nicholas didn't like the familiar way one or two of them eyed

Mr. Milton. It was obvious to Nicholas that Mr. Milton had been trifling with them. God, what a place he'd brought Penelope and young Stephen to!

He excused himself from the parlor as soon as he decently could and took a long ride around the fields. What he saw discouraged him. The bailiff's presence was sorely missed.

The crops were stunted. Obviously, the seed had not been put into the ground early enough in the spring. It would take years to right the damage Mr. Milton had done with his inept management.

Discouraged, Nicholas returned to the house. The mediocre dinner set before the company was evidence that the excellent cook who had ruled the kitchens on his last visit had departed, but the wine was excellent.

"I am certain you will want to retire early because of your long journey," Mr. Milton said, his cheeks flushed from the quantity of wine he had drunk.

No one argued, although Nicholas suspected that Mr. Milton's consideration stemmed from a desire to get everyone abed so he could pursue whatever dalliance he enjoyed with one of the maids.

Later that night, Nicholas was reading by the light of a candle in his bedchamber when he heard a commotion outside the door. His sensitive nostrils discerned the aroma of smoke. He hastily donned a dressing gown and ran into the hall, where some of the rest of the household in various states of undress had already collected.

"What is it?" he asked.

"Fire," said one of the servants distractedly when Nicholas stopped him on his way to the scene of the trouble. "In the east wing."

"The nurseries!" shrieked Diana, who had just emerged from her chamber. She ran down the hall to find her son, and Nicholas was right behind her.

They came to a hallway filled with smoke, but Diana plunged through, ignoring Nicholas's command to stop as he followed her. Along the way they saw fleeing nursemaids. Not one of them had Stephen.

"We couldn't find him, my lady," cried one small maid. "He wasn't in his bed. We thought one of the others must have taken him out, so we ran to save ourselves."

Diana brushed by her and plunged into Stephen's bedchamber.

"Stephen!" she cried. "Where are you?"

Her voice broke off in a cough.

"Mama!" bleated a small, scared voice from deep inside the room.

"Go back!" bellowed Nicholas, capturing her wrist. "I'll find the boy."

"No! He'll be frightened," replied Diana, managing to get away from him when he banged his knee on a low table. "He'll want his mother."

Swearing under his breath, Nicholas ran into the blinding smoke after her. He supposed it was a good sign that he saw no actual flames in the room, but smoke, he knew, could be just as deadly. After what seemed like an eternity of searching, Nicholas heard a small, whimpering sound. He dropped to the floor, and his hands encountered a soft, trembling little body. Stephen had curled up in the way of all small, frightened animals awaiting death.

"I've found him!" he shouted, scooping up the boy in his arms. Stephen clung to him like a monkey.

Diana didn't answer, although he could hear her cough as she made her way to his side. With the boy's face tucked against his shoulder, Nicholas reached out and touched her. She was doubled up, fighting for air.

"Take Stephen to safety," she rasped. "I'll follow in a moment."

"You'll come now," Nicholas insisted. He grabbed her arm and yanked her upright. They made their way out of the smoke and into the hall, where the servants had organized themselves into a bucket brigade to throw water on the flames. Others were attempting to beat the fire out with blankets.

Nicholas brushed by them, but he was arrested by Penelope's scream of horror.

"Diana! Your gown is on fire!" she shrieked.

When Diana looked behind her and saw the thin flames that licked at the hemline of her voluminous dressing gown, she began to run again. Nicholas pitched Stephen into Penelope's arms and ran after her. When he caught her, she fought him like a tigress in her panic. He wrestled her to the floor, smothering the flames.

He ended up on top of her, staring straight into her watering, bloodshot eyes. Mercifully, sanity had returned to them.

"You have soot all over your face," he said gently as he brushed her cheek with his thumb.

"You should see yours," she said tartly. "Get up. You are crushing my ribs, you big ox!"

"Ingrate." He levered himself off of her and reached for her hand to pull her to her feet. She shrank from him.

"Are you hurt?" he asked in concern.

"I don't think so, but I am wondering how much is left of the back of my dressing gown."

He laughed in sheer relief.

"I didn't think of that," he said, as Penelope, Edith, Mr. Milton and a small knot of servants approached.

Diana laughed, too, as if struck by the absurdity of her dilemma. Her eyes were on her son, who was struggling in Penelope's arms.

"She's hysterical. Someone ought to slap her," Edith suggested eagerly.

Everyone ignored her.

"Penelope, is Stephen all right?" Diana asked.

Before she could answer, Stephen unexpectedly leaped out of Penelope's arms and landed on top of his mother, who winced at the impact and held him tightly as she strained to sit up. It was the first time anyone had seen him dirty, and Diana kissed the top of his sooty little head.

Diana's maid stepped forward with quiet authority and took Diana's arm. She'd had the foresight to bring a blanket, and she placed it around her mistress to protect her modesty. Diana refused to relinquish Stephen to her.

"Come with me, my lady," Bessie said firmly.

Diana turned wrathfully on the head nurse and nursery servants, who shrank from the expression on her face.

"All of you will be out of this house by sundown tomorrow," Diana said angrily.

"If Nurse was good enough to take care of my son, she's certainly good enough to take care of yours," Edith shouted.

"Well, she's not going to take care of my son any longer," Diana shouted back.

Diana's maid and Penelope put their arms protectively around Diana and started to lead her away, but Diana shook them off and turned to face Nicholas.

"Thank you, Nicholas, for saving my son's life," she said softly as she raised up on tiptoe and kissed his cheek. Stephen reached out and patted his face.

Nicholas couldn't trust himself to speak.

Then Diana turned to follow Bessie and Penelope.

"How dare she!" Edith exclaimed furiously.

One of the servants came up at that moment to report that the fire was out. Nicholas talked with Mr. Milton about what repairs should be set in motion and where the servants could set up rooms for Stephen now that his old rooms were uninhabitable. He had to concentrate very hard on these practical matters to keep from running after Diana and clasping her and Stephen in his arms to keep them safe.

What a fool he was. Diana would be absolutely appalled if he did any such thing. And everyone would stare.


Nicholas came down to breakfast the next morning to find Penelope bursting with eagerness to discuss the fire.

"Wasn't Diana magnificent?" Penelope asked him between mouthfuls of buttered toast and bacon. He noticed with some amusement that her appetite had returned with a vengeance now that the fire had distracted her from her disgrace.

"Yes," Nicholas agreed as he accepted the cup of coffee she poured for him. "Thank you, my dear."

"You were magnificent, too, Nicholas," Penelope added generously.

"Anyone would have done the same," he said, helping himself to ham from a chafing dish. "I suppose we won't see Diana and Aunt Edith until at least noon."

Before Penelope could reply to this, they heard a commotion and went to investigate. Diana was standing by one of the side entrances to the house giving instructions to a half-dozen servants who were making a cheerful racket with brooms, mops and buckets. She was dressed in a simple cotton gown, and her hair was confined in a single plait down the back. She looked about sixteen. She had Stephen balanced on one hip.

Mr. Milton was remonstrating with her.

"Dear lady," he said. "I beg you to reconsider. You will want your family with you at a time like this—"

"You are perfectly right," Diana said, interrupting him. "Unfortunately, my family is on the continent now."

"Diana, what are you doing?" asked Penelope, her eyes bright with curiosity.

"I am moving to the Dower House with my son," Diana said. "By rights, my mother-in-law should occupy the Dower House while Stephen and I remain here, but since the manor apparently isn't big enough or safe enough for all of us, I am happy to go."

"Dower House hasn't been lived in for decades," Mr. Milton pointed out.

"Well, it's going to be lived in now," Diana said grimly. "Forward!"

She came back after the servants were on their way.

"Penelope, dear," she said, "you are welcome to live with us in Dower House if you think you would be more comfortable with Stephen and me. Think about it."

Six hours later, Nicholas found Diana alone in the dining room at Dower House. The servants had all gone back to their usual duties at the manor. She was sitting with Stephen in her lap on the floor drawing on a piece of paper. She was covered with dust and had a smut on the end of her aristocratic little nose. She had drawn a diagram of the room, and she was putting in little squares and circles that apparently symbolized the furniture she would bring here.

"If the *ton* could see the elegant Lady Diana now," he teased.

"Scoff if you like," she said, grinning up at him. It occurred to him that she was one of the least vain women of his acquaintance. "What do you think?"

"About what?" he asked, distracted by the warmth of her smile.

"The house, of course. We gave it a thorough cleaning, and I don't think it looks too bad. Rupert bought all of the furniture in my bedroom and sitting room for me when we were married, so I can bring it here. I wish I could bring the rose silk draperies as well, but they will not fit these walls."

"You are serious about living here, aren't you?"

"Quite serious," she said, giving him her hand so he could assist her to her feet. "My son is not spending another night at the manor. The servants will bring our furniture after their dinner."

"Surely you do not think the fire was deliberate."

There. It was out in the open.

Diana gave a long sigh.

"It seems hysterical to suspect such a thing, does it not?" she said. "Whether the fire was deliberate or the result of carelessness is irrelevant. My son could have died in that fire if it were not for you, and the people I trusted to take care of him would have permitted it."

"You're right, of course," he said. "This place might be rather uncomfortable for a while. Will you take your dinner at the manor?"

"Yes. I'm afraid I must until I see what condition the stoves are in. I hope I can find my old cook somewhere in the village. Mr. Milton fired her in a fit of temper months ago. I wonder if Penelope will come to Dower House, too."

"I'm certain she will," Nicholas said with a glimmer of humor. "She and Aunt Edith have clashed rather badly since you left, I'm afraid. I don't think Aunt Edith bargained for the timid, obedient schoolgirl developing a mind of her own."

"Penelope is a darling, isn't she?" Diana said warmly. "She'll make you a charming wife."

"Of course she will," he said after a small hesitation. "If you like, I'll go back to the manor to make sure Aunt Edith isn't harassing the servants about the furniture."

"Will you, Nicholas? I would appreciate it. I wish I could offer you accommodation here, too, but that wouldn't be at all the thing."

"That's all right. Aunt Edith and I get along well enough when you aren't there to stir her up."

"*I* stir *her* up!" Diana exclaimed indignantly. Nicholas laughed and took his leave, giving her a careless wave.

In a shorter amount of time than anyone would have guessed, the drawing room at Dower House was set to rights. All Diana needed to complete its jewel-like perfection was new draperies, and she knew a shop in the village that had silks brought from London for important customers.

Little did Diana suspect on that beautiful May morning when she embarked upon her shopping excursion that she would meet and steal the heart of the most eligible bachelor in the neighborhood.

# Sixteen

"That's exactly what I need!" exclaimed Diana, pointing to the bolt of delicately patterned blue silk propped against the wall behind the counter.

"I regret, my lady, that the blue silk is already sold," the shopkeeper said. "I ordered it special from London for a customer. Now, this other pattern is very similar—"

"No. Too green," she said, frowning at the bolt he had laid on the counter. "Does your customer need *all* of it? My house is small, and perhaps—"

"I'm sorry, my lady. My customer—"

He was distracted by the opening of the door, and Diana looked up to see an imposing man of about forty years enter the shop. The merchant was suddenly wreathed in smiles.

"Sir Richard Iversley," he whispered to Diana in a tone that suggested she should be impressed.

Diana turned to look at the customer with a polite smile on her lips.

The gentleman's thick red-gold hair was a lion's mane, and his eyes were deep sea green. He was dressed informally, but no one could have mistaken this tall, elegantly turned-out man for a mere country squire.

Diana had thought her old blue muslin gown quite good enough for an excursion to the village, but suddenly she felt very dowdy. The gentleman seemed to find nothing amiss with her appearance, however, and he smiled back at her with friendly interest.

"Good morning," he said in a cultured voice that reminded her of thick, warm velvet.

"Good morning, Sir Richard," she replied.

His smile grew.

"Have we met? I'm certain I would have remembered you."

"No," she said, slightly embarrassed. "Mr. Purley told me your name just now and—"

"Then perhaps you will tell me yours."

"Diana Milton, sir," she said, using her married name.

"I am honored, my lady," he said. "Our neighbors have told me about the beautiful Lady Diana. I see they did not exaggerate."

"You are very kind." She managed to break her gaze from his brilliant eyes. She wondered what else the neighbors had told him as she smiled an end to the conversation and busied herself in looking at the bolts of fabric on the end of the counter. Sir Richard took his dismissal like a gentleman.

"Well, my good man," said Sir Richard affably to the shopkeeper. "I've come to see if my blue silk matches the fabric samples I've brought with me."

"It is here, sir," the shopkeeper said as he picked up the bolt of blue silk Diana had coveted. He put it on the counter in front of Sir Richard and smoothed it with loving fingers. "I'm sure it will match your samples, since they were a perfect match with the pattern card."

"Perhaps, but I know that sometimes there is a great deal of difference between a pattern card and a subsequent dye lot."

Diana smiled regretfully.

"I advise you to buy the silk without delay," she told him. "I would have bought it myself if Mr. Purley had been in the least cooperative, I promise you."

"Then, my lady, you must have it," he said at once. "Mr. Purley can order another bolt for me."

"Oh, no, Sir Richard," she said, embarrassed. "I couldn't possibly—"

"Of course you can! Perhaps you will invite me to call on you one afternoon to see if I approve your choice."

"But—"

He ran a careless finger down the other bolt of fabric.

"Perhaps I will have the green instead to bring out the pattern of my upholstery. So, my lady, you have done me a very great favor by taking the blue silk off my hands."

Diana was dubious, but he insisted with such charm that she couldn't refuse. After she arranged for the bill to be sent to her at Dower House, Sir Richard raised her hand to his lips.

"You will permit me to call on you very soon, will you not, my lady? I have just bought Thornwood, which is very near your manor."

"I shall look forward to it, Sir Richard," she replied, "but I live in the Dower House on the opposite side of the gardens."

"Indeed?" he said, looking surprised. "I had thought . . . but you shall enlighten me when I come to call on you."

Diana's maid, Bessie, who had reached over to take the bolt of cloth for her mistress, only caught a glimpse of the dazzling smile Sir Richard directed at Diana, but she was so bemused by it that she almost got into the wrong carriage.


When the day that Sir Richard was expected to call on her arrived, Diana looked about her perfect drawing room with satisfaction. The dainty furniture Rupert had purchased for her was scaled admirably to the small proportions of the room, making it look larger than it was. The rather ordinary chandelier had been polished until it shone, and was revealed to be not so ordinary after all. The blue silk draperies, which had left the seamstresses' hands just hours before, were opened to admit the glorious sunlight.

Only one thing was missing, and before long Nicholas came to announce its arrival.

"It's coming, Diana," he said, looking winded. "I had to help the men bring it down from your sitting room myself for fear they would break it. Where do you want it?"

"In that corner," she said, pointing.

"All right." He stepped to the door and addressed the men

who had come with him from the manor. "Bring it in, and watch the wainscoting, if you please!"

The rosewood pianoforte was soon set in its place, much to the relief of the harassed workmen. They escaped with alacrity when Nicholas dismissed them.

"That's just right," Diana said with satisfaction as she checked the instrument to make certain it was still in tune. "I am much obliged to you, Cousin Nicholas."

"My pleasure, Cousin Diana. What is the occasion?"

"Occasion?"

"Penelope has been dropping hints about a mysterious visitor."

"Oh, Penelope!" she said, laughing. "Sir Richard Iversley is calling on us today. Nothing will convince Penelope that she is not about to play a part in a grand romance. Is it not diverting?"

"Yes. Very diverting," he said grimly. "Tell me about this Sir Richard Iversley. I don't believe I've met the fellow."

"He lives at Thornwood, which was owned by Lord and Lady Marple before he purchased it. He is renovating the manor house, for the place was sadly run down."

"Elderly gentleman, is he? With a periwig and a cane?" Nicholas suggested.

"No. A gentleman in his prime, I should say. In his early forties at the most. Red-gold hair. Green eyes. Very handsome. Dresses magnificently."

"Ah. Foppish sort, then."

"Not at all," she said, her eyes glinting with amusement. "Perhaps you would like to join us this afternoon and satisfy your curiosity."

"I should be delighted. Penelope said she met him when she went to the village with you one day."

"Ah, now I see the reason for this sudden interest in our neighbor," she said, amused. "I shouldn't think he would try to cut you out with Penelope. I doubt that his taste runs to very young ladies."

"How very fortunate," Nicholas said lightly.

"At about two, then," she said.

"I'll be here," Nicholas said, taking the hint to leave. He wondered if she intended to spend the entire three hours until the appointed time primping for her visitor.

When he returned to Dower House, it was to see that Penelope had spent a considerable amount of time primping as well. Penelope wore a demure white muslin dress decorated with scalloped lace he hadn't seen before, and Diana looked deliciously cool and elegant in pomona green with her golden hair arranged in long ringlets cascading from a psyche knot high on the crown of her head.

Nicholas had dressed a bit more carefully than usual, but there was something about Sir Richard Iversley that made him feel vaguely threadbare.

Sir Richard walked straight to his hostess and raised her hand to his lips.

"My dear Lady Diana," he said. "The room is a perfect setting for your beauty, as I knew it would be."

Nicholas's lip curled slightly, but to his disgust, both Diana and Penelope seemed entranced by this trite sentiment.

"And the delightful Miss Chalmers," Sir Richard added, kissing Penelope's hand as well. Her reply was inarticulate, but she returned the smile.

"Lord Arnside," Diana said politely. "May I present Sir Richard Iversley, our new neighbor?"

"A pleasure, sir," said Nicholas, shaking hands with Sir Richard. The gentlemen inspected one another with great interest.

"Ah, the fortunate fiancé of the delightful Miss Chalmers! You are to be congratulated, my lord."

"Thank you," was all Nicholas could think to say.

"I was telling Lord Arnside about your monumental task in setting Thornwood to rights, Sir Richard," Diana said in an attempt to get a conversation started.

"Yes. I enjoy nothing quite so much as a challenge," Sir Richard said, favoring Nicholas with a bland smile.

"How long have you lived at Thornwood?" Nicholas asked.

"A few weeks only," he said. "I had intended to use it only as an occasional retreat for house parties and so forth." He glanced warmly at Diana. "But that was before I became acquainted with the many charms of the neighborhood."

"I see," said Nicholas, who did, all too clearly.

After that, the conversation over tea and cake seemed to be dominated by Diana and Sir Richard, who discussed the fascinating subject of house renovation with so much animation that neither Nicholas nor Penelope had anything to contribute.

"We are boring Miss Chalmers and Lord Arnside," Sir Richard said with a gleam in his eye that convinced Nicholas that he was excessively pleased with himself for monopolizing Diana's attention for a half hour.

The talk turned to general topics, and before long Sir Richard took his leave.

"I had a charming time, Lady Diana," he said. His eyes were warm as they rested on her slightly flushed countenance. "Perhaps all of you will visit me when my house is fit to be seen."

"We should be delighted," she said, pleased. "But I fear we will be going back to London soon, possibly before you are ready to receive guests."

"A pity," he said, "but perhaps you will return for the summer."

"Perhaps," Diana said. Nicholas, who knew that Diana had intended to take Penelope to one of the resorts for the summer months, was not pleased by this evasive answer.

"Isn't he wonderful!" Penelope exclaimed when Sir Richard was gone and Diana had excused herself to check on Stephen.

"He seemed quite respectable," Nicholas said.

"He is so elegant and distinguished," Penelope persisted, oblivious of Nicholas's reserve. "Wouldn't it be charming if he and Diana fell in love and got married?"

"*I* don't think it would be so charming," he said repressively.

Penelope stared at him in surprise with a question forming on her lips, but Diana returned to the room before she could speak.

"He's asleep," Diana announced. "Well, Nicholas. What do you think of our new neighbor?"

"He's a pleasant fellow, I suppose," he said.

"Don't you think he is very handsome?" Penelope prompted, plainly expecting him to do his part to promote a romance between Sir Richard and Diana.

"Yes," Nicholas agreed, "for an older sort of man."

"Fudge," said Diana, her eyes glinting with amusement.

"I don't suppose we will be seeing him much," Penelope said regretfully, "since he will be so busy with his house."

It appeared, however, that Sir Richard wasn't so busy with his house that he couldn't spare what Nicholas considered an immoderate amount of time escorting the ladies into the village and to the homes of their neighbors. Penelope proudly confided to Nicholas that they entertained almost as much at Dower House as they had in Mount Street.

Nicholas saw that this was true. The neighboring gentry rode past the manor without a single glance and beat a path to Dower House, where Diana entertained one and all with quiet elegance in her beautifully turned-out home. To Nicholas's dismay, Sir Richard had gotten into the habit of making informal visits in order to advise Diana on the decor of the remaining rooms. Since one of them was her bedroom, Nicholas thought this a most improper development.

"Fusty," Penelope said airily when he said as much to her.

"I might have known you would say that," Nicholas grumbled. "Although why you should be so anxious to promote a match between Diana and a man who is a stranger to us—"

"He is not a stranger to *me*," Penelope pointed out.

Diana went about in a glow of high spirits, her head busy with plans for adding shrubbery and papering walls.

One day Nicholas arrived at Dower House to find Diana and Sir Richard, both dressed in old clothes, gleefully mixing paints in one of the empty bedchambers to arrive at the desired color for the walls. Diana, who had somehow acquired a smudge of yellow paint on her cheek, was laughing up into Sir Richard's eyes when Arnside came into the room.

"Good morning, Cousin Nicholas," said Diana, flushing slightly.

Sir Richard, as usual, was unperturbed.

"Your servant, Lord Arnside," he said. "I understand you are going to take Miss Chalmers to the village today. I hope you will have a pleasant outing."

"I am certain we shall," he said as Penelope hurriedly came into the room drawing on her pelisse.

"We're not in that much of a hurry, my dear," Nicholas said, helping her into this garment.

"Yes, we are," she said, hastily bidding goodbye to Diana and Sir Richard. "I want to go to the bakery before all the seed cakes are gone."

"I didn't know you were so fond of seed cakes," Nicholas said as he helped her onto the box of the carriage.

"I'm not," she said with a mischievous grin. "I couldn't think of anything else at the moment. The whole idea is to leave Sir Richard and Diana alone, of course."

"What an idiotic notion!" Nicholas exclaimed in annoyance.

"Don't be so fusty, Nicholas," Penelope told him. "Isn't it a wonderful coincidence that Sir Richard moved into his house just as we came into the country? I am persuaded it was *meant.*"

"Such *rot,* Penelope!"

"Oh, Nicholas," Penelope said with a sigh.

At Dower House, the precise shade of yellow had been determined when Sir Richard, standing behind her, startled Diana by putting his arms around her waist and drawing her back against his chest as she stood up from the table.

"Sir Richard," she said softly. "Please don't spoil it."

"I wouldn't dream of it, my dear," he said, his lips against her hair.

"No," she said, struggling against his strong arms. He released her immediately.

"It is too soon," he said, standing back to give her some distance. "Will you forgive me?"

"Of course," she said, avoiding his eye.

"You must have loved your husband very much."

"I did," she said, biting her lip.

"So, we have found the elusive shade of yellow," he said lightly. "Perhaps you will come to my house one day to give me the benefit of your exquisite taste in redecorating my dining room."

She remained silent.

"You mustn't be alarmed," he said gently.

"I know," she said, flushing with mortification. She had reacted like a silly schoolgirl.

He apparently thought a change of subject would put her at ease.

"And when am I to have the honor of meeting Lord Dunwood, my lady?"

Her face relaxed at once.

"Now, if you like," she said. "I usually spend this time of the morning with him."

"Excellent."

"I should warn you, though, that he is excessively fond of gentlemen's neckcloths."

"Indeed? It is a good sign when one so young begins to take an interest in matters of dress."

"He doesn't want to wear them, I'm afraid. He likes to rumple them."

"How barbaric. I shall take good care to keep mine out of his reach, then."

He needn't have worried.

Stephen answered all of Sir Richard's friendly overtures with a bright-eyed, curious look, but, to Diana's embarrassment, he wouldn't cross the room to shake Sir Richard's hand at his invitation. In fact, he wouldn't move from the safety of Diana's lap for the entire interview.

"He's like you, my dear," Sir Richard said when she accompanied him back to the parlor. "Cautious."

Sir Richard gave Lady Diana a humorous look and took his leave. He would have enjoyed staying longer, but he thought it unwise to prolong his visit.

He had erred in embracing her, but he sensed she was not indifferent to him. He was satisfied. She had said "no," but he was confident she only meant "not yet."

# Seventeen

Contrary to his usual experience in the country, Nicholas did not sleep well while he was in Kent. Sir Richard Iversley had become most particular in his attentions to Diana, and Arnside half expected an Interesting Announcement to be issued from Dower House any day.

He disliked everything about Sir Richard. His elegant, well-formed person. His deep, pleasant voice. His striking sea green eyes. And his charm.

Most of all, his charm.

He was contemplating these repellent qualities at the ungodly hour of two o'clock in the morning and finally got out of bed in his frustration. The moon was full, and he stepped out onto the balcony to let the wind blow the cobwebs from his mind. The cold felt good on his bare, sweat-soaked chest.

Soon his eyes adjusted to the moonlight, and he was astonished to see a slim white shape, suggestive of a human body, on the path below. It appeared to be wearing a loose, shroudlike garment. Its draperies lifted in the breeze.

He wondered if he had seen the ghost at last. The fact that he was a sensible man of six-and-twenty did nothing to allay his excitement.

Everyone at the manor and in the village knew about the ghost. Supposedly, it was the shade of an early-eighteenth-century Lady Dunwood who had met an untimely end, presumably at the hands of her violent husband.

Nicholas and Rupert had spent most of their early adolescence prowling the gardens at midnight in the hope of encountering this ghoulish apparition.

According to legend, the lady moaned and wrung her hands and, on at least one occasion, turned eyes of blue fire on her horrified victim, who spent the rest of his natural life babbling incoherently in an asylum.

Well, it stood to reason that anyone would want to see *that!* Perhaps the ghost was a natural phenomenon. Whatever it was, it certainly resembled a woman as it stood so still on the path that led to Dower House.

Nicholas hastily donned his dressing gown and pushed his feet into his shoes. Then he ran to the terrace door, grabbed a lantern from a hook, lit it and went out. When he got to the path, he could see the apparition quite clearly.

It *was* a woman. He recognized her.

"My God," he breathed as he approached her cautiously. He stopped on the path before her and held the lantern aloft. Her eyes were open, but their expression was perfectly blank. No intelligence whatsoever. She did not even blink in the light.

Nicholas put the lantern on the path behind him and wondered what to do. He had always heard it was dangerous to awaken a sleepwalker too abruptly.

His hair stood up on the back of his neck when her lips parted.

"Rupert," she said. It was an anguished cry from the heart. Her arm rose slowly as if she were reaching for something and encountered Nicholas's chest.

A ragged gasp tore from her throat as she awoke.

"It's all right, Diana," Nicholas said soothingly as he put an arm around her shoulders. She was shaking.

"What on earth am I doing out here?" she asked in a surprisingly strong voice.

"You were walking in your sleep. Don't be frightened."

"I'm not frightened," she said. "I'm cold."

He was at a loss for a moment. Her nightgown was an extremely modest one, made high to the throat with long sleeves, but its muslin folds were no protection against the brisk night wind. Her feet were bare, and the ground was wet from a recent rain. Her hair had been confined in a braid, but part of it had worked loose in the wind and was tangled around her face.

Diana was cold. She needed his help.

That broke the spell.

Nicholas bent for the lantern, then scooped Diana up in his arms and began carrying her toward Dower House. He hoped he could accomplish this without setting her gown on fire. The lantern cast dancing shadows before them.

"What are you doing?" she protested.

"Taking you home." His voice sounded normal, he thought in relief. Perhaps he would manage not to make a fool of himself, after all. "Of course, it would be more convenient to take you to the manor, but I haven't the gall to walk into Aunt Edith's lair, bold as brass, with a half-naked woman in my arms—"

"*That* would cause a fuss," she agreed with a sigh.

"It would help if you would hold on. I don't bite."

"All right, but you'll probably be sorry when you sprain your back," she said, putting her arms around his neck. "I'm not exactly a dainty little thing."

"Well, you *are* tall, but you're not fat," he said with a glimmer of humor.

"How *very* kind. At any rate, you don't have to carry me. I can walk."

"This path is made of loose stones, and you aren't wearing any shoes," he told her. Diana had been cold to his touch at first, but now he could feel her body warming in his arms. After tonight, Nicholas would never again have an excuse to hold her this way. He could feel every curve through the thin muslin of her gown. This was killing him, but he couldn't have released her now if his life depended upon it. "Your feet are probably like ice, if they aren't already cut and bleeding. The least I can do is spare you further damage."

"But—"

"No, don't thank me," he said dryly. "Any gentleman would do the same."

"Any gentleman would feel his obligation discharged with the loan of his coat, I imagine," she pointed out.

"Perhaps he would," Nicholas said, "if he happened to be wearing anything underneath it."

He felt her body stiffen and he tightened his arms around her. If she started squirming, he was a dead man.

"Careful," he warned. "I should hate to drop you."

"This is *not* funny, Nicholas," she said indignantly. He realized that she mistakenly had attributed the careful neutrality of his voice to stifled laughter.

Thank God.

"No," he agreed. The thought of what could have happened to her, alone and vulnerable in the dark, effectively took his mind off his present dilemma. "You might have walked into the pond. You weren't far from it when I found you."

She digested this in silence for a moment.

"It isn't deep," she said. "I would have awakened immediately."

"Yes, and caught an inflammation of the lung," he pointed out. It was a terrible thought. "Have you walked in your sleep before?"

"Not until after Rupert died. But I hadn't done it for months now. I've never gotten outside the house before."

"You said Rupert's name."

"I've done that before, too."

When he would have spoken, she interrupted him.

"I may as well tell you now, Nicholas," she said bitterly, "that references to Lady Macbeth will not be well received. Believe me, Edith has exhausted all the possibilities."

This was sensitive ground, and Nicholas retreated from it.

"You almost scared me witless," he said. "I looked out from the balcony, and there you were in that white thing, looking like a wraith. You are fortunate I didn't hide under the bed instead of coming outside to investigate."

"The family ghost," she guessed. "Rupert told me about it when he brought me here after our wedding."

"Yes. For a glorious instant I dared hope."

"I am sorry to disappoint you," she said. He could hear the smile in her voice.

They arrived at Dower House. Nicholas had shifted Diana slightly so he could try the door, but it opened against his hand and Diana's maid stepped outside.

"Thank heavens," Bessie said, relief plain in her voice. She took the lantern from Nicholas's hand and held the door for them. "I was about to rouse the household, my lady. Are you hurt?"

"No," Diana said as Nicholas reluctantly set her down. "Lord Arnside saw me from his balcony and was kind enough to carry me home because I have no shoes on. I was walking in my sleep again."

"I am sorry to hear it, my lady. You must be chilled to the bone. I will make you a cup of tea directly."

She bustled away, and Diana turned to Nicholas.

"Would you like some tea, Cousin?" she asked.

"No, I thank you," he said. "I must go."

If he had any sense at all, he would get out of this house immediately. Instead, he just stood there, looking down into her eyes. She shifted self-consciously on one bare foot like a child. The next time he saw her, she would be dressed with her usual cool elegance, and her hair would be beautifully arranged.

Nicholas didn't know how he would bear it.

"I'm sorry about your ghost," Diana said, putting an end to the awkward silence.

"That's all right," he said, smiling. "I'd never seen a sleepwalker before. You were almost as interesting as a ghost."

"Why, thank you!" she replied, giving a silvery laugh.

Nicholas walked slowly back to the manor, thinking over the night's events. He supposed that only deeply disturbed persons walk in their sleep. Diana gave every appearance of having adjusted to her bereavement. Yet she had said Rupert's name in that anguished voice. What was it about his memory that troubled her?

Then he had a most unwelcome thought. Maybe Diana was feeling guilty about her late husband because she was seriously contemplating a second marriage.

The next few days were enough to confirm this reasonable theory.

Diana and Sir Richard were almost continually in one another's company, but they never invited gossip by going alone on excursions to the village or places of historical interest. They always assembled a party composed of neighboring gentry. Quite often Penelope and Nicholas were invited to accompany them.

It was the third week in May when Diana announced it was time to go back to London in order to salvage what was left of the season. Penelope needed to complete the ordering of her brideclothes. Nicholas was relieved that the journey was not postponed in order to give Diana and Sir Richard more time together. Gossip in the neighborhood had them as good as married already.

Two nights before they were due to leave for London, Sir Richard hosted a sumptuous dinner in their honor and invited not only the neighboring gentry but members of his family as well. It was clear to Nicholas that the purpose of the dinner was to introduce a prospective bride to Sir Richard's relatives. Most of them had journeyed far for the occasion, and they certainly would not have done so for an evening party in the country, no matter how grand, unless there was a good reason.

Nothing could have been more distinguishing than the attention shown to Diana that evening by Sir Richard's relatives, and it was obvious that Diana liked them, too. They were all very handsome, cultured, well-mannered people just like Sir Richard, damn his eyes! Diana blushed when Sir Richard toasted her as the guiding genius behind the decor in his dining room.

Later that evening, the ladies entertained the company on the pianoforte and the harp. After several of the younger ladies had given competent but uninspired performances, Penelope's beautifully executed sonata was well received. Diana followed Penelope, and she seemed embarrassed when the simple ballad she sang was applauded with much more enthusiasm than Penelope's vastly superior performance.

Diana's audience demanded another, but Sir Richard, noticing her reluctance, immediately went to her side.

"Delightful, my dear," he said, kissing her hand. "But you must not strain your lovely voice. Now we will go into the gardens for refreshments."

The gardens, the only part of the manor that had not been neglected by the previous owners, were magnificent, and they were illuminated by lamps set on little poles. The silver and crystal on the refreshment tables gleamed in the candlelight.

"You have a maze!" Penelope exclaimed. "How wonderful! May we go inside?"

"I'm afraid not," Sir Richard told her. "It could be dangerous after dark. One might not be found until morning."

Penelope looked so disappointed that Sir Richard at once invited Diana to bring Penelope the next afternoon so she could inspect it.

"And Lady Dunwood and Lord Arnside, too, of course," Sir Richard added with a correct little bow that made Nicholas irrationally long to plant him a facer.

The next day, Lady Diana, the dowager, Penelope and Nicholas returned to Thornwood for the promised treat. Sir Richard once more proved himself a gracious host. After Penelope and Nicholas had meandered in the maze for the better part of an hour without finding the key, Sir Richard rescued them and graciously offered the company a tour of his picture gallery.

"You will have refreshments first, of course," Sir Richard said with a courteous smile. "I am sure you are quite thirsty after your exercise."

Nicholas gritted his teeth. He and Penelope were both soaked with perspiration because she had stubbornly refused to let him call for help in negotiating the maze. Sir Richard, Diana and the dowager looked annoyingly cool. After a quarter of an hour in the maze, Sir Richard had guided Diana and Edith out of the labyrinth and entertained them until he deemed it necessary to rescue Penelope and Nicholas.

The party then spent what was to Nicholas an excruciatingly dull half hour looking at the depressingly faded images of Sir

Richard's long-dead forebears. The only impressive portrait in the gallery, to Nicholas's disgust, was a magnificent one of Sir Richard himself as a young man in his twenties astride a black stallion. The place beside it was empty, as if waiting for a companion piece to be set there.

Penelope commented on this.

"My wife's portrait will be put there when I marry," Sir Richard said, glancing at Diana, who blushed.

"Are you engaged, sir?" Penelope asked innocently.

"No. Not yet," he answered. "But one never knows what will happen, does one?"

To Nicholas's annoyance, Penelope gave Diana a look pregnant with significance.

The dowager was every bit as annoyed as Nicholas.

She was only five years Sir Richard's senior and she remembered well the days when he was a handsome young man and the despair of every matchmaking mother in London. Edith thought it too exasperating that her hussy of a daughter-in-law should manage to captivate Sir Richard when many a lady of superior birth, fortune and breeding had failed.

"Isn't it romantic? Sir Richard is *so* handsome, and Diana is so beautiful," Penelope unwisely said to Edith later that day when she was visiting with her godmother at the manor.

"Don't count on it ever coming to anything," Edith said with a bitter laugh.

"Whatever do you mean?"

"Only that your precious Diana can't resist sending out lures to every man of her acquaintance. But I doubt that marriage is what very many of them have in mind."

"That is not true," Penelope said indignantly.

"Is it not, miss? You'll sing a different tune when she's managed to steal Nicholas out from under your nose."

"She wouldn't!"

"No? I shouldn't be at all surprised if she wants him for herself. Why else would she saddle herself with the two of us? She despises me as much as I despise her. She probably only agreed to play propriety for you because it brings Nicholas into her house at all hours of the day."

"Diana is my friend!"

"Do you really think so?" Edith asked maliciously.

It said much for Penelope's new maturity that instead of leaping to her feet and running home to Dower House, she finished drinking her tea, ate some iced cakes and made polite conversation with her hostess on a number of indifferent topics until an acceptable interval had passed and she could take her leave.

On the way back to Dower House, Penelope told herself that her godmother must be mistaken. Diana *wouldn't* try to cut her out with her fiancé. Why should she, when she could have any other gentleman in London she wished? Although Diana never mentioned it, Penelope knew that she had rejected the suit of a handsome and wealthy earl just before they came into the country.

Penelope knew that Edith's spiteful words were the product of a suspicious mind, but she still caught herself watching Nicholas and Diana carefully when they were together.

She soon came to the conclusion that Edith had been mistaken. Diana and Nicholas rarely conversed together in company, and when Nicholas came to Dower House, he always asked for Penelope. Most of the excursions he proposed did not include Diana.

Penelope was relieved. Nicholas might not be romantic, but he was very kind, and she was certain he would never deliberately mistreat her. If only everyone would stop telling her she had to be so very *good* to deserve the honor of being his wife, she thought resignedly.

Had she but known it, matters would come to a head between Diana and Nicholas the very next day.

Diana had gone to the village with Sir Richard, and on the way back he stopped his curricle in a secluded lane.

"Why are we stopping here?" she asked in surprise.

"Because it appears to be the only way to have a private conversation with you, my dear."

He took a small square box out of his pocket and opened

it. Diana gasped when she saw the magnificent ruby ring inside.

"It is an heirloom, handed down in my family through the generations. The ruby itself is said to have been given to one of my ancestors by Queen Elizabeth. The diamond band was added in the last century. But that is unimportant. Will you marry me, Diana?"

"Richard, I am stunned. I never expected . . . that is, I didn't think—"

"—It would be so soon," he finished for her. "Neither did I. We have known one another for only a few weeks. But they have been the happiest weeks of my life."

She opened her mouth to speak, but he put a finger across her lips.

"Please don't tell me you are sensible of the honor I have done you, et cetera, et cetera," he said humorously.

"I am sorry, Richard," she said, hanging her head. "I *do* like you so very much, but I never thought to marry again. I don't know what to say."

"Are you definitely saying 'no,' my dearest?"

She shook her head.

"Then I am satisfied. I will just keep this for you until you are ready for it, shall I?" he said, pocketing the ring.

"Thank you," she said gratefully, relieved that he was taking it so well. "You are so kind to me."

He kissed her lips very sweetly, and she forced herself not to draw away.

"Your husband," Sir Richard said, caressing her cheek before he took up the reins, "was a very fortunate man."

Within a short time they stopped at Dower House, but Sir Richard declined Diana's invitation to go in.

Penelope and Nicholas, meanwhile, were in the parlor discussing where they would go for their wedding trip when they heard a mischievous giggle coming from behind a low chest of drawers.

"What was that?" asked Nicholas.

Penelope put her finger to her lips and stealthily made her

way to the chest. Then she reached behind it and lifted Stephen aloft in her arms.

"Got you, little rascal," she said triumphantly. "I'll wager the new nurse and nursery maid are looking for him. They know Diana will have a fit if she comes home and they don't know where he is."

Stephen giggled and pulled one of Penelope's dancing curls. She shrieked and put him down hastily. She made a face at Nicholas, who was laughing.

Free again, Stephen dashed over to Nicholas and held up his arms. Absurdly flattered, Nicholas picked him up, and the child made a grab for his neckcloth, destroying its crisp folds.

"You little devil," Nicholas said, giving Stephen the hug he plainly expected. Nicholas had to smile. It was impossible to be annoyed with such a sweet-natured child.

"Quick, isn't he?" Penelope said, laughing merrily as she took Stephen away from him.

"I wonder how he got down here," Nicholas said, patting Stephen on the head.

"He's a devious little fellow. No!" Penelope shifted the child on her hip and gave him a straight look when he seemed about to pull her curls again. "Back to the nursery with you, little monster," Penelope added fondly as Stephen giggled at her. "I'll be back in a moment, Nicholas."

The smile faded from his face when Diana, looking thoughtful, entered from another door, slowly peeling off her gloves. When she saw the damage done to Nicholas's neckcloth, she gave a forced laugh.

"I can tell Stephen has been here," she said.

"Penelope took him back to the nursery."

"I suppose I had better go to him," she said, averting her eyes as Nicholas looked searchingly at her.

His voice stopped her when she would have left the room.

"He has offered for you, has he not, Diana?" he asked.

She did not insult his intelligence by pretending to misunderstand.

"How did you know?"

"I would have to be blind not to see it," he said, grasping

her shoulders and compelling her to face him. "What did you tell him?"

Her voice deserted her as she looked up into his intent face.

"What did you tell him?" he repeated, pulling her closer.

"Nothing. It was too soon," she said. "I know that sounds dreadfully coy at my age, but—"

"You can't marry him!"

"I fail to see what business it is of yours, Nicholas," she said defiantly.

"He doesn't love you. You are nothing to him but another decorative object to display with the rest of his trophies!"

She turned her face away.

"I know it," she whispered.

"Then why didn't you refuse him outright?" he asked angrily. "Surely you aren't entertaining his proposal. He's twenty years older than you. You can't do it!"

"Why can't I?" she cried, her voice throbbing with indignation.

He bent his head, and his demanding lips met hers. She lifted her hands to push him away, but instead her fingers curled against him, twisting in the thin fabric of his fine cambric shirt to draw him even closer as she responded passionately to his kiss.

When he released her at last, she stared at him, dazed.

"So, now you know," he said with a self-deprecating smile.

"Oh, Nicholas," she said, resting her head on his shoulder. "What are we going to do?"

"Do?" he said bleakly, staring straight ahead at the wall. "What *can* we do? Diana, I love you to distraction, but I could never betray that sweet child. Lord, when she sees her friends, all they talk about are her brideclothes and the wedding. No gentleman of honor can cry off from a betrothal once it has been announced in the newspapers."

"I know it," she said huskily.

"I am going to my estate in Surrey. And I am going to work night and day until I drop from exhaustion. I don't know how much longer I can see you every day without . . . but I must get over you, and you must get over me. In a few weeks I will return to London. I will continue to see Penelope, but whenever possible I will avoid seeing you."

"You make me sound like a contagious disease," Diana said sadly. "How vastly flattering, my lord."

"You will be besieged by suitors. You will forget me, and you will marry one of them."

"Or I could still marry Sir Richard."

"Diana," he said softly. "Don't say that. Please."

She looked down at her hands, but not before he saw the sheen of tears in her eyes.

"Very well, madam," he said, hardly trusting his voice to speak. "I will come in the morning to take leave of Penelope."

"I will not be present," she said. "Have a safe journey home, Nicholas."

Leaving Diana—knowing he could never have her—was tearing his heart out, but he turned on his heel and walked away from her with all the dignity he could muster.

# Eighteen

Diana, Penelope and Edith were delighted to receive an invitation to a *ton* party almost as soon as they arrived in Mount Street. Everyone who was anyone would be there, and this told the ladies in Mount Street that Penelope's recent notoriety had been lived down.

It was an ill omen, however, that the very first person Diana encountered at the party was Count Antonio Zarcone.

"My lady," the count said, bowing, as a wicked smile played across his well-cut features.

Unsmiling, Diana returned his greeting and moved on.

"Well, what have we here?" Caroline asked when the count stared thoughtfully at Diana's retreating back.

"Mrs. Benningham," he said, his eyes bright with malice as he turned to her. "One of my *oldest* friends."

"Charming as always," she murmured, preparing to follow Diana.

"No. Don't go," he said, detaining her.

"But I must, darling. I always have a nip of brandy this time of night. Does my gout worlds of good."

The count tightened his grip on her arm.

"Please, Caroline," he said with a disarming smile.

Caroline's eyes widened in mock surprise.

"Are we on Christian name terms now? I hadn't known it."

"Yes, if you please."

"Very well. What do you want, Antonio?" she asked suspiciously.

"Just your astringent company. I am so bored."

"The more fool you for coming," she replied heartlessly.

"I have never been pursued by so many wide-eyed, innocent debutantes in my life. They are all too cloyingly sweet and wholly devoid of the essential spice. It must be something in the English climate."

"Some women find elderly rakes irresistible. I can't see it, myself."

The count's eyes gleamed, but he let her blatant provocation pass.

"She doesn't look happy," he said, indicating Diana with a motion of his head. "Maybe she needs some companionship."

"On the contrary, she's invited everywhere."

"And her friend Lord Arnside?"

"Is marrying Miss Chalmers, as you already know."

"I would give something to see the gentleman humbled," he said pensively.

"Fiddlesticks!" Caroline said, unimpressed. "You made a cake of yourself, and that's the plain truth. Lord Arnside was merely a witness to your folly."

She would have said more, but a flurry of activity near the door caught her attention. A tall, handsome blond man became visible in the throng, and Caroline's eyes immediately sparked with interest. Upon seeing him, Diana put one hand to her throat, and her eyes locked with those of the stranger.

"Hmmm. This is interesting," Caroline said speculatively.

"Who is he?" asked the count.

"I don't know, but you can be certain I will find out," she said.

The blond man walked straight to Diana.

Nicholas, who was talking to Penelope at one side of the room, recognized Sir Lawrence Windom, an adventurous society physician who traveled extensively in foreign lands. Nicholas had known him rather well at one time, for they'd attended the same school as boys. His father was a viscount and had disapproved when his younger son insisted upon joining a profession his family considered unworthy of his breeding.

His name had been on poor Rupert's death certificate.

Diana looked distressed, and Nicholas could see his aunt approach the interesting couple with a burning light in her eyes that portended nothing good. Nicholas went at once to intercept Edith.

"Let me go," she said when he barred her way. "He attended Rupert in Greece."

"I know. Aunt Edith, you don't want to—"

"I *must* know how my son died, and he can tell me. At last I will find out what that little hussy has been hiding from me all these years."

Dr. Windom appeared about to take his leave from Diana after a few whispered words when Edith darted around Nicholas and accosted him.

"Tell me," Edith demanded, her fingers clutching the startled doctor's sleeve to keep him from escaping. "Tell me how my son died."

"No," Diana gasped in horror. A flurry of shocked whispers surrounded them.

"Yes," Edith cried. "Tell me what part she played in my son's death!"

The doctor stared at her.

"You are . . . Lady Dunwood?" he asked.

"Yes," Edith hissed. "I am his mother. She killed him, didn't she? He died in a duel over *her!* Or he contracted some terrible foreign ailment because *she* forced him to go racketing about even though she knew his health had been poor lately."

"Come with me," Nicholas said, taking command of the situation. He took his aunt's arm and led her and the doctor to a private room. Fortunately, he knew the house well. Diana followed.

"My lady, I do not understand," said the doctor, totally bewildered. "Are you suggesting that Lady Diana had something to do with her husband's death?"

"Yes! And I demand to know how he died!"

"Lady Diana?" Sir Lawrence asked, as if requesting permission.

She nodded slowly. Then she turned away.

"Lord Dunwood did not wish for his family and friends to know the cause of his illness," Dr. Windom said, "so he asked his wife to accompany him to Greece. He had contracted a particularly virulent strain of the French pox, and he did not want his mother or his friends to witness his physical deterioration. He died in great pain, and Lady Diana nursed him devotedly until the end. She deserves your gratitude and not your censure for her care of him. He made us promise him not to tell anyone how he died, because he feared the manner of his death would cause you embarrassment. Until now we have honored that promise."

"I had a right to know!" Edith said, dissolving into tears. "He was my only son."

Her fingers curled like claws, and she charged at Diana as if she might do her an injury. It was plain that Diana would not defend herself. Nicholas imprisoned his aunt in his arms and tried to comfort her.

"I ask your forgiveness, Lady Dunwood," Diana said softly. "It was wrong of me not to tell you, although it seemed the most humane course of action at the time."

"Humane," Edith said, biting off her words. "More humane for *you,* perhaps. If you had been a better wife, Rupert would not have turned to those *creatures—*"

"So I have told myself many times," Diana said.

Blinded by tears, Edith stumbled from the room. When Nicholas tried to go with her, she bared her teeth at him.

"You are all of you alike," she sneered. "Ready to take her part against me."

"I am . . . sorry," the doctor said to Diana, looking uncomfortable. "I had no choice but to tell her."

"Of course," she said, smiling tightly. "I am sorry for the embarrassment this must have caused you, Dr. Windom. And, again, I thank you for your care of Rupert. I don't know what either of us would have done without you."

She shook hands with him, and he clasped hers a bit longer than was strictly necessary.

"I shall accompany Lady Dunwood home," she said unexpectedly.

Nicholas straightened.

"Diana, do you think that's wise?"

She smiled sadly.

"Do not worry so much, Nicholas," she said, leaving them. "It is my duty as her daughter-in-law to see her home safe."

"I am shocked that anyone would suspect that Lady Diana had anything to do with her husband's death," Dr. Windom said to Nicholas when she was gone. "No man could have asked for a more devoted wife to care for him in his last days."

"His mother is not quite sane on the subject," Nicholas said uncomfortably.

"I am sorry to have caused her this grief," the doctor said. "If I had known this would happen, I would not have come."

"You could not have known," Nicholas said, thinking that Diana was the one who had been wronged. She had behaved with perfect generosity toward a husband who obviously had betrayed her with other women. She had left her infant son behind to nurse him in a foreign country in his last illness, which must have been heartbreaking for so devoted a mother. Yet all the time the members of her late husband's family—himself included—were thinking the most dreadful things of her.

He wanted to fly to Diana's side, but he knew that would only make matters worse. Instead, he went in search of his fiancée.

The next morning, Diana hastily excused herself to find Penelope when Nicholas called at Mount Street and was ushered into the parlor.

"Diana."

He put a hand on her shoulder to stop her from leaving him. She couldn't quite look him in the eye, and he was sorry for it.

"You have nothing to be ashamed of," he told her.

"If I had been a better wife—"

"Nonsense! Rupert, and only Rupert, is responsible for what happened."

Her shoulders slumped, and he couldn't stop himself from taking her into his arms.

"I love you so much," she said with a sigh of what sounded almost like relief as she rested her head on his shoulder. "I am trying so hard to be strong."

"So am I," he said wryly, kissing her brow. "We are going to have to do much better than this, love."

He felt her relax in his arms for a bittersweet moment. Then he released her to stand by the window.

"I am going to Surrey for most of the summer," he said. "I'll tell Penelope I have to prepare my manor house to receive her. She'll think it odd when I don't follow you to Brighton, but it can't be helped. It would be better if you and I don't see one another until autumn."

"The wedding," Diana whispered. "I don't know if I can bear it.

"No," she added when he would have taken her in his arms again. "I'll send Penelope down to you."

Diana left the room, and Penelope presented herself within a few minutes. Her innocent, cheerful face and the trusting way she put her hand in his made Nicholas feel like a blackguard.

"I know you have an appointment with your dressmaker, but can you spare me a few minutes, my dear?" he asked her.

"Certainly, Nicholas," she said, obviously puzzled by his grave expression.

When they were seated, he took her hand.

"I will not be able to accompany you and Diana to Brighton," he said. "I have some business to take care of at my estate."

"Nothing is wrong, I hope," she said, surprised.

"No. But the manor house has not had a mistress for a very long time, and I wish to get it in some sort of order before I take you there. You do understand, don't you?"

"Of course I do," Penelope said.

"Then I'll take leave of you, my dear."

Because she plainly expected it, Nicholas kissed her cheek. Then, shyly, she offered him her lips.

Well, he thought grimly. He had to kiss her sometime if he was going to marry her. He touched her lips briefly with his, and he could sense her disappointment. He knew the experience had hardly been thrilling for her, but he couldn't help it. He felt disloyal to Diana, which he knew perfectly well was absurd under the circumstances.

"There," he said, standing back and smiling kindly. "I won't keep you, my dear. I must leave tonight."

"When will we see you again?"

"I am not certain," he said evasively. "I will try to visit you in Brighton, and I promise you I will be back in London in plenty of time for the wedding."

He kissed her again quickly and left, but not before he saw the troubled look in her eyes. He felt the imprint of her soft, innocent lips against his for hours.

# Nineteen

Caroline burst into peals of laughter when Diana grimly dragged the muddy urchin into their rented house in Brighton.

"Well done, bantam," Caroline said, her eyes gleaming with mischief.

The urchin, lifting its head of copper curls, favored Caroline with a grateful smile.

"It's all very well for you to laugh, Caroline," Diana said, exasperated. *"You* aren't responsible for the naughty minx! Penelope, how *could* you?"

Penelope had the grace to hang her head, but to Diana's indignation, she didn't look at all repentant.

The culprit looked adorable despite her grubbiness, since not all the enterprising damsel's arts had been successful in making her look in the least like a stripling despite the loan of a set of boy's clothes.

The clothes, Penelope confessed under duress, had been recently outgrown by a slender young gentleman who had embarked on the grand tour with his tutor.

Diana had no difficulty in assigning much of the blame for this escapade to the young man's hey-go-mad sister, the Honorable Miss Emily Wraxham, and she looked forward to a frank discussion of the young lady's iniquities with her long-suffering parents.

"I know it is very bad," Penelope said, "but I have never seen a cockfight and I've always been curious."

"So you and Emily dressed up in boys' clothes and made

a spectacle of yourselves," Diana said bitterly. "You would do it in *Brighton,* of all places. All the world is here!"

"No one recognized me," Penelope argued. "I was dressed as a boy."

"Very true, but your disguise might have been a trifle more convincing if you had not worn those slippers," Caroline pointed out.

"Robert's shoes didn't fit me," Penelope explained. "They were too big and kept falling off—"

"Those shoes are the least objectionable part of the costume," Diana snapped. "You should be dead of shame."

Puzzled, Penelope turned to Caroline for a translation of this cryptic utterance.

"She means the pantaloons and stockings," Caroline explained kindly. "Your legs are rather too shapely for a boy's. I suspect she doesn't like the way you fill out young Robert's shirt, either."

"Is it very dreadful?" Penelope asked, crestfallen.

"Yes. You look *very* fetching dressed as a boy, dear," Caroline said. "We might keep this in mind for the next time you are invited to a masquerade—"

"Caroline, I'll thank you not to encourage the brat," Diana said with a sigh.

"I never thought you would be so *missish,* Diana," Caroline said. "Lord, some of the things we did were quite as bad, if not worse, than this."

"We *never* did anything so shocking," Diana said, looking Caroline straight in the eye. If she said one word about Naples, Diana was going to do her an injury. "At my wildest, I would never have dreamed of displaying my legs in men's pantaloons!"

"Very true," Caroline agreed. "However, I remember that perfectly *divine* Grecian gown you wore to the theater right after you were married. It was the most ravishing thing, Penelope, in a style that was all the crack in Paris. It bared one shoulder, and it would have been practically transparent even *without* being dampened, which it most certainly was. You could see Diana's red slippers laced almost to the knee right *through* the thing. Rupert banished you to Kent for that bit of whimsy, if I am not mistaken."

"How *dashing, Diana,*" Penelope exclaimed rather unwisely.

"You are incorrigible, both of you," Diana said in despair. "Now go wash that grime off, you little hoyden. If you even *dream* of doing this again—"

"I won't," Penelope said sunnily, "for it was quite horrid watching the birds peck at each other. The managers actually *lick* them to get them ready to fight. Ugh!"

She left the room with a jaunty little prance.

Caroline threw her hands up in surrender as Diana rounded on her with furious eyes.

"I couldn't resist! I'm sorry," Caroline admitted. "Good Lord, Diana, what's happened to your sense of humor?"

"In case you haven't noticed, Penelope has been impossible since we came to Brighton," Diana said severely. "If she isn't kicking up larks with that set of madcaps she's cultivated, she's making a spectacle of herself by flirting outrageously with every scarlet coat in town."

"And you, of course, *never* flirted with officers when you were just out," Caroline said with a straight face.

Diana favored her with a disapproving look.

"You are making a great deal of fuss over nothing," Caroline continued soothingly. "Of course she's flirting with officers. She's just trying her wings. Everyone knows she's marrying Lord Arnside next month. No one would *dare* trifle with her."

"Have you forgotten that *wretched* Captain Burnside?"

"No. Not at all. Penelope won't make *that* mistake again. Of all the innocents, to fall for that 'marry me or I'll kill myself' fustian. She's much more up to snuff now."

"Well, if you call it up to snuff to dress like a boy and go to a cockfight—"

"She promised she wouldn't do it again."

"No, but it's not much consolation when she and that little wretch Emily Wraxham seem to have limitless scope for inventing new mischief!"

"Take courage, love," Caroline said. "Soon Penelope will

be married, and it will be Lord Arnside's problem to deal with her pranks. Then you can pick up the thread of your own life. Just think how agreeable that will be."

"Very true," said Diana, biting her lip.

A few weeks later they were in Mount Street, where Diana ran distractedly from room to room with her hands trailing long lists of tasks that must be accomplished before the wedding. The dowager had decided to return to Kent after she learned the truth about Rupert's death and would only return to London briefly to attend the nuptials, so all the arrangements rested firmly on Diana's shoulders.

The day the bridal gown arrived from the dressmaker, Diana was barely paying attention when Penelope told her that she had been invited to spend the night with Emily Wraxham.

"Her parents will take us to a ball," Penelope said. "I will be home tomorrow afternoon."

"That sounds harmless enough if Miss Wraxham's parents will accompany you," Diana said absently.

"If only Nicholas would come back to town," Penelope complained. "People are always asking about him when I go to parties, and I don't quite know what to say."

"He promised he would come to London in plenty of time for the prenuptial parties," Diana said kindly.

Penelope bit her lip. She was so nervous about the finality of her marriage to Nicholas that she thought she would jump out of her skin, but she could hardly be ungrateful enough to say so to Diana when she was working so hard to make her wedding day memorable.

It was still unfashionably early for a young lady to be up and about the town, but Emily specifically had asked Penelope to come to her in the morning. As she was about to leave the house with one of the maids, Diana hurried after her.

"My dear, would you mind fetching a few things for me from town on your way to Emily's?" she asked. "I know I won't have time to go myself."

"Certainly, Diana," Penelope said. "I'll send them back with the carriage. Will that be all right?"

"That would be very helpful. Thank you," Diana said, smiling at her.

Penelope had just selected the items on Diana's list at the shop when she looked up to see Mr. Rivers standing beside her with a sheaf of drawing paper in his hand.

"You look distressed, Miss Chalmers," he said in concern when they finished their transactions and left the store. He took both her hands in his. "Has something happened?"

"No, nothing like that," she said, seeing that she had alarmed him. If only Nicholas were this sensitive to her moods, she thought, chiding herself at once for her disloyalty. The warmth of Mr. Rivers's hands was so comforting that she returned the pressure of his fingers convulsively. She gave the maid a straight look, and the girl backed away to stand at some distance so she would not overhear their conversation. "I'm so nervous about the wedding. Nicholas visited us twice in Brighton, and he has written to me several times over the summer, but—"

"Is that all?" Mr. Rivers asked. He was smiling, but his eyes were sad. "He was detained in Surrey, but he will arrive in London this evening."

"I don't know what is wrong with me lately," she said, fighting tears.

"As you said, you are only nervous about the wedding. Don't worry. He'll be here in time. It isn't for another week. May I escort you home?"

"No. It is kind of you to offer," she said, turning away hastily, "but I—I must go to Emily's house. We're going to a ball tonight."

When she would have entered her coach, he put his hand on her arm and looked into her eyes. "Miss Chalmers, there is something I wanted to tell you."

"Is it something dreadful?" she asked, daunted by his grave expression.

"I just wanted to tell you I won't be here for your wedding. I'm going to India rather sooner than I expected."

"I'll miss you," she said wistfully. "I wish I could go, too."

He looked startled for an instant. Then he gave her a smile of great tenderness.

"So do I," he said. "Maybe Nick will bring you to visit me after you're married. I might not see you before the wedding, so I'll wish you great happiness now."

"Thank you, Mr. Rivers," she said, as he handed her and the maid into the carriage and gave the coachman the order to start.

At that moment, Captain Burnside was ushered into Emily Wraxham's parlor. Her parents were absent, but for propriety's sake her aunt sat doing needlework in one corner. Fortunately for the captain's scheme, the aunt was quite deaf.

"I shall never forget your role in securing my future happiness," the captain said emotionally as he bowed over Emily's hand.

"How could I refuse to help my dearest friend?" she replied. "When you told me she was being constrained to marry Lord Arnside, I—"

"You know what you are to do?" he interrupted, casting a furtive eye toward the aunt who nodded at him, smiling.

"I will tell her I want to show her my new horse. When I lead her out to the stables, you will be waiting with your carriage."

Emily's brow furrowed in thought.

"But why is it necessary to trick her? If she truly loves you—"

"She does," the captain said, throwing himself into his role. "But she is helpless to fight her guardian or her fiancé on this matter. Between them they have bullied my poor love into submission, but with your help, dear lady, I will save her."

"But Lord Arnside seems so—"

"He is ruthless. Penelope is afraid to defy him."

Emily gave a little shudder.

"Do not worry, Captain. I shall not fail!"

"Bless you, my dear." He took her hand and almost kissed it. But the aunt looked over with a frown on her face at this intimacy, so he hastily straightened up.

"I must go," he whispered. "Remember, not a word to anyone."

"I promise."

Penelope arrived a half hour later, and Emily, seeing the strain on her face, was reassured that she was doing right in helping her elope with Captain Burnside.

"Do come out to the stables and see my new mare," Emily said, stopping the footman with a tiny negative shake of her head when he would have taken the young lady's pelisse. The maid carried Penelope's ball gown up the stairs in the housekeeper's wake. "She is a beautiful stepper."

"Won't your mother think it odd if I don't pay my respects first?" asked Penelope in surprise.

"No. She won't expect us to stand on ceremony today."

Penelope shrugged and obediently followed Emily toward the stable. She drew back when Emily led her to a carriage drawn by a rather elderly pair of horses waiting in the yard.

"Do come along," Emily said, happily anticipating the reunion of the lovers.

When they drew close to the carriage, Captain Burnside got out and seized Penelope's arm.

"No! Don't touch me!" Penelope cried as she struggled to break away from him.

"Be quiet," the captain barked, withdrawing a pistol from his coat. He pointed it straight at his beloved's heart. "Now get in!"

"Wait!" shouted Emily, aware that she had made a very great error. Penelope looked terrified.

"Back in the house, you silly chit," the captain snarled at Emily. "And if you say a word about this to anyone, you'll be sorry."

"Nicholas will come after me," Penelope said defiantly.

"By then it will be too late, even if he does care enough to ride after a little ninnyhammer who has run away with another man twice!"

"I hate you!"

"That is really beside the point, my dear," he said, grinning evilly. "Now get inside or it will be all the worse for you."

When they were under way, the captain kept the pistol close at hand and took a large swig of gin. They were going much too fast.

"Stop the coach, please!" Penelope begged.

"No," he said, wiping his mouth with the back of his hand.

"But I'm going to be sick!"

"Put your head out the window," he said callously.

When the carriage was out of sight, Emily ordered her family's carriage readied immediately. Unfortunately, her father's stable master was used to Miss Emily's outlandish tales, and he didn't believe her wild story about an abduction at gunpoint for a moment. Nor did he think her father would approve of his allowing the girl to go off by herself in the carriage.

The stable master was a family man, and he had no intention of losing his post over some nonsense of Miss Emily's. He capitulated only when the desperate girl threatened to take a hack alone into the city if he would not obey her.

By the time Emily reached Lord Arnside's town house, Captain Burnside had a good hour's start on his desperate flight to Scotland. Emily was distressed to find that Penelope's fiancé had not yet arrived from the country.

Some time later, Bernard returned to the house and found the distraught young lady wringing her hands in his cousin's bookroom and the servants agog with curiosity. It wasn't every day that an unattended young lady presented herself on their master's doorstep, sobbing hysterically and demanding to see His Lordship on a matter of dire importance.

"I am Lord Arnside's cousin, Bernard Rivers. May I be of assistance, miss?" Bernard asked politely.

"Captain Burnside has abducted Penelope!" she cried, bursting into tears.

"When? Tell me at once," Bernard demanded, alarmed. Then he forced himself to be calm, realizing that it would do no good to shout at the already distraught girl.

"Take a deep breath," he said in a milder tone as he handed her his handkerchief. "That's better. Now. Tell me what happened."

"I thought she loved him," Emily sobbed. "But it was no such thing. She didn't want to go with him. He pointed a pistol at her."

"Good God. Listen, what is your name, anyway?"

"Emily Wraxham."

"Miss Wraxham. Are they bound for Gretna Green?"

"Yes. I'm sure of it. *He* said she was being constrained to marry Lord Arnside, and I believed him. I thought—and now Lord Arnside isn't home, and—"

"It will be all right. Truly," Bernard said as he took Miss Wraxham's arm and escorted her to her carriage. "You have done well to come to me. I will go after them at once."

After he had seen her on her way, he appropriated one of his cousin's fastest horses and left a note for Nicholas before flying to Penelope's rescue.

He rode through most of the morning and afternoon before he saw a coach matching the description given to him by Miss Wraxham. He veered dangerously close to it.

"See here, young fella!" shouted the coachman. "You're going to put us in the ditch!"

"Stop, then, blast you!" Bernard shouted back.

The coachman pulled over, muttering something under his breath about drunken young scamps, and Bernard immediately reined in and ran up to the coach.

"Miss Chalmers," he shouted. "Are you in there?"

"Mr. Rivers, don't come any closer!" squeaked Penelope, showing herself at the window. Her face was streaked with tears. "Captain Burnside has a pistol, and he's forcing me to go to Gretna Green with him."

The next thing Bernard saw was a pistol pointing straight at him. Penelope screamed. "If you're smart," Captain Burnside said with an evil grin, "you'll get back on your horse and forget you ever saw us."

"Not without Penelope," Bernard said stubbornly, expecting to feel the bullet enter his body at any moment. He hurried to the coach and pulled the door open just as the captain gave a shout of pain. Penelope tumbled into Bernard's arms, and as she fell, she dropped the heavy pistol. It disappeared into a mud puddle by the side of the road.

Bernard set Penelope on her feet as Captain Burnside leaped out of the coach and faced them with an angry scowl on his face. His wrist bore the distinctive imprint of a set of small teeth marks.

"Run into the woods," Bernard ordered, giving Penelope a little nudge in the appropriate direction.

"What are you going to do?" she asked, her face anguished.

"I'm going to fight him, of course."

Captain Burnside looked him up and down and laughed uproariously.

"You can't," she exclaimed. "He's bigger than you, and he's a *soldier.*"

"Don't worry about me," Bernard said grimly. "Go. Now."

Penelope ran to the captain and pulled on his sleeve.

"I'll go with you," she said. "I'll *marry* you, only don't hurt Mr. Rivers."

"Miss Chalmers," Bernard said, his voice like steel, "get away from him."

Insolently, Captain Burnside grabbed Penelope and kissed her full on her unwilling lips. Then he gave her a hard shove and she went sprawling into the grass.

"Wait for me, sweetheart," he said, laughing drunkenly. "This won't take long."

As soon as he turned back to face his opponent, Bernard's fist hit him in the face, splitting his lip. The men pounded each other relentlessly until the captain lay winded and bleeding on the ground.

Bernard hastily grabbed Penelope and pulled her toward the coach, eager to get her away before the captain recovered. He was already showing signs of rousing.

"Mr. Rivers, your poor face," she said, putting her hand to his cheek.

"No time for that," he said, wheezing for breath. "Get inside."

He handed her in and had a short, terse conversation with the coachman, who agreed to drive them back to London in exchange for Bernard's silence on the matter of his accepting a bribe to help the captain kidnap a young gentlewoman.

Bernard got into the coach beside Penelope and gave the order to start. Through the window he could see Captain Burnside gingerly lever himself into a sitting position.

"You are not hurt, are you?" Bernard asked Penelope. "He pushed you pretty hard."

"Your face is bleeding. Here, let me help you," she said, extracting a dainty, scented handkerchief from her pocket and dabbing his face rather ineffectually with it.

"That's enough of that," he said, wincing as he caught her hand.

"Bernard, you were wonderful," she said with adoration in her voice.

"I don't think there's anything so very wonderful about beating a drunken man," he said harshly.

"But you saved me! How can I ever repay you?"

"You can't. Nor do I expect you to."

His manner was curt because it was all he could do to refrain from gathering her into his arms and kissing her until they were both breathless out of sheer relief that she was safe.

Penelope burst into tears of reaction.

"You're probably disgusted with me for crying," she sobbed, "but, truly, I could not help it."

"Penelope," he exclaimed, reaching for her. She threw herself into his arms and cried all the harder. When she was finished, she looked at her bloodstained handkerchief dubiously.

"I'm afraid I can't help you," he said, amused. "I gave mine to Miss Wraxham. The good captain well and truly pulled the wool over her eyes."

"And mine as well," Penelope said with a shudder. "I knew he wanted to marry me for my fortune, but I never dreamed he would resort to violence. I could *kill* him for hitting you."

"Well, I hit him first. And I would say he's lucky I did, for it would have gone far worse for him if Nick had caught up with him before I did."

The mention of her betrothed caused Penelope to sit up abruptly within the circle of Bernard's comforting arms.

"What will Nicholas say?" she asked plaintively.

"He will only be glad you escaped injury."

Before he could stop himself, Bernard smoothed a wayward curl from her brow and kissed it.

"He won't want to marry me after this," she said quietly.

"Of course he will. Any man in his right mind would want to marry you," he said, gently releasing her.

# Twenty

Nicholas returned to London from Surrey, determined to make the best of his marriage to Penelope even though his heart still yearned for Diana.

How could he help loving a woman so generous that she mothered and protected every frail and misguided soul that instinctively gravitated to her? Stephen. Caroline. Penelope. She had even tried to protect the dowager from the tragic truth that her son had perished from a horrible, disfiguring disease when she had shown her nothing but contempt.

Well, Nicholas was not going to impose upon her tender heart as well. Let her believe that his time in Surrey had cured him of his dangerous obsession for her. He would present every appearance of being a happy bridegroom when he married Penelope, and Diana would soon find someone worthy of her.

He entered his study with a heavy heart, glancing at the pile of invitations on his desk. The last thing he wanted was to embark upon a series of parties, but his fiancée had a perfect right to expect him to dance attendance on her after his neglect of these past months. Lady Diana would have a ball in their honor the day before the wedding.

Then there would be the wedding itself.

Heaven help him.

"My lord," his butler said, breaking into these dismal thoughts. "Mr. Rivers left this for you. He seemed very anxious that you read it immediately upon your arrival."

All thought of the ordeal before him fled as he crushed Bernard's note between his hands and ordered his stallion brought around.

Riding neck or nothing to the rescue, he alternated between concern for his fiancée's virtue and alarm that the desperate fortune hunter might put a bullet through his favorite cousin.

It was almost nightfall when he saw an unfamiliar coach coming toward him and Bernard's cut and bruised face suddenly protrude from the window. Relieved, he reined in as Bernard waved his arm at him.

As soon as the coach stopped, Bernard opened the door and jumped down.

"Bernard!" exclaimed Nicholas, dismounting. "By all that's wonderful, are you all right? You look like you took a pounding. Where is Penelope? Is she safe?"

"Penelope is asleep inside," Bernard said in hushed tones. "She's worn to a thread, poor thing, but otherwise she's perfectly all right."

"Thank God!"

"Let's go over there, and I'll answer your questions. I don't want to wake her. She was very upset." They walked to the back of the coach.

"What happened?" Arnside asked impatiently.

"I fought him and won."

"Did you, now?" Nicholas said, impressed. "I'm beginning to think I've underestimated you."

"You haven't," Bernard said grimly. "He had been swilling from a bottle of blue ruin all the way from London to give himself Dutch courage, so he was foxed by the time I caught up with him. Then Penelope bit him and got his pistol away from him, so—"

"Apparently I've underestimated Penelope, too."

"You aren't going to scold the poor girl, are you?" Bernard asked, looking belligerent. "That Burnside was a pretty ugly customer and—"

"Certainly not! She's suffered enough, I should think," Nicholas said. "She must have been terrified."

"Bernard? Where are you?" Penelope called, sounding frightened.

"I am here, Penelope," Bernard said.

There was something in the way he pronounced her name that made Nicholas look sharply at him.

Penelope pushed open the door of the coach and looked about anxiously. Bernard ran over to help her.

"Nick is here," he told her as soon as he lifted her to the ground without bothering to let down the steps.

Penelope approached her betrothed slowly, her eyes huge with trepidation.

Nicholas took both of her hands in his and was about to express his relief that she was safe when she drew back and squared her shoulders.

"No. Don't touch me, Nicholas," she said, her lip trembling. Then she blurted out, "Nicholas, I cannot marry you!"

It was the last thing he expected from her. His mouth dropped open, and he couldn't think of a thing to say.

Bernard put a gentle hand on her shoulder, and she turned her head to rest her cheek against it.

"She doesn't mean it, Nick," Bernard said.

"I *do* mean it. I love *you,* Bernard. If I marry Nicholas, I will make him a *wretched* wife."

"Penelope, no!" Bernard gasped, making it apparent he had not expected this. "Nick, I—"

Nicholas couldn't believe it. Penelope was jilting him!

Thank God.

He wanted to grin like an idiot. Instead, he tried very hard to look crushed.

"Penelope, you must not do this," Bernard said earnestly. "Your reputation will be ruined. I can't let you throw yourself away on a penniless—"

Leave it to Bernard to try to talk the girl out of it, Nicholas thought in disgust.

But Penelope silenced him by suddenly throwing herself into Bernard's arms and kissing him on the lips.

"No . . . Penelope . . . you can't . . . *we* can't," Bernard gasped, but his arms cradled her of their own volition, and soon he was returning Penelope's fierce kisses with such fervor that Nicholas was satisfied his persuasive ex-fiancée would soon talk her reluctant cavalier around.

When they emerged for air, Nicholas hastily wiped the relieved grin off his face.

"My dear, you know I would never stand in the way of your happiness," he said solemnly. "If you wish to announce to our friends that we have decided we will not suit, I shall support you."

"I had not hoped for such generosity," she said with a little catch in her voice.

"Penelope, you haven't considered—" Bernard said.

Nicholas fixed Bernard with a stern glare, and his astonished cousin fell silent.

"I will ride ahead to Mount Street and prepare Diana for the news," Nicholas said.

He could hardly wait.

"Diana!" Penelope cried, conscience-stricken. "She has been put to such a dreadful amount of bother for the wedding."

"Pray, do not regard it," Nicholas said. "Like me, she will only want your happiness."

"Nicholas, I don't know what to say," she said tearfully.

"Say nothing," he said gravely. "Bernard, I will trust you to see Penelope home safely."

Bernard put a protective arm around Penelope's shoulders and opened his mouth to object to this impropriety, but Nicholas hastily ran for his horse to make his escape before his annoyingly conscientious cousin could voice any more objections to his future happiness.


Diana was sitting alone in the darkness of the parlor, staring straight ahead and wondering how she could watch Nicholas marry Penelope without disgracing herself, when she heard footsteps approach.

"I was just going up to bed, Jasper," she said without turning her head. If she did not dissuade him, he would insist upon lighting the room properly, and she needed the darkness to-night.

"I will not keep you long then."

Diana gasped and peered at Nicholas in the dim light of the single candle that burned on the low table at her elbow.

"Penelope is at Emily Wraxham's house, Nicholas," she said, looking away from him. He had just arrived in town, she supposed. Naturally, he would call on his fiancée first thing despite the lateness of the hour. "She will be sorry she missed you."

"No, Penelope is *not* at Emily Wraxham's house."

"Whatever do you mean?" she asked in surprise.

"Penelope was abducted by Captain Burnside today."

"What? She was supposed to be with Emily—"

Diana was absolutely horrified. "Why are we standing here! We must save her!" she cried.

"Steady, my girl," he said, blocking her path when she would have rushed from the room. "The damsel has been rescued and she's on her way here. I only came ahead to prepare you."

"Prepare me?" Diana clutched her heart as her imagination conjured up a terrible vision of her darling Penelope's lifeless body being borne into the house. She got a grip on her emotions. Nicholas would not be smiling if Penelope was dead. "Is she unharmed, then?"

"Yes. Perfectly. But she has decided to jilt me."

Diana stared at him. "She doesn't mean it," she said slowly, denying the leap of hope that rose within her. "She was upset."

Nicholas gave her a look of pure exasperation.

"I *do* wish people would stop saying that! She looked and sounded very much to me as if she *did* mean it, and I will thank you to refrain from trying to talk her out of it!"

Diana put her hands on her hips. How like a man! Despite her own hopeless passion for Nicholas, her sympathy was all for her innocent young friend at the moment.

"If Penelope has cried off from such an advantageous match, it is because *you* were beastly to her. How *could* you, Nicholas? That poor girl must be suffering agonies!"

At that moment they heard the door knocker, and Nicholas stepped quickly into the hall. Diana followed him.

"I will open the door," Nicholas said to the butler, which Diana thought was pretty high-handed of him in *her* house. Then she let out a cry of dismay when Mr. Rivers and Penelope, both looking bedraggled, came inside. Mr. Rivers's arm was around Penelope, but it was unclear to Diana who was supporting whom.

"Mr. Rivers!" Diana cried when the light of the candle in the hall illuminated Bernard's bruised face. "I shall send for a doctor at once!"

"No need, Lady Diana. I am perfectly well," he said, sounding remarkably cheerful. He exchanged an affectionate look with Penelope. "I couldn't be better."

"But what—" Diana sputtered. "I don't understand. Mr. Rivers, how did you come to—"

"Penelope is exhausted," Nicholas interrupted. "Why don't you take her up to her room, Diana, and return to me in the parlor?"

"Well, all right," Diana said dubiously. "Come along, my dear."

To Diana's utter astonishment, Penelope turned to Mr. Rivers and kissed him full on the lips.

"Thank you, Bernard, for rescuing me," Penelope said, smiling shyly at him when she released his shoulders.

"It was my pleasure," he said gallantly. Diana noticed that Bernard's clothes were rumpled and muddy, but his face was not battered quite as badly as she had at first supposed. He had a foolish grin on his face.

Nicholas, by contrast, looked as if he had just left the hands of his valet.

Could it be true that the mild, scholarly Mr. Rivers had rescued Penelope?

Still puzzled, Diana led Penelope off to her room while Penelope regaled her with a colorful account of Mr. Rivers's heroic rescue of her person from the dastardly Captain Burnside. Further, the girl insisted that she would marry Mr. Rivers and not Nicholas. Nicholas had taken his disappointment quite well, she said innocently.

When Diana returned to the parlor, Nicholas stood up from where he had been sitting in the shadows by the fireplace.

"Where is Mr. Rivers?" she asked, a little dismayed at finding herself alone with him.

"I sent him away."

His eyes were so ardent that she backed away from him a little when he approached her. He pulled her into his arms.

"Kiss me, love," he said.

"But Penelope—"

"—would infinitely prefer Bernard to me."

"Prefer Mr. Rivers to you?" she said incredulously. "What utter nonsense!"

"Thank you, my darling," he said, kissing her cheek. "And to think I was once quite set up in my own esteem. Dare I hope *you* will marry me? The thought of facing the gossips as a rejected bridegroom quite unmans me."

"I could conjure up a trifle more sympathy if you did not look so abominably well pleased with yourself," she said, her eyes glowing.

"You have totally misread my expression. I am in a quake that you won't have me. I wish you would."

"Of course I'll have you, you silly man," she said fondly.

Suddenly she gave a muffled scream.

"What is it?" he asked in concern. "Did I hurt you?" He had been holding her tightly.

"No," she said. "But, Nicholas, what are we going to do about the wedding? Most of the guests from the country have already begun their journeys by now."

"You will marry me instead," he said promptly. "That way, at least *my* relatives won't have made the journey for nothing. In the morning I shall go at once to procure a special license."

"That is the most ridiculous scheme I have ever heard! You cannot invite people to a wedding and substitute a different bride at the last minute!"

"No?" he asked softly, bending to kiss her.

She emerged from his embrace flushed and a little shaken.

"It *would* be a pity," she said breathlessly, "to waste all of the staff's preparations."

Bernard was tying the straps to one of his trunks when Nicholas's butler announced that an unattended young lady had arrived and desired immediate speech with him.

"Penelope!" he exclaimed when the veiled lady revealed her face to him. "What are you doing here?"

"Nicholas said you still intend to go to India in two days!" she said accusingly. "Is it true?"

"Yes, it's true," he said, his eyes solemn. "You shouldn't be here. It is not at all the thing for a young lady to visit a gentleman's home unattended—"

"Never mind that rubbish! You were going to leave without even saying goodbye, weren't you?"

"I was going to call on you tomorrow."

"I see," she said, crestfallen. "You did not mean what you said last night, then."

"I meant every word," he said earnestly as he put his hands on her shoulders. "But, love, consider. I'm a younger son of a younger son. I am totally ineligible."

"You are not! Your birth is as good as mine."

"My birth, but not my fortune. I am obliged to make my living."

"Not if you marry me," she pointed out with a gleam of mischief. "*I* have forty thousand pounds."

"Penelope, you little wretch," he said, his eyes warm.

"You could take me to India with you," she suggested. She traced the angle of his jaw with one slender finger, and he caught her hand and kissed the inside of her wrist. "You do not have to marry me if you had rather not."

"My beautiful innocent, I would *definitely* have to marry you if I take you to India. What *will* you say next?"

"Don't you want to marry me?"

"You know I do," he said. "But if you marry me, you'll regret it later."

Penelope wasn't listening.

"My guardian would *have* to consent if I ran away with you," she said thoughtfully.

*"No,* darling! I can't take you with me."

"You don't *want* to take me with you," she said angrily.

"That isn't true! Do you think I want to leave you behind? But what if you meet someone who is worthy of you and you are encumbered with me?"

"I won't! Why won't you believe me when I say I love you?" she asked plaintively. "I believed *you* last night."

He held her close for a moment.

"You are so young. I can't take advantage of you."

"I am no younger than I was when I agreed to marry Nicholas. No one said *he* was taking advantage of me," she pointed out as she wound her arms around his neck and pressed her cheek to his.

"It is not the same, my dear. You had better go now," he said when he had released her. "Goodbye, Penelope. I promise I will come back for you if you feel the same way in a year."

"Bernard Rivers, you are the most stubborn man I have ever met," she cried, reminding him very much of an infuriated kitten. "Goodbye! I won't change my mind, and you had *better* come back in a year or I'll come after *you!"*

"I'll hold you to that," he said, smiling tenderly.

She made a face at him and flounced out the door.


When Penelope returned to Mount Street, she nearly collided with Caroline Benningham, who was just leaving after calling on Diana.

"I beg your pardon, Penelope," Caroline said. "I wasn't watching where I was going. Are you all right, dear child? This must be very awkward for you, living with the woman who is going to marry your fiancé in three days."

"Ex-fiancé," Penelope corrected her. It was perfectly obvious to her now that Nicholas and Diana had been in love all along and had denied their feelings to spare hers. She supposed she should be grateful to them for caring so much about her happiness, but she only felt stupid. And now Bernard was being stubborn.

"As you say," Caroline conceded. "I must admit I find it all very depressing. I feel as if I am losing my last friend. There is certainly no reason for me to stay in London with Diana going on her honeymoon to Paris for a month."

Penelope gave her a speculative look, and Caroline's eyes narrowed.

"What are you thinking of, brat?" Caroline asked warily.

Penelope drew Caroline back inside the house and took her to her bedchamber. Within a quarter hour they were laughing conspiratorially.

# Twenty-one

The wind was cool and brisk as it ruffled Bernard Rivers's hair and made his eyes water. Soon the ship would take him away from England and the woman he loved. He was staring out to sea, watching the gulls circle overhead, when he imagined he heard Penelope calling his name.

"Bernard!" the voice repeated, sounding impatient.

He turned quickly and captured a small, fragrant bundle of orange blossom scent and blue merino cloak as it propelled itself into his arms.

"Darling, you shouldn't have come," he said, holding her close. "This is no place for you. It is kind of you to see me off, but—"

"I am not seeing you off," she interrupted. "I am going to India, too."

"No!" he cried. "My love, I won't let you compromise yourself—"

"I am not compromising myself. I am compromising *you!*" She said gleefully. "You will *have* to marry me or your reputation will be in shreds."

He blinked when Mrs. Benningham came to his rescue. He had been so intent upon Penelope that he hadn't noticed her standing there in an excessively becoming jonquil yellow traveling costume.

"Don't let the naughty minx tease you, Mr. Rivers," Caroline said in amusement. "Neither of you will be compromised. I will accompany Penelope to India, where I have the permission of her guardian to launch her upon colonial society.

"And *you,* Penelope," she continued, fixing that young lady with a mischievous grin, "should be dead of shame for the way you terrorized that poor man."

Penelope blushed.

"Well, I had to tell him *something* to make him let me go to India," she said defensively.

"I agree, but to boast about jilting Lord Arnside in that shockingly brassy way, and to tell him that if he tried to inflict another unwanted fiancé on you, you would cast your reputation to the winds and seek a career on the stage was the outside of enough!"

"Well, it worked," Penelope said, unrepentant. "I daresay if I hadn't made him so anxious to get me off his hands, he might have sent me back to Bath."

"Penelope, you are an unprincipled brat," Bernard said with admiration in his eyes. He grew solemn. "You may meet someone else in India. If you do, I won't stand in your way."

She gave Bernard a saucy smile.

"Isn't he sweet when he's being noble?" she asked Caroline as Bernard shook his head in amused resignation.

"Come along," Penelope said, taking his arm and leading him toward the ship. Then she stopped dead in her tracks and gave him a look of dismay that was almost comical. "I never thought. Do you suppose I shall be sick?"

"Yes," he said resignedly, "but I will do my best to distract you."

She smiled and tucked her arm happily in his as they walked toward the ship. Caroline sighed heavily as she followed them.

"To think of me," she said in a tone of self-pity, "playing duenna to a pair of youthful lovers. I never thought I would come to this."

She stopped suddenly, staring into the sea of faces waiting to wave farewell to the passengers.

"You go ahead," she said to the blissful couple.

"But, Caroline—" Penelope protested.

"I'll be with you in good time. Don't worry," Caroline told her absently.

The couple hurried away as Count Antonio Zarcone approached Caroline with his long, regal stride and stopped before her, legs apart and shoulders squared as if he were a monarch about to grant an audience.

"Well, Caroline," he said, smiling roguishly at her.

"Have you come to see me off, Antonio?" she asked. "Good of you."

"Not precisely. I came to talk you into abandoning this mad scheme and seeing Italy with me instead."

"I have seen it," she said.

"Only Naples. I have a villa outside Rome. We will eat grapes from my vineyard and warm our bodies in the sun."

"No, Antonio," she said firmly. "I have no wish to be your *chère amie*. I am going to India."

"Venice, then. We will go for long rides by gondola in the canals and drink lovely cool wine in the moonlight—"

"Antonio, are you by any chance asking me to marry you?"

"No, my dear," he said with regret in his tone.

"Good," she said briskly, "for I am done with that sort of thing. I am going to have a grand adventure, probably my last before I grow quite decrepit. Consider yourself fortunate that you won't be compelled to witness my sad deterioration."

"And you will not abandon your grand adventure for me," he said, tracing the angle of her jaw with one lazy finger. "Not even if I ask you to marry me."

"No," she said without hesitation. "I am going to shoot a tiger and ride an elephant or two before I cock up my toes."

His lips were inches away from hers.

"Then will you share this so-grand adventure with me instead?"

"What are you talking about?" she asked, staring at him suspiciously.

His secretary, a dapper little man in a black suit, walked up to them at that moment. He was directing two servants laden with heavy trunks.

"I have procured our passage, Your Excellence," the secretary said, glancing at Caroline. "We must go now, or the ship will go without us."

"It wouldn't dare," the count said tranquilly. "However . . . Caroline, will you take my arm?"

"Antonio!" Caroline exclaimed.

"Do not look so alarmed, my dear, for I am merely a fellow passenger," he said. "I am not so young myself, you know. I shall not interfere with your desire to shoot tigers or ride elephants—"

"Or flirt with maharajas?"

"Why should you, when you can flirt with me instead?" he asked, genuinely surprised.

Caroline laughed and took the proffered arm.

"I shall probably regret this," she said. "What would you have done if I had agreed to go to Italy with you?"

"I knew you would not," he said, his eyes crinkling with laughter. "You amuse and infuriate me in equal measure, my sweet, but you never disappoint me."

Elizabeth Carson, Lady Banks, shed sentimental tears as she watched her sister and her new husband receive the congratulations of their guests. Diana looked ravishing in glimmering ivory silk, and Lord Arnside couldn't take his eyes off her. Neither could anyone else.

"Wasn't she the most beautiful bride?" Elizabeth sniffed, clinging to her husband's arm.

"No," Robert said. "You were."

"Darling," she said, her usual mischievous smile touching her lips. "Oh, look! There is Stephen! Doesn't he look sweet?"

The child, released from his nurse's charge, ran up to his mother and pulled on her ivory silk skirts. She stooped to kiss him, and Nicholas hoisted him up in his arms.

Stephen giggled happily and pulled Nicholas's neckcloth out of its meticulous folds.

"Oh, Stephen!" exclaimed Diana, horrified. Nicholas merely sighed.

"Do not worry, my love," Nicholas said, smiling warmly at her as he held his new little son close. "I shall become accustomed."

# ABOUT THE AUTHOR

Kate Huntington lives with her family in Illinois. She is the author of three Zebra Regency romances and is currently working on her fourth, *Mistletoe Mayhem,* which will be published in October 2000. Kate loves hearing from readers and you may write to her c/o Zebra Books. Please include a self-addressed stamped envelope if you wish a reply.

# BOOK YOUR PLACE ON OUR WEBSITE AND MAKE THE READING CONNECTION!

We've created a customized website just for our very special readers, where you can get the inside scoop on everything that's going on with Zebra, Pinnacle and Kensington books.

When you come online, you'll have the exciting opportunity to:

- View covers of upcoming books
- Read sample chapters
- Learn about our future publishing schedule (listed by publication month *and author*)
- Find out when your favorite authors will be visiting a city near you
- Search for and order backlist books from our online catalog
- Check out author bios and background information
- Send e-mail to your favorite authors
- Meet the Kensington staff online
- Join us in weekly chats with authors, readers and other guests
- Get writing guidelines
- AND MUCH MORE!

**Visit our website at
http://www.zebrabooks.com**

# More Zebra Regency Romances

# Celebrate Romance With Two of Today's Hottest Authors

## Meagan McKinney

| | | |
|---|---|---|
| __In the Dark | $6.99US/$8.99CAN | 0-8217-6341-5 |
| __The Fortune Hunter | $6.50US/$8.00CAN | 0-8217-6037-8 |
| __Gentle from the Night | $5.99US/$7.50CAN | 0-8217-5803-9 |
| __A Man to Slay Dragons | $5.99US/$6.99CAN | 0-8217-5345-2 |
| __My Wicked Enchantress | $5.99US/$7.50CAN | 0-8217-5661-3 |
| __No Choice But Surrender | $5.99US/$7.50CAN | 0-8217-5859-4 |

## Meryl Sawyer

| | | |
|---|---|---|
| __Thunder Island | $6.99US/$8.99CAN | 0-8217-6378-4 |
| __Half Moon Bay | $6.50US/$8.00CAN | 0-8217-6144-7 |
| __The Hideaway | $5.99US/$7.50CAN | 0-8217-5780-6 |
| __Tempting Fate | $6.50US/$8.00CAN | 0-8217-5858-6 |
| __Unforgettable | $6.50US/$8.00CAN | 0-8217-5564-1 |

---

Call toll free **1-888-345-BOOK** to order by phone, use this coupon to order by mail, or order online at **www.kensingtonbooks.com**.

Name _____

Address _____

City _____ State _____ Zip _____

Please send me the books I have checked above.

| | |
|---|---|
| I am enclosing | $_____ |
| Plus postage and handling* | $_____ |
| Sales tax (in New York and Tennessee only) | $_____ |
| Total amount enclosed | $_____ |

*Add $2.50 for the first book and $.50 for each additional book.

Send check or money order (no cash or CODs) to:

**Kensington Publishing Corp., Dept. C.O., 850 Third Avenue, New York, NY 10022**

Prices and numbers subject to change without notice.

All orders subject to availability.

Visit our website at **www.kensingtonbooks.com**.